BANANA BOTTOM

CLAUDE McKAY

ecco
An Imprint of HarperCollins*Publishers*

HarperCollins books may be purchased for educational,
business, or sales promotional use. For information,
please email the Special Markets Department
at SPsales@harpercollins.com.

Originally published by Harper & Row Publishers, Inc., in 1933.
Reprinted by Harcourt Books in 1974.

FIRST ECCO PAPERBACK EDITION PUBLISHED 2023

Library of Congress Cataloging-in-Publication Data
has been applied for.

ISBN 978-0-06-335771-6

ScoutAutomatedPrintCode

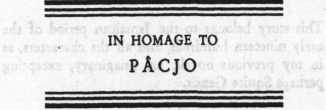

IN HOMAGE TO

PÂCJO

AUTHOR'S NOTE:

This story belongs to the Jamaican period of the
early nineteen hundreds, and all the characters, as
in my previous novels, are imaginary, excepting
perhaps Squire Gensir.

1

THAT SUNDAY WHEN BITA PLANT PLAYED THE OLD
straight piano to the singing of the Coloured Choristers in
the beflowered school-room was the most exciting in the
history of Jubilee.

Bita's homecoming was an eventful week for the folk
of the tiny country town of Jubilee and the mountain village of Banana Bottom. For she was the only native Negro girl they had ever known or heard of who had been
brought up abroad. Perhaps the only one in the island.
Educated in England—the mother country as it was referred to by the Press and official persons.

Bita had had some seven years of polite upbringing.
And she had never had any contact with her home and
her own folk during those years. And now she was a
real young lady wearing a long princess gown and her
hair fixed up in style.

The Reverends Malcolm and Priscilla Craig were responsible for that. They had taken Bita like a child of
their own. As a child of their own. The achievement was
impressive. And those who had bright in their minds
the picture of the hoyden girl in a plain knee frock and
two ribboned stumps of pigtail who had left Jubilee at
fifteen were speechful with admiration before the return
of the developed brown beauty.

With Belle Black, the first soprano leading them, the

Coloured Choristers were in no way intimidated by Bita's years of higher and foreign culture. Indeed they were united on testing it. And so Belle Black, tall and haughty like a black thatch, started a race with the piano regardless of time and beat with the rendering of the first piece of the cantata. And she kept that up from the beginning to the end. Bita was able to keep up the pace although she had only run carelessly through the score once and had not practised with the Choristers. She had arrived the Saturday before only. But the music was a simply arranged thing.

The Choristers thought it was grand. They had a local reputation for excellent singing and were unitedly proud. So when the cantata was over and finished they ringed around Bita with congratulations.

"You played fine!"

"Perfect accompaniment!"

"Welcome to Jubilee!"

"Welcome back home!"

Bita had passed *their* test.

And supported by her father Jordan Plant she went from one ring to another to shake hands and kiss the Jubilee folk and some from her native village of Banana Bottom who had come to town to hear her and the cantata.

Bita was a girl with a past. Between the years of twelve and thirteen she had been raped. She had been raped by Crazy Bow Adair.

Crazy Bow was a descendant, third generation, of a strange Scotchman who had emigrated to Jamaica in the eighteen-twenties. This Scotchman bought the vast mountain estate of Banana Bottom, liberated the slaves and married one of the blackest of them. Before the coming of this strange liberator, many slaves had been allowed to cultivate lots on the estate. The Scotchman sold these lots outright to the tillers and set a policy of cutting up his thousands into small holdings for the blacks who wanted to buy.

His Negress bore him plenty of children. And his children begat a lot of children. His progeny in Banana Bottom and the surrounding villages numbers a score of families. A variegated multitude from coffee-brown to café-au-lait. And there are many unnumbered.

Of the great property, a dilapidated long, oblong flat house (called by the peasantry 'State House—*i.e.*, The Estate House) with ten acres of land is the only integral part left of the original. The rest is now a hill-and-valley village of thatched and shingled homes housing black and brown families.

The Highlander's blood has flowed down into a dark-brown stream deep sunk into the soil. His children's children are hardy peasants. Some are reliable artisans. The wheelright and cooper of Gingertown is one. Also the cabinet-maker of Jubilee whose finely carved whatnots are locally renowned. And a gold-and-silver smith of the city.

None of that breed may be found among the little politicians and preachers of the island. The rude progenitor was a passive enemy of word-mongering people and it was as if the power of his will had persisted as a restraining element in his blood.

In the island there are still extant a species of white humanity who cling to the belief that the Act of Emancipation was a bad thing and the mixing of different human strains. And they may point out to you the village of Banana Bottom and the descendants of the last owner of the original estate as a picture of decadence and degeneracy.

Crazy Bow was the last child of a large brood of the Adair stock that lived in the crumbling 'State House. He had been a precocious child and the first Adair to show signs of an intellectual bent. The village schoolmaster encouraged his parents to give Crazy Bow the benefit of a secondary education. He thought the boy would be good for an official job some day. Or make a mark for himself in the bigger life of the island.

Besides his precociousness Crazy Bow had the external qualities that carried candidates to success in the limited mundane affairs of the exotic conglomeration of West Indian life. While most of his blood relatives were dark brown, Crazy Bow was the colour of a ripe banana. And that with a modicum of intelligence and push could assure him one of the little polite places that were always the plums of the lighter-skinned coloured people.

For the island colony was divided into three main groups in a political and social way. The descendants of the slaves were about three-fourths of the population and classified as black or dark brown. The descendants of Europeans and slaves were about one-fifth of the population and classified as coloured or light brown. The rest were a few thousand East Indians and Chinese and perhaps the same number of pure European descent.

The demarcations were not as real as they seemed. East Indian and Chinese blood were mingled in the dark-brown group and obviously there were thousands who were drawn in from European stock. One could easily pick out individuals by texture of hair, contour of face, shape of nose. But a strong transfusion of black African blood had determined their pigmentation and group. In the coloured group were many of a light complexion distinguished by Sudanese features and hair, while others of original coloured stock had approximated to and turned white.

But the social life of the colony was finely balanced by the divisions. The "coloured" group stood between the mass and the wealthy and governing classes and all the white-collar jobs of business and government were reserved for it.

Crazy Bow was the first of his clan to go to a higher school. From the village school he was sent to a private institute for boys at Jubilee. It was expensive enough for a peasant boy. But his folks' land was good for banana and sugar-cane. Besides they raised pigs and goats and ran the village grocery shop. The whole clan was proud of Crazy Bow and kept him supplied with clothing and money.

The first year he was a brilliant student, amenable to work and discipline. But after that he shot right off the straight line and nothing could bring him back. As a boy Crazy Bow was full of music. He made flutes out of bamboos and blew new joys into the village tunes. He was an imitating wonder. Once he heard a tune played he could pick it up and play it through, often surpassing the original performer. He could play any of the instruments found among the peasants in the hill country: fiddle, banjo, guitar.

But what turned him right crazy at the school was a piano that he taught himself to play there. It knocked everything else out of his head. Composition and mathematics and the ambition to enter the Civil Service. All the efforts of the headmaster were of no avail. The boy could not be got back to the routine of studying. And so after a few months he went back home.

There was no piano in the hills, so Crazy Bow's favourite instrument was the fiddle. He wasn't steady enough to keep one of his own, but he played all the village fiddles. The owners were glad to let him. For he knew all kinds of music: village tunes, hymns and anthems, jubilee songs and snatches of high music. The village accepted his harmless insanity and called him Crazy Bow.

The village also accepted his strange apparitions.

Unheralded he would thrust his head into the doorway of a house where any interesting new piece of music was being played . . . There were no pianos in Banana Bottom but there were a few organs to be found in the homes of the more cultivated villagers. . . . Crazy Bow would appear when the village choir was rehearsing in the schoolroom, but could not be induced by the choirmaster to participate in a regular manner. Sometimes he would sit down to the organ for a spell of anything from anthems to dance tunes. Then the choir practice would be ended for that evening, but no one wanted to stop him, everybody listened with rapture.

He was more tractable at the tea meetings, the unique social events of the peasantry, when dancing and drinking and courting were kept up from nightfall till daybreak. Then Crazy Bow would accept and guzzle pint after pint of orange wine. And he would wheedle that fiddle till it whined and whined out the wildest notes, with the dancers ecstatically moving their bodies together to follow every twist of the sound. And often when all was keyed high with the music and the liquor and the singing and dancing

Crazy Bow would suddenly drop the fiddle and go. And no one could stop him.

Bita's people and Crazy Bow's were near neighbours. Her great-grandfather on her mother's side had been the first to acquire five acres of the Banana Bottom property when it was cut up for sale. But the land had been used for cultivation only until Bita's father built his house there.

The Plant house was on the same plateau strip as the 'State House, with both pieces of land sloping off parallel down to the Cane River. Along that part of the river there were thick patches of the long guinea grass growing under mango trees and rose-apple trees overhung with stout climbers.

As a child Bita had been given lots of rope to roam around and had developed tomboyish traits. She was a seven-months baby. The village folk said that she had killed her mother. That was the way the black peasants referred to a child that survived when the mother had died in giving birth to it. She was a fragile baby and much petted by her father and her aunt Naomi who took her sister's place and became Bita's stepmother.

But as she grew out of babyhood she became remarkably strong and self-reliant. She learned to climb all the mango and star-apple and naseberry trees on her father's place to pick fruit. And she could swim, and ride a horse bareback.

Crazy Bow was a frequent visitor at Jordan Plant's, often eating with the family, when he could be persuaded to sit down to table. And whenever Crazy Bow was in the mood he would take the fiddle down from the wall and play. And sometimes he did play in a way that moved Jordan Plant inside and made tears come into his eyes—tears of sweet memories when he was younger down at Jubilee and fiddled, too, and was a gay guy at the tea-meetings. Before the death of his father. Before he became a sober member and a leader of the church.

Ah, Crazy Bow could play. Every fiddler in and around Banana Bottom called him master. Those who had been to the city and heard a little high music said he was a virtuoso. The schoolmaster called him a coloured Paganini. And the Rev. Malcolm, who kept up the family tradition of appraising native accomplishments, said, when he heard Crazy Bow play, that he was a sinful, drinking lunatic but a great musician. The peasants took Crazy Bow as a fine fiddler for the hill country, but laughed at the idea of greatness in him. Greatness could not exist in the backwoods. Nor anywhere in the colony. To them and to all the islanders greatness was a foreign thing. The biggest man in the colony was the governor. But not even the most ignorant peasant thought him great, nor that he possessed any personal attributes of greatness besides that belonging to his office. They knew that he represented a great person who was their king. And that that king lived in a far country surrounded by other great persons, none of whom could possibly live in a little island colony.

Bita was often with her father when Crazy Bow played. Some of the village children were afraid of him, but she was not. She sometimes met him when she went down by the riverside to get mangoes. And one day they romped together in the soft brown fox grass that grew upon the slope. And after that she grew very familiar with him when he came to the house or when she met him down by the riverside, mostly on Saturday when there was no work.

Then Crazy Bow was twenty-five and Bita past twelve, and neither Jordan nor Naomi Plant nor even the wags of Banana Bottom gave the slightest thought to that companionship. Crazy Bow was harmlessly light-headed and none could imagine him capable of any natural aberration. Besides, the village was sentimental about Crazy Bow because of his antecedents. Every Banana Bottom child was acquainted with the origin of the Adair family, the story of which had been told from generation to generation. Of that taciturn tradition-breaking European who by one great gesture created Banana Bottom and placed it among the first of independent expatriate—Negro villages. The village would have been proud if Crazy Bow had been able to make good at books and go into the Civil Service, the place where all the intelligent light-coloured young men went. So many black boys had pushed up out of the canefields from under the fat spreading bananas and forced their way into clerical and scholastic places, it would have been most fitting and admirable if a mixed-blood descendant of that unpuritan liberator who helped to give the black boys their chance had made the grade himself.

One Saturday noon Bita and Crazy were romping together in the caressing fox-tail grass sloping down to the Cane River. The Cane River for about ten chains was the natural boundary of Jordan Plant's property.

As they romped, Bita got upon Crazy Bow's breast and began rubbing her head against his face. Crazy Bow suddenly drew himself up and rather roughly he pushed Bita away and she rolled off a little down the slope.

Crazy Bow took up his fiddle, and sitting under a low and shady guava tree he began to play. He played a sweet tea-meeting love song. And as he played Bita went creeping upon her hands and feet up the slope to him and listened in the attitude of a bewitched being.

And when he had finished she clambered upon him again and began kissing his face. Crazy Bow tried to push her off. But Bita hugged and clung to him passionately. Crazy Bow was blinded by temptation and lost control of himself and the deed was done.

In the late afternoon when Anty Nommy (so the village affectionately named Bita's stepmother and aunt Naomi) called Bita to go to the grocery shop she noticed that she did not run off skipping as usual, but that she waddled painfully. Anty Nommy called Bita back and examined her and found blood upon her shift.

Anty Nommy discovered that Bita had had her first sexual affair. "Befoh de time!" she exclaimed in a panic. Jordan Plant was away with his dray at the far market. So Anty Nommy ran to the house of the midwife of Banana Bottom, Sister Phibby Patroll, who could only certify that the deed had been done and Bita confessed to her that it was by the person of Crazy Bow.

Sister Phibby Patroll was a member of the famous Delgado clan of the Banana Bottom region and combined with her efficiency as midwife had the reputation of being preeminently the village looselip. She boasted that she could tell the symptoms of a female with child before she herself knew her own condition, and to many of Banana Bottom's babies she had given fathers other than the recognized ones. When Jordan Plant got back home the deflowering of his daughter was the talk of the countryside. He would have liked to hush the matter up, but it was too late. Crazy

Bow was arrested, tried in the criminal court, and sent to the madhouse.

The pride and joy of the Reverends Malcolm and Priscilla Craig in Bita as a development of their idea were full and unconcealed. After the cantata they held a reception on the veranda of the mission-house, shaded and heavy-scented with Jamaica evergreens and flowering plants: variegated tanias and crotons, wild plaintains, hibiscus, bell-flowers, bluebells and honeysuckle.

The announcement of the performance of the Coloured Choristers with Bita at the piano had brought out all the lesser local élite. A lawyer, a shopkeeper of Spanish-Jewish descent, the postmaster, the druggist, the dentist, the schoolmasters of four denominational schools and their wives, all trooped elegantly up the broad low wooden-slabbed staircase with sweet "welcome home" on their lips for Bita. And after them the common church folk crowded in. The members of the choir in gay prints, the young men in drills and stiff-starched collars, and the women of the older generation beaming under gleaming bandanna head-kerchiefs.

This day celebrated the sum of joy in the clerical career of the Reverends Malcolm and Priscilla Craig. They were happy in a praise-Godly humble way over their handiwork. The transplanted African peasant girl that they had transformed from a brown wildling into a decorous cultivated young lady.

Bita was one precious flowering of a great work. Not only the work of Malcolm and Priscilla Craig. But of the pioneers who had preceded them in that field and whose tradition was the living breath of their work. In that glorious epoch that marks the end of the eighteenth and the beginning of the nineteenth century a band of zealous nonconformists went forth to the famous and fertile slave belt of the New World to preach the Word to the Quashees. To bring to the jungle creatures Light. But they were soon aware that to preach the Light it was also necessary to teach. But the men who waxed rich upon black folk in the dark were opposed to the Light. That started the great crusade for Freedom and Light for jungle folk. While some assailed the strongholds of nonconformists of religious and social slavocracy in Europe, others set forth to labour in the fields. Generally they were called missionaries. But upon examination the best of them will be found to be very different in spirit from the popular idea of missionaries prevailing today.

Many of those crusaders enrolled as missionaries because it was in that way only they could strive for the ideal then that fired the world: universal human freedom. They came from all ranks. Enlightened scions of historical families and others that were poor in means but rich in spirit, all fighting shoulder to shoulder like men pressed pellmell together in a conscript army.

Malcolm Craig was directly descended from that crusading line. His grandfather had founded the Jubilee mission around which had grown the town. By blood he was not connected with any of the great names green in native legend. But his wife was straight out of one of the first of the historical families, from which had sprung a famous gentleman abolitionist.

The island colony was rich enough in suchlike personages. And the local newspapers often dug down to serve them up as interesting colonial items. Creoles who claimed unquestionable blood relationship to men and women who were famous in varying degrees in European annals: in war, politics, letters and high society.

"Praise God, from whom all blessings flow."

The choir sang, joined lustily by the congregation at the end of the cantata. And standing in the first row, supported by deacons and leaders, Malcolm and Priscilla Craig sang with the people. Praise God for all things. For the cantata. For the choristers. For the mission. For the natives' love of religion. And for Bita.

Tiny beside her well-built husband, the always austere face of Priscilla Craig was flushed with an almost beatific light as she sang, thinking of the work and the result.

2

"You may wrap her up in silk,
You may trim her up with gold,
And the prince may come after
To ask for your daughter,
But Crazy Bow was first."

THE RAPE OF BITA AND THE CONFINEMENT OF CRAZY
Bow had inspired the native musicians to make a sugary
ditty, and soon the countryside was ringing with rakish
singing.

It was a toothsome tale for reasons unrelated to the deed
itself. Jordan Plant was a leading peasant. He had acquired
the best acres of any small proprietor in Banana Bottom.
He was a leader in the church and the preferred friend
of Malcolm Craig, whose grandfather had founded the
Banana Bottom mission. And Bita was his only child, surely
destined for nice bringing-up. When she finished the village school at fourteen she was certain to be sent to some
sort of girls' school, low or middling class. And before she
was thirteen she had fallen into the profound pit that
yawned between the plane of the peasantry and higher
achievement.

Young Africa, expatriate, emancipated, turning out of
barracoons and huts, pressing forward, eager eyes fixed
upon the Light held high by a white hand, tripping and
falling ingloriously in the sweet snare of the flesh.

Bound on a preaching or a teaching way, the main civilizing professions for the dark peasantry, and almost unawares dropping down in the pit, never to reach out and press on again. Pretty dark damsels and brilliant bucks face townward, cityward. Turn back to the cane-fields to rearing little pickaninnies under the long cool banana shadows.

But poor Bita hadn't even known the bitterness of hope and defeat. . . .

Sister Phibby Patroll succeeded in being the first to take the story to the Craigs at Jubilee. The Craigs had an interest in Banana Bottom sentimental as much as Christian. Crazy Bow's great-grandfather had given the lot to Malcolm Craig's grandfather when he founded the mission. The old giant was opposed to preaching people on principle, but he did admire the work of the nonconformist pioneers in the West Indies.

Sister Phibby started overnight for Jubilee, walking the way. The town was fifteen miles from Banana Bottom. Since Jubilee was not a regular market town for everyday going, Sister Phibby made a pretense of taking a dozen of nice sugar-heads to the Craigs. So with the sugar basketed on her head and her shoes slung on top she started out, burning to deliver herself of the news, her figure remarkable in the road and much broader than actual from the two stiff-starched brown calico petticoats under the spreading and noisy print frock.

So Sister Phibby told the tale to Priscilla Craig. And although she thought it was a sad thing as a good Christian should, her wide brown face betrayed a kind of primitive satisfaction as in a good thing done early. Not so that of Priscilla Craig's. It was a face full of high-class anxiety, a face that generations upon generations of Northern training in reserve, restraint and Christian righteousness had gone to cultivate, a face fascinating in its thin benevolent austerity.

If there was anything that Priscilla Craig and her fellow workers in Christ were agreed on in discussing the qualities of the natives, their faults and their virtues, it was the lack of restraint among them. Where the law of the land was concerned they were quite docile in obedience. But in the moral law generally they were so lax. They did not seem to grasp the meaning of the high social significance of existence. Sex was approached too easily. And for that reason some of the most promising young men and young women who had been chosen or had chosen the preaching and teaching professions often found themselves halted and worthless in the midst of their career. It wasn't because these people were oversexed, but simply because they seemed to lack that check and control that was supposed to be distinguishing of humanity of a higher and more complex social order and that they were apparently incapable of comprehending the opprobrium of breeding bastards in a Christian community.

"Poor child!" said Priscilla Craig.

"Yes, poor child," echoed Sister Phibby. . . . "But she was ober-womanish ob a ways the folkses them say."

"That's no reason she should have been abused," said Priscilla Craig.

"Temptation, Missis," sighed Sister Phibby, "and the poor fool was mad! What kyan a poah bady do ag'inst a great big temptation?"

"Pray to God, of course, Sister Phibby," said Mrs. Craig.

Jordan Plant was making preparations to send Bita to

a relative in the city. But before he was ready Malcolm and Priscilla Craig drove up to Banana Bottom to see him. To Jordan Plant their visit was a surprise and their proposal an amaze. They had come prepared to take and educate Bita, bringing her up as their own child. And Jordan Plant would have the right to take her whenever he liked. That very day Bita drove in the Craig carriage to Jubilee as their adopted child.

Mrs. Craig had suggested to her husband that they might do something for Bita. Her whole being was moved with compassion for the girl. She felt hurt to the quick that a child, apparently a promising child, should be blunted in the blood like that. The incident gave her the idea of taking Bita to train as an exhibit. It was easy to imagine what would become of a girl like Bita if she were just allowed to drift along with the stigma upon her. The countryside was overrun with runts of girls who had been wantonly introduced to the ways of womanhood before maturity. Mrs. Craig wanted to demonstrate what one such girl might become by careful training . . . by God's help.

For Malcolm Craig, frank, hearty, God-praising soul, it was not impossible to scent something of God's mysterious ways in the rape of Bita and her subsequent coming under his mission roof. It was giving him an opportunity to demonstrate in full the measure of the family friendship that began with his father between the Craigs and the Plants, the white man and the black. The sentimental friendship began from the time when Jaban Plant, Jordan's father, took his stand with the Reverend Angus Craig, the father of Malcolm, during the coffee scandal.

Jaban was a native son of Jubilee and, having a job as

local agent and purchaser of native produce, chiefly coffee, he used to explore the most inaccessible backwoods to get the beans and bring them donkeyback into Jubilee.

The flush season for coffee used to be just around Christmas time. And then the price was always lowest. Later, in the winter and spring the price would mount up sometimes to over twice the original amount. But the poor peasants living with immediate needs from crop to crop had perforce to sell during the flush season. And they always complained, believing that the big white dealers kept the price low at the opening of the season because they knew the peasants were bound to sell.

One year the price of coffee soared from threepence a pound during the flush season to ninepence in the spring. The peasants made a lot of sad noise about their misfortune. That touched the Reverend Angus Craig and caused him to think out the scheme for the next year. Getting the bigger peasants to pool collectively their coffee and hold it over for the spring selling season.

It came as natural to Angus Craig to act for the peasants in practical matters as to pray for them, for he felt and presided over Jubilee like a patriarch. Wasn't the place founded by his father who had built a temporary palm booth to worship God with the slaves on the site that was now occupied by the spacious grey-stone building called the Free Church?

Since then, after the emancipation, the Wesleyans had come, the Presbyterians and even the Anglicans who the nonconformists had named AntiChrist in the tropical heat of the anti-slavery conflict. The Free Church was nearer perhaps to the Baptists among the nonconformist sects. But it was free. About the time of the founding of the mission there was a movement among the nonconformists making for unity to stand serried together against the slavocracy and the Anglican Church. For in the old days the pious aristocratic slaveowners had their Anglican chapels upon the great estates.

The founder of Jubilee, more abolitionist than sectarian, and backed by a wealthy layman, had made his church nonsectarian as a practical contribution towards unity. But he had not been much imitated. In the whole colony there were only three other Free Churches. In the Free Church there were no rigid sectarian rules. Immersion was practised. But persons from other denominations who adhered to sprinkling and who wanted to enter the Free Church were admitted without being obliged to undergo another baptismal rite.

Even the name of the town originated with the ardent abolitionist who, to celebrate the Declaration of Emancipation, christened the mission, The Jubilee Free Church. Before it was a nameless Quashee appendage of the Goldenrun estate. . . .

The proposal of the preacher was eagerly accepted by the natives and became known as the Free Church coffee pool. A campaign was started exhorting all the peasants to store their produce. All the peasants who could fill an export-price bag of coffee brought it in. Some of the prosperous peasants turned in as many as ten.

That late autumn the price for coffee began fairly well, better than the two preceding seasons, with a few cents more. The peasants exulted over that, taking it as a sign that coffee would make a record price in the spring. But as the spring drew near the price of coffee diminished until it touched the lowest level in the history of the bean as West Indian commodity.

Dismay struck the hearts of the peasants. Many of them were put to sore pecuniary efforts to hold their coffee over, renouncing the Christmas feasting of pig and fowl and wheat bread, and doing with green-boiled bananas and salt herrings.

The reverend Angus Craig went among the peasants encouraging them to wait and hope. And his confident honest presence inspired assurance. They waited, trusting in God and believing that the market would turn better. But the price went down and down until it touched half of what it was at the beginning of the early coffee season.

Some native persons, chiefly those who were employed in minor posts by the whites as shop clerks, foremen on estates or domestics, and who delighted in putting on airs over those who tilled the soil, made a pretence of a fundamental knowledge of city and business affairs. . . . And they put out the story that the big buyers had deliberately slumped the price of coffee because they were infuriated by the peasants' audacity in coöperating to hold their produce over for higher prices.

The coffee had been stored in the big stables of the mission. The Reverend Angus Craig thought the only thing to do was to hold the coffee over for the next year, when the price might improve. He advised the peasants to do this and borrowed money and loaned sums to those who needed it.

The next year came. The coffee crop was a huge one with the slight trees laden to earth with the red berries. And many more bags were brought to the pool than the previous year. But there was no improvement in price.

And with the after-Christmas season the price went even lower down.

What had happened was the spreading on the world market of Brazilian coffee, competing with West Indian coffee, just as years before cheap beet sugar had challenged West Indian cane sugar, made the large-scale operating of many estates unprofitable and was a chief factor in the emancipation of the slaves.

Angus Craig counselled the peasants to sell. It was a bitter thing for him to do. His prestige, the tradition he had inherited from his father as champion of the blacks, his position as the most important preacher, because he was the son of the founder of Jubilee—all was involved in the affair.

The peasants murmured against him. Some time before that happened, Angus Craig had had to discharge his new assistant, Jacob Brown. For lack of integrity, it was said. The assistant was a new type of missionary who was ignorant of the spirit and work of the abolitionists. He was a product of an English institution for waifs and strays and was sent out to the colony when his charitable Christian training was ended.

Turned out of the Baptist fold and unable to place himself among the other Christians, Jacob Brown did not see happily into the future, having no foothold among the natives. It was then that the idea came to him of exploiting the grievance of the natives against Angus Craig. Jacob Brown gave encouragement to the murmuring of the natives; he added to it by whispering innuendoes. And soon it was being said among the credulous natives that Angus Craig had made an underhand deal with the produce-dealers and that he had persuaded the people to pool their produce and thus suffer loss for some obscure reason.

The next thing that amazed Jubilee was Jacob Brown beating a big drum and singing salvation hymns and calling the people to follow him. They did. First and second generations of slaves they had trusted in simple faith to a man who had inherited the leadership that had been devoted to their freedom. They had trusted him in spiritual and in material things. He had failed them. They had suffered loss. Their faith in him was shattered.

The Free Church folk had never known why Jacob Brown was dropped as assistant. The thing had been done quietly after a consultation between Angus Craig and members of the executive of the Baptist body who were responsible for Jacob Brown's appointment. Among the church members it was whispered vaguely that it was an affair of mortal sin involving one of the best native families of the congregation.

To the people Jacob Brown was a warm-speaking young white man, appearing very nice. And now that he was preaching to them such homely truths concerning their material existence, things that Angus Craig never mentioned from the pulpit, there was no doubt that he was wise.

Jacob Brown led the people to an open lot in the town and under a grand trumpet tree he roused them to revival frenzy with that strange mixture of social aphorisms and celestial analysis that became his principal weapon throughout his career of holding the natives under his spell.

" 'Some trust in chariots and some in horses, but we will remember the name of the Lord our God.'

" 'All ye like sheep have gone astray. . . .'

"You have been led astray by men who were not God-appointed to lead. Men who got their positions easily. Men who have never suffered hardship themselves so that they could understand your own suffering. Jesus said: 'Feed my sheep,' but you have been robbed of your food for the wolves.

"Which of us is fit to lead? How can we know the true leader from the false? Only by praying to God and waiting for His answer. We can all pray, black, brown and white, learned and ignorant. There is no difference before God. The prayer of a poor ignorant person may reach him quicker than that of a great wise man. Let us ask him for a leader. All of us altogether. We need a true leader for these trying times. A leader sent by God. Let us ask him for one. Let us pray. . . .

"I have seen the vision with the people and I feel I am called to lead and I will lead. I will be your leader in the name of the Lord.

> " 'Lord Jesus, build upon me too
> As upon Peter as a rock,
> And help me ever be a true
> And worthy leader of your flock. . . .' "

Jacob Brown beat the drum and sang to the easy swinging tune. And the dark voices joined him, swelling lustily.

" 'Upon this rock I will build my church!'

"And upon this place I would build a church to the glory of God for the worship of God. And I would call it the Ark, dedicating it to the faithful, those who flee from pain and sorrow, deceit and loss in harvesting and exchanging, buying and selling, to find refuge and solace in the Ark of the Lord."

Upon that open lot in Jubilee the foundation of the Ark

was laid in the shape of a monmouth palm booth. There the people deserting the Jubilee Free Church flocked under the big drumming of the self-ordained Reverend Jacob Brown. And in spite of the pecuniary pinch they were undergoing and which had reduced them to salted-herring-and-green-banana rations they forked up pennies and shillings for the material sustenance of Jacob Brown. Right then even it was suggested that that lot was consecrated ground and efforts made to purchase it. And the first money was subscribed by the enthusiastic black rebels in religion. And today the Ark may be visited in Jubilee, a little monument to the springing of a new faith from black despair under the involuntary shifting of material values.

A Sunday came when only one native presence in the Jubilee Free Church beside his own family saved Angus Craig from preaching to an empty house. That broke the will of Angus Craig. His father had bought the Jubilee property and so it was his by right. Angus Craig mortgaged it to pay the peasants the difference that was lost between the price available during the season when they stored the coffee and the price for which they sold.

Although his will was broken, Angus Craig kept his faith. And it was strengthened by the only worshipper who remained believing in him. That worshipper was Jordan Plant's father. As a small produce-purchaser Jaban Plant's business had been almost ruined by Angus Craig's pooling scheme. For the peasants up in the high hills and the woods whom he used to hunt down for produce had all refused to sell. They were attracted by the pool. But as agent for a city dealer Jaban Plant knew that the fall of coffee was real and a little of what was the cause of it. When he tried to convince the peasants of the truth they accused him of being the accomplice of Angus Craig. But he maintained his position and was the only officer left in the Free Church. And thus was sprung the close sentimental friendship between the Craig and the Plant family.

Angus Craig was succeeded in his work by his younger son Malcolm. He lived long enough after the coffee crisis to see one-half of his members sneak back shamedfacedly to the Free Church. But the Ark had a successful time drumming up the natives (it was the only church that used a drum Salvation Army fashion) and gained many new adherents with the opening up of the American market for the banana and the natural growth of the town.

After the coffee crisis Angus Craig made a resolve to train a native to succeed him at the Free Church. But he did not live to do it. Three things he urged Malcolm to remember: the bond of friendship between the Craig and the Plant family; to help forward by all means whenever and wherever he could the training of black and brown folk to lead themselves; the paying off of the mortgage on the Jubilee church property.

He died hating Jacob Brown and bequeathed his hatred to his son Malcolm. Once when he was attending a meeting of ministers for hurricane relief Jacob Brown walked in among them. And Angus Craig walked out. He never veiled his animosity by hypocrisy. When Jacob Brown grew strong and pushed himself to a prominent place in the secular life of the colony a few business men, friends of both preachers, tried to bring about a reconciliation. But Angus Craig refused to stoop to a dirty reconciliation when his heart held a clean hatred. He was reminded of the Christian exhortation: Love your enemies. And in reply quoted Israel: I have hated the unjust; and have loved Thy law.

Native leadership became his mania after the coffee trouble. He preached it from his pulpit and wherever he went in the colony assisting at missionary meetings, harvest festivals and church conferences. He even said that the black folk having been freed from the bondage of unrewarded toil they needed also to be freed from white magic so that they might develop as a people. He thought it was the magic of the white skin that made possible the easy conquests of the Jacob Browns. If the leaders were of their own tribe the people might be less gullible and more sceptical, quicker to question the neat phrases of a ready tongue. And even if they were betrayed by their own, it wouldn't be such a soul-sickening thing as the sheer banditry without subtlety of execution passing legitimately under the popular hypotheses of white superiority and dark inferiority and the "survival of the fittest." Let them be fooled and exploited by their own. It would be more tolerable, more human.

Jordan's father had five children, all boys. Two by his first concubine and three by his second concubine, who, after his conversion to Christianity, was made his legal wife by the Reverend Angus Craig. The two first boys had emigrated to Colon to find work during the first attempt to cut the Panama Canal. The eldest of the second woman had gone Panamaway, too, to find his brothers after his failure to qualify as a schoolmaster. And they never communicated with their island folk again. The second of the second woman had followed his father's *métier*, travelling from town to town and village to village, buying and selling native produce, but not making enough to settle down, in disgust he had at last ended up in the city by enlisting in the army.

And Jordan after his father's death had gone back with his mother to the village of Banana Bottom, where she was born and where she had a lot of land. That lot he began cultivating and adding to until he became the most prosperous peasant of the village.

Rooted in the soil, Jordan then was obviously the one thriving Plant. Besides its incidental basis, the friendship between him and Malcolm was linked closely with the time when they both played together as boys on the mission land, swimming, marbles, bird-hunting, fruit-gathering, foot-racing.

Malcolm Craig had wanted to adopt Herald Newton, the son of Deacon Day and train him for the ministry, eventually to succeed him at Jubilee. For the Craig line, clerically, was running out with Malcolm. He and Priscilla had only one child, that could not talk and had developed into an adult without getting beyond the creeping stage. The natives called him Patou, which was the dialect word for screech-owl, because he was subject to recurring crises when he would suddenly double up and make an eerie noise like a screech-owl.

But Mrs. Craig could not stand the idea of adopting a boy, with her own son living in a cripple-idiot state. Her intellect was partial to her husband's plan, but the failure in making a son of her own made her heart revolt. With a girl it was different. A girl could never arouse in her that inexplicably bitter resentment that a boy would.

And besides she was something of a feminist. A relative in England was a crusading suffragette. She sympathized with the movement and subscribed to its literature. As an ordained clergywoman (of whom there were two only in the colony) carrying on her work successfully and in harmonious coöperation with her husband, she believed that women were quite capable of political action and filling positions that were concentrated in the hands of men.

At Jubilee Bita surprised the Craigs themselves by straightly taking their hearts and brightening up the family life of the mission. Surprised them in that they didn't have to make any special Christian effort to regard her as their own child.

When she joined them at the breakfast table in the morning she had to kiss first Malcolm and then Priscilla Craig. And it was as natural to them as kissing Patou and more pleasing, for Patou often resented kissing with an impish reaction. Priscilla Craig's austere face would relax pleasingly at Bita's climbing a cashew tree. Her husband seemed to enjoy Bita's being a little tomboy outdoors, especially as she was so correct in the mission, fitting into the life of the place like one of his books of sermons on the shelf in his study. She was as apt at learning croquet as she was at the piano. Priscilla Craig herself carried forward her instruction in books and Bita's progress was such that at the end of two years Mrs. Craig was seized by the idea of giving her the benefit of a thoroughly English education.

She could afford it because she belonged to one of the wealthiest of the abolitionist families and had plenty of money of her own. She had paid off the mortgage on the Free Church property. And the premises having fallen into disrepair, at the time of her marriage to Malcolm she had provided the funds for the reparation of the church and the building of a gallery and the remodelling of the mission house.

The more the Craigs thought of sending Bita to be educated in their motherland, the more they grew in love with the idea. During the slavery era many masters had educated their mulatto children, and some were sent to England for that purpose. It was mainly from them that had developed the efficient light-coloured middle class of the colony. And after the emancipation some of those mulattoes and quadroons that had succeeded to the estates of their parents sent their own children abroad to be educated.

Also before the emancipation an English nobleman had sponsored the education of a pure black student at one of the great English universities. The student won high honours and wrote poems in Latin. But when he returned to the colony and his patron tried to experiment with him by placing him on the basis of his education, the social obstacles proved insurmountable. And the Negro became a very wretched man with his high English education between his contemptuous English masters and their slaves. But after the emancipation black and brown men had gone abroad to be educated as professional men returning to work among their people. But it was an unique thing for a Negro girl to have that splendid privilege.

Tabitha Plant going away to be educated abroad! (Tabitha was the full name, but the village had abbreviated it to Bita. And the Craigs had liked that better, as everybody did; so Tabitha was dropped for Bita.)

Bita going abroad. The peasants were stunned by the news and gossiped about nothing else. And there was not a dark family in Banana Bottom and that gorgeous stretch of tropical country that did not wish one of their children had been in Bita's shoes and had been instead the victim of Crazy Bow.

30

And the song was remembered in the hills again, but with all honour to Bita.

"You may wrap her up in silk,
You may trim her up with gold,
And the prince may come after
To ask for your daughter,
But Crazy Bow was first."

3

BITA HAD HAD SEVEN YEARS' SOUND EDUCATION. PRISCILLA Craig had conceived the idea of redeeming her from her past by a long period of education without any contact with Banana Bottom, and at the finish she would be English trained and appearing in everything but the colour of her skin.

And so during her years of higher education and refinement Bita had never come back home to a vacation among her native people and things. Twice Priscilla Craig had visited her at the school. At the end of the third year and the summer before that of her coming home. On that second visit Priscilla had taken Bita to Germany as a holiday gift and to round out her education. It was the time when that country was something like a hobby among serious-minded and right-thinking people. Even in a far-away little British colony.

Little children, even little coloured children, were given books of German fairy tales for Sunday-school and elementary-school prizes, and at Christmas time with Santa Claus there were German picture tales of starry Christmas trees and quaint little pink-cheeked children in mufflers and sabots, with strange little things like myriads of white moths wind-blown about them that were named snow, and they waving to one another and crying: *Auf Wiedersehen!*
Auf Wiedersehen!

And some that grew older and went a little farther from Sunday-school and grade to more entertaining literature learned also more of the country of quaint Christmas tales and the pretty *Auf Wiedersehen*. If they reached as far out as reading Shakespeare, they might have heard that there was a great poet whom cultured Englishmen put next to Shakespeare and that his name was Goethe. And that that great man had lived in the very century in which they were born. And if they were curious about higher music, they would know that a race of musical giants had sprung from that country.

So Priscilla Craig, a proud descendant of militant Protestants, had never felt so rare travelling as when she took her brown ward of Protestantism voyaging through the Fatherland of the founder of that cult. And Bita had been introduced to the charms of Munich and Dresden and Leipzig, the Rhine towns and the birthplaces of Goethe and Beethoven.

. . . .

At eight o'clock Bita entered the study of Malcolm Craig for the morning prayer. Priscilla Craig was already there, perusing her Bible, and raising her eyes to say sweetly, "Good morning, Bita," immediately was absorbed in the pages again, reading silently but with her lips in motion, thus preserving whole that feeling of sanctity that always inspired her from the moment of rising to the hour of prayer.

In a few minutes Malcolm Craig stepped lightly in, saying in a low tone, "Good morning," and seating himself in his armchair before the large red-edged Morocco-bound family Bible set in a mahogany frame that was well polished by Rosyanna's hands.

He was a tall man, finely-proportioned, and might have cut a handsome figure as an army officer. He was a little stoop-shouldered (perhaps deliberately trained), but it went right with his presence as a parson. His lean face had that wistful and sometimes irritating look of a person who made a hobby of humility and was always in communication with God. His manner of walking was remarkable, as if he thought he was always treading on holy ground and afraid of exhibiting by strong strides the natural strength of his body. Such a strapping, robust man might have seemed almost incongruous as a humble follower and preacher of Jesus if it were not for the fact of his unshaken belief in the Word he preached, in the black peasants, and in the mission and its spiritual and social influence over them, which revealed him in perfect harmony with his work and his environment.

A song from Sankey was sung. Malcolm Craig opened the Bible and read a psalm of praise. As he finished, Rosyanna shuffled in wiping her hand on her apron, and took her unchanging seat near the door. While her ear was attuned to prayer, her face betrayed the fact that her heart was in the kitchen, occupied with the breakfast which she had already prepared, carrying it to the point where it would be ready to be served right after the morning's devotion was over.

"Let us pray," said Malcolm Craig, and they knelt down against their chairs, closing their eyes while Malcolm prayed for all—for the mission and the flock. And when he was finished all repeated together The Lord's Prayer.

.   .   .   .

Sitting on the back veranda of the mission, Priscilla Craig conversed with Bita about the work of the place and her new duties. It was generally understood that Bita would be an auxiliary at the mission. Her training had been directed towards that end; therefore it came to her quite natural to fit into place. The secretary-treasurership of the Sunday school was now hers. And she would share the job of organist with Priscilla. And help the schoolmaster with the Band of Hope.

From the porch it was a precious view of the community that had sprung up around the church on the hillock. Below there were three neat parallel streets containing the oblong edifices of the Wesleyan Church, the courthouse with its big yard, the post office, the dry-goods store, with one street curving uphill suddenly, at the top of which was the rectory half hidden by tree ferns and lime trees, and in between the grey-white gable-end cottages set in their flower gardens. And winding out away towards a little banana port a chalky macadamized road passing tilled fields of coffee, yams and sweet potatoes, with pimento and avocado pear and naseberry trees and little white-washed shingled houses. The pimento trees were straight, long and silver-brown coloured, and so many in that region that the parish was called the spice-field of the colony.

Priscilla remarked that she had once thought of disbanding the Band of Hope. For when she first settled in Jubilee she had considered it superfluous. The natives were contented with mild drinks like orange wine and ginger beer. But now so many of them were getting the habit of the hot Jamaica rum. The parsons and all the pious people were alarmed at the change.

"It's the Panama Canal," said Priscilla. "Our Negroes

are not the same after contact with the Americans. They come back ruder."

Bita replied, "But they make more money there, though. The least two dollars a day, they say. And here they get only a shilling. Eight times more gain over there."

"And a loss of eight times eighty in native worth. They come back hard-drinking and strutting with bad manners, loud clothes and louder jewellery.

"I don't like it," continued Priscilla. "Times may be hard here and our black folk terribly poor. But I like them better so than when they come back peacocks from Panama."

"Money makes a big difference, though," said Bita.

"There was quite a stir about a blade from Banana Bottom called Tacky or some such name. He got in wrong with the police here drinking mad. They say he respects nothing and nobody. He talks Yankee, the nasal accent with the Negro dialect. And they say it's as funny as it's awful. He has been to Panama three times, and each time comes back with more money. Don't know how he does it, for he doesn't seem to stay long enough to work for it. Your father says all the up-country lads want to imitate him. They all want to go to Panama."

"They say the construction is a mighty work and the black labour the best down there," Bita remarked pridefully, "especially the Jamaicans and Haitians."

"Yes, but it is a pity that that Canal is swallowing up some of our best native lads who might be better here using their talents as preachers and teachers," said Mrs. Craig. "Deacon Day's younger son has just gone that way, too. He was a promising lad. As much as his brother. The schoolmaster said he was the best monitor he ever had."

Jerry Muggling, the coachman, appeared with the mail from the post office. There was a big batch of English newspapers and magazines, most of which had been subscribed by friends and well-wishers of Priscilla Craig and the mission. And conspicuous among the letters were two bright picture post cards from the city of Kingston bearing greetings for Mrs. Craig and Bita from the elder son of Deacon Day, Herald Newton, who was a theological student.

Herald Newton Day came largely into the plan of the life that lay before Bita. Although Malcolm Craig had not adopted the son of his senior deacon, he had been assiduous in suggesting and promoting his career, and it was thought locally that Herald would succeed Malcolm Craig at Jubilee some day. Also it was local talk that Bita was being educated for Herald or Herald trained for Bita. Bita was aware of it. And the Craigs were partial to the idea. An idea which they were only too conscious of having created. A cultured native couple succeeding to one of the finest missions in the colony. That in the minds of the Craigs would be the best tribute to their labour, the most fitting fulfilment to the pioneer purpose that lay behind the founding and building of Jubilee and the perfect crowning of Angus Craig's thought.

"A very worthy young man," Priscilla Craig said, fingering his card. "Sometimes I am assailed by wicked doubts about our work here, but I regain confidence when I think of a type of young man like Mr. Day. The hope of the colony lies in his type."

"He was nice coming to the boat to meet me," said Bita.

"He *is* nice and I am glad you think he is. No doubt he will succeed us here some day when we retire—or die. If that is the will of God. Deacon Day is always talking about you two together." Mrs. Craig affected a trifling smile.

"Everybody seems to be," Bita laughed.

"How people will tattle!" said Mrs. Craig. "But that is not so bad when it is about a good thing."

Patou crept through the light bamboo swinging door and pathetically blinked his big brown owl's eyes at the women. For an instant Mrs. Craig's face was changed by a shadow of revulsion, but she called cheerily to her son and went quickly to him.

Bita left them together and went round to the kitchen. That morning she was going marketing with Rosyanna.

From the front veranda of the mission one could look down on the market. It was a vast square where the peasants used to come down from the mountain to barter and sell in the open before Jubilee grew to be a town. Now it was fenced in, half stone wall, half wire. At one end a long shingled shed with stalls for meats and poultry, grain, sugar and other native products, and at the other another shed packed with donkeys, mules and horses hitched close together and biting, scratching and kicking one another, and in between the wide uncovered ground, where the majority of the peasants sat together dispensing with the cost of stalls and crying their stuff under the merciless blazing sun.

The market was the centre of the town. A main macadamized road from the city, another from the little fruit port, and one coming down sharply from the mountains over Banana Bottom picked up the footways and mule tracks winding out of the greeny blue and fruiting little villages, and converged upon the market.

Rosyanna, broad, dark blue and spreading like a pruned orange tree, was joyful to go marketing with Bita for a change, anticipating some novel first-hand news which she could retail to the sisters of her set. Rosyanna was the low-down news agent between the mission and the town. She emphasized the importance of her being a servant of the mission by getting hold of first news, such as what preacher was exchanging pulpit with Malcolm or Priscilla Craig on such a Sunday, what church member was going to be invited to dine with the visiting preacher, and what date was fixed for a harvest festival or missionary meeting. But of the private life of the mission she had little to say, for outside of the household items, Mrs. Craig was as uncommunicative as she looked.

So Rosyanna rocked and dropped splay-footed along beside Bita, swinging her basket and chattering about Jubilee in a general way, with Bita nodding neutrally and absentmindedly to all she said, for Bita was thinking other thoughts. But soon Rosyanna gave her a jog by asking pointedly if Bita had seen Herald Day in town and did Bita know when he would be coming over to Jubilee. Bita said no to the second part only of Rosyanna's question, and not very pleasantly.

"But you no know one day him's gwinea take Revrin' Craig place hyah at Jubilee? Eberybody know dat."

But Bita said she was uninterested about that in a manner that made Rosyanna think that she was going to be as uncommunicative outside domestic matters even as Mrs. Craig, and set her down as haughty and putting on white folks' airs.

Just outside the gate of the market Bita met Belle Black, who had already done her marketing, having taken a basket of eggs to sell and finishing early. She was now going home provisioned with meat and sugar and yam. With her was a thin-made young man of a banana-bark-brown colour locally known as Hopping Dick. He was the son of Amos Delgado, the slickest horsedealer of Jubilee, and got his nickname from his curious habit of stepping hoppingly like a bird called Hopping Dick. He had a reputation of being wild.

Belle Black exclaimed joyfully over Bita, and Hopping Dick, standing by expectantly, got introduced to her. Now Hopping Dick was not well thought of among nice church people, although he was always with Belle Black, the leading treble of the Coloured Choristers. But Belle's position was a little equivocal also. She was the daughter of the drummer Nias Black and his concubine, Emma. Her parents lived comfortably together and had resisted all persuasion to get married and become church members. Nevertheless, as a maker and expert player of drums Nias Black was often the chief performer at picnics and other festivals connected with the churches. And as he was thus always mingling with the church people, they took him kindly as a good sinner. Belle was accepted like her father because she had a high thrilling voice, but like many of the choir girls she was not a church member nor a candidate to be. The good sisters of the church wished that Belle's home life was as good as her voice. They thought it was over-slack. For Nias Black played the drums for all the tea-meetings and yard dances and weddings, and the ungodly set often met and caroused in his house.

Hopping Dick was an outstanding member of the ungodly set. He assisted his father in his profession, and that profession was considered as tricky as gambling. The shrewd swapping of horses and mules, donkeys and oxen, and the palming off of sick and worthless beasts. And Hopping Dick was a dandy thing, a great and ever-welcome dancer and buyer of things at the tea-meetings, and fine-strutting in the peg-top clothes that were then the fashion.

Bita did slow marketing. For there were many Free Church people at the market, some selling eggs and cakes and buns; others cocoanut drop, banana fritters, ginger nut, and pindar cakes and suchlike titbits that they had fixed up out of the raw stuff the country people had brought down and were selling back to them. Some bartered outright, dispensing with quatties and tups, bits, shillings and florins, they exchanged chickens and ducks, cocoa balls and fish from the bay against cockstone and Congo peas, yams and yampies, breadfruit and the unrefined cane sugar that lay caked rich brown and sweet in upright oblong tins.

Three times more women than men higgling and pedlaring; broad warm faces of all colours between brown and black, sweating comfortably, freely in gay calico clothes, the full hum of their broad broken speech mounting and falling in strong waves under the sheer downright sun.

Bita mingled in the crowd, responsive to the feeling, the colour, the smell, the swell and press of it. It gave her the sensation of a reservoir of familiar kindred humanity into which she had descended for baptism. She had never had that big moving feeling as a girl when she visited the native market. And she thought that if she had never gone abroad for a period so long, from which she had become accustomed to viewing her native life in perspective, she might never had had that experience.

Many young natives had gone to the city or abroad for higher culture and had returned aloof from, if not actually despising, the tribal life in which they were nurtured. But the pure joy that Bita felt in the simple life of her girl-hood was childlike and almost unconscious. She could not reason and theorize why she felt that way. It was just a surging free big feeling.

The noises of the market were sweeter in her ears than a symphony. Accents and rhythms, movements and col-ours, nuances that might have passed unnoticed if she had never gone away, were now revealed to her in all their striking detail. And of the foodstuff on view she felt an impulse to touch and fondle a thousand times more than she wanted to buy.

Some of the church folk detained her for a few pleasant words. And she was such a long time getting done with her purchases that Rosyanna was fairly rebellious. At last they were ready to go back to the mission. Rosyanna's basket was packed and her hands full. At the moment of departure Bita spied a splendid sugar-pineapple. She bought and carried it herself, Rosyanna protesting. For at Jubilee and similar towns nice persons did not carry packets nor anything heavier than a fan or a cane. There were number-less little brats always ready to run errands and tote things. Among the aspiring native youth who got away from the soil and were being trained to use a pen profitably and read and figure fluently, it was considered quite disgraceful to use those same fingers to tote a little bundle.

One day Malcolm Craig carried a bunch of bananas on his shoulder from the market to the mission. And Priscilla could often be seen in the streets insisting on carrying a packet of her own. Thus they desired to set an example to the native population. For they believed and preached that education and material progress should not preclude the possibility of simple living.

The great founder of Jubilee had declared that the idea of his work was to help make men free and materially independent, but not in the image of their white masters. But as humanity is prone to be inspired by the imitative rather than the initiative qualities of life, there was a tendency in many who had been freed from the slavery toil and soil to efface the traces of their origin and past servitude from a sense of shame and to approximate, not to the rugged principles of the pioneers of the struggle, but rather to the antedated patterns of the vanquished class.

Swinging her pine through the main gate of the market, Bita was accosted by Hopping Dick, who, pretending that it was accidentally, struck a gallant attitude and said: "Such hands like yours, Miss Plant, were trained for finer work than to carry common things like pineapples."

"Do you think this will spoil them?" laughed Bita, who was instinctively coquettish and not the sort to turn sour over a compliment.

"Too much will, indeed," said Hopping Dick. "There's more big-foot country gals fit to carry pines than dunkeys in Jamaica. Please give me the pleasure to relieve you, as I am walking your way."

So Hopping Dick insisting, Bita allowed him to take the pine, while Rosyanna's face under her basket was heavy with disapproval. Annoyed by Hopping Dick's remark, being a country woman and barefooted, she was also amazed at his audacity in offering to walk along with Bita and her permitting it. She was a servant of the mission and a sister of the church, and Bita was too much identified with both to walk the street with a grogshop customer, a horse-gambler and a notorious feminine heart-breaker.

Hopping Dick turned on his dandiest strut walking up the main street with Bita. Out of the corner of his eye he saw a group of his set in the door of the grogshop watching him open-mouthed; but apparently unseeing he strutted more ornamentally, ostentatiously absorbed in conversation with Bita. He was as much astonished himself at what he was doing, for although he had the reputation of a fast worker and successful, it was not with girls of Bita's standard. He would never have approached Bita alone. It was just his famous luck being with Belle Black that morning and getting introduced on it. It was no wonder that people stared. After the first compliments Hopping Dick was stumped of what to say. He was very ready-tongued with the local girls in the market and at the tea-meetings, but he felt he could not use the same talk upon a person like Bita, and he wanted to shine. So the few minutes between the market and the mission were mostly spent in perfecting his strut.

Once he said: "That was one beautiful performance that you gave for the benefit of Jubilee, Miss Plant, and we all proud and talking about it."

"Oh, you were there!" said Bita.

Hopping Dick hesitated: "No I missed out, but Miss Black told me all about it. Never been much to church meetings, but I'll be going from now on whenever you play."

Now they were at the gate of the mission and Rosyanna, who had puffed out to balloon proportions in the meantime, rocked testily through without a word, leaving Bita, who stopped a moment to exchange formalities with Hopping Dick. She thanked him, taking the pine.

"You will find Jubilee too small to live in after living abroad," said Hopping Dick.

"I don't think so. I believe I could live anywhere there's air to breathe and space for free movement."

"There's not enough here. This place is too small. The whole island's too small."

"Oh well, small things are better for comfort, sometimes," and Bita said good-bye.

"Good-bye, Miss Plant. I hope I shall have the honour of more conversation with you. You're so intelligent. There aren't any intelligent young people in Jubilee."

"Not any? Not even you? Then we must find some," she said.

Whether Rosyanna informed Mrs. Craig that Bita was at the gate with Hopping Dick or Mrs. Craig had spied them from the front veranda, which gave a good view of the gate, Bita was never sure. But as soon as Mrs. Craig was alone with her she said:

"How did you meet that man? I'm sorry you've been talking to him."

"Oh, I met him with Belle Black and he offered to carry my pine."

"He's not a fit person for you to be seen in the street with, Bita. And he had no right to take advantage of your ignorance and force his company upon you. He is a brazen bad young man."

"He didn't force himself on me. He asked me if he could come and I said all right."

"Of course I excuse you. Since you're quite like a stranger here after so many years away. There are lots of things we have to talk about. You know there are certain things we just can't do, simply because they reflect on the mission."

"But I don't think walking and talking a little with Mr. Delgado could have anything to do with the mission. Even if he's not a person of the best character."

"Bita, my child! Don't try to be ridiculous. A mere child even could see the right thing to do. You have received an education to make you see and do the correct thing almost automatically. Even Rosyanna feels a certain responsibility because she is connected with the mission. And Mr. Craig and I—we put the mission first in everything. We never forget we are living examples of right conduct. That we are public servants."

Bita retired to her room. And the more she thought of the incident the more resentful she became. She wondered, now that she had come home to it after all the years of training, if she would be able to adjust herself to the life of the mission.

She had been given a good Christian education, but there had been nothing mission-school about it. For the school had undergone many changes since it was founded as "a religious institution for girls from God-fearing homes." It had a national reputation famous for its sound educational principles. And Mrs. Craig, who was very tribal underneath had preferred to give Bita the benefit of a sound national institution. Many girls were sent to that school because their mothers and grandmothers had gone there. But it was a long time gone since grandmother's days.

Now was a time of inquietude. Queen Victoria had died with the nineteenth century. And the times were full of ideas. Socialist and Feminist and Freethought. Bita remem-

bered that her aunt Nommy had written to her upon the
Queen's death, asking the truth about the rumour among
the natives, that women would have their hair cut off and
slavery reëstablished under the new king. An Englishman
running against a native politician for the local legislature
had had a hard time going against his opponent, who used
the rumour among the ignorant and superstitious peasantry
for all he could make out of it. The Englishman informed
his constituents that the king was too sensible to the charms
of all women to deprive them of any.

Bita read that part of Anty Nommy's letter to some
of the girls and it provided a great deal of merriment.
They asked her many curious questions about her native
land. In what part of the Congo it was situated. Were the
cannibals very ferocious? And would they eat white flesh
too or was their appetite restricted to dark? And when
Bita said her home was in the West Indies, they said, Oh
yes it was India and not Africa and was it North or South
India and how did she feel the first time she changed from
a fig leaf or straw apron and put on manufactured clothes
to go abroad.

That night Bita went to bed with a new book that had
arrived for Mrs. Craig. It was a novel by a Mrs. Humphry
Ward and the motif was the conflict between Faith and
Reason. She tried to read it, but could not get into the
spirit of the book and be carried away. So she lay thinking about herself and her future. Everybody among the
natives, from her father down, thought it was a magnificent and unique chance for her to have been adopted and
given a high-class education and come back to the Jubilee
Mission practically the heiress of the Craigs. But she was
full of doubt about the future. Would she be able to stand

that spiritual atmosphere—go through with what was expected of her and finally reap the material reward? There was that talk about Herald Newton Day. Would she like him enough to marry him? And would she be able to live with satisfaction the life of the mission? There was no doubt that Mrs. Craig had her own rigid ideas about the correct things that she should do. Would she be able to live up to them?

4

EMANCIPATION DAY, THE 1ST OF AUGUST! ALL OVER the island there was ringing of joybells from churches and schools for the great West Indian holiday. It was the great holiday season. More stimulating to the blacks than Christmas. And there were many festivities, sacred and secular. Harvest festivals, cantatas, picnics, pageants, horse-racing, concerts and tea-meetings. A week of rejoicing, chiefly at night among the country people, who held as many tea-meetings as at Christmas time.

For this high holiday Bita was going home to visit Banana Bottom. She had made the most careful preparation for toilet, appearance and poise, for as much as she tried to ignore it she was more apprehensive about revisiting her obscure village than she had been going abroad to Europe and visiting famous places.

She had been specially invited to Banana Bottom. The first of August had come on Sunday, and Monday was declared the official holiday. On that Sunday the Banana Bottom Church was holding its annual Sunday-school rally and Bita had been asked to play the organ and distribute the prizes to the children at the end of the performance.

On the Saturday afternoon Bita left Jubilee in the Craigs' buggy, driven by Jerry Muggling, the coachman. With her was Belle Black. Mrs. Craig didn't like Belle Black going in the buggy with Bita, but as she wasn't able to put an objection in a plausible manner she allowed it. For Belle had asked the favour of Mrs. Craig after the buggy had been given to Bita and Bita had said she would like to have Belle's company. It was the first time Belle rode in the mission carriage. Church members or their relatives were sometimes accommodated in the carriage but nearly always in cases of serious accidents or illness.

Bita spent a lot of time over her dresses, more than ever she did since her return to Jubilee. Princess gowns were the vogue in women's wear then. And she picked for the rally a copper-red one, the exact colour of the under side of a star-apple leaf. She had also made a two-piece print frock full of flowers for the Sunday-school picnic on Monday. She loved bandanna colours, like all the peasant folk of the West Indies. And although she was now too cultivated to riot in them on all occasions like the rest of the country girls (she had to wear a sort of uniform dark blue as organist at Jubilee) she anticipated with happiness the freedom of going bandanna on a picnic day.

Banana Bottom was prepared for a week of festivities. There were two other picnics besides the Sunday school's. The elementary school had announced a gala day and the rum-shop keeper a barbecue dance. And there would be about five all-night tea-meetings. These tea-meetings were the best, but Bita wouldn't be able to go, for they were discountenanced as low and rowdy affairs among the respectable church elements.

Bita started at sundown. Mrs. Craig had chosen the time. She wanted to save the horses from the heat. She was a member of the Society for the Prevention of Cruelty to Animals and had imposed upon Jerry gentleness in driving. And the way was mostly uphill.

Belle was as fluttering as a blue quit about going to the mountains. For her Jubilee, with its few hundred souls, was a great town and Banana Bottom backwoods. She teased Bita for looking so grave as if Banana Bottom was important.

They arrived with the dusk. The journey was like climbing a winding path up a straight mountain and zig-zagging down again, dropping into a long oblong valley fenced by a river on one hand and ferny hills on the other. That was Banana Bottom.

At the foot of the valley the main road came up from Gingertown to meet that from Jubilee. Right there was the hub of the village, consisting of a rum shop, a little general store, a baker shop, a tiny pharmacy, a large thatched shed for drays, a paddock for temporary feeding of mules and horses, and a big barbecue belonging to the produce-dealer for the drying of coffee and cocoa and ginger that were not perfectly dried when purchased. The village houses were not clustered together, but spreading around and along up the slope were little fields of tropical plants (yams twining upon poles, coffee, cocoa, cassava, arrowroot, ginger, and erect over all the banana) and in the midst of them little thatched and shingled, chiefly gable-end houses.

Jordan Plant's house stood midway up the slope overlooking the river, a little below the dilapidated old State House. It was a frame house of six rooms and a veranda around and fixed upon stout cogwood pillars sunk deep into the earth. Set a little way back from the village road, there was a flower-garden front full of heavy-scented hot-country flowers growing untidily thick together, bellflowers and bluebells, the night jasmine and the creeping jasmine contesting the ground with the running bramble, crotons of many colours, the climbing sweet-william trailing its tiny but strong vermilion bloom along the veranda, and the exquisitely speckled tania flowers and the delicate variegated painted-ladies.

Anty Nommy loved flowers and had a wonderful hand with them, but she had no sense of space and patterns in a garden, so the flowers grew all ways, struggling and blooming over and under one another. From the back of the house Jordan's vegetable and fruit garden went sliding green and fat down to the river.

The village was aware of Bita's coming and there was a crowd down at the Crossroads, with Jordan and her cousin Bab Plant to meet her. But if Bita was a little timid the village was quite intimidated. For in their eyes she was now a grand lady who had been to the high white folk's country and was learned in their ways, just like one of them with only the difference of pigmentation.

It was Bita who had to call those she remembered to approach her. The village and the older folk didn't seem much changed with the passing of seven years, but it was difficult to remember some of her schoolmates. Many of the girls had had children, one, two, three, some as many as five, without the benefit of a steady mate and were now heavy-footed and flabby-breasted and worried under the weight of motherhood.

What a difference between them and Bita, so neat and sweet-faced, a miracle of gentle upbringing and nice clothes. Some of them had swayed and skipped to the ditty,

"Crazy Bow was first,
Crazy Bow was first."

But the best of them had wished afterwards that what Crazy Bow had done to Bita had been done to them. The village had long ago buried and forgotten the tune. But it had remained in Bita's life and often came humming in her head at the most unexpected moments.

The dinner was ready at home. It was a good dinner, although Anty Nommy was reserving the best for Sunday, the big day. Anty Nommy was expert in the kitchen. She was working as a cook for the owner of the General Store at Gingertown when Jordan married her. The village had gossiped much about Jordan's marrying his sister-in-law. Because when Jordan was courting Bita's mother, Anty Nommy became with child and gave birth to a boy. Anty Nommy named one of the near-backra of Gingertown, but the father disowned the act, so Bita's mother had taken the child to Banana Bottom to leave her sister free to work. It was called Barnaby, which had been abbreviated to Bab. Gossip tried to make out that Bab was really Jordan's child. And it was renewed when Bita's mother died in childbirth and Jordan married Anty Nommy one year after. But the fact belied the theory. For Jordan was black, Anty Nommy the colour of a young cocoa-plant leaf, and Bab was as ripe as a banana.

The table was spread for six. Bita and Belle, Jordan and Anty Nommy, Bab, and Jerry the coachman. There were a girl and a boy who brought in the food from the kitchen, which was a separate building from the house. The poorest natives, especially girls with illegitimate children, who were legion, had a custom of placing such children in better-off homes where they became as one of the family, doing little household and field tasks for their board and keep. There were three such in the Plant home.

Anty Nommy, tall, straight and thin-faced, with a bandanna wound cone-shaped around her head, served the thick Congo-pea soup, seasoned with salted beef and scallion from a big long-bottomed bowl. Then followed stewed goat meat, the sauce high-coloured with annatto, and a large flat dish with an assortment of native vegetables, the yellow and flowery afou yam, bourbon-pink cocoes and fine mashed cho-chos.

It was pure native cooking and serving, home cooking such as Bita was used to as a girl, and it tickled deliciously her palate. It was native food, of course, she had been eating since her return to Jubilee. But it was not just the same at the mission table. The Europeans had many of the native foods prepared in their own way, different from the native style.

After the dinner she went out on to the barbecue with her cousin. Bab twitted Bita about her officiating at the Sunday-school rally the following day. Like other people in Jubilee and Banana Bottom, he thought that Bita's college training had been exclusively for religious service.

"I hope you won't be treating us to a sermon," he said.

"I didn't have the time yet to learn any at Jubilee."

"I don't mean the Jubilee kind, but a real English one like you were used to at college."

"At college I was used to reading French and playing the piano and dancing," Bita said laughing.

Bab, like all the peasants, had had a different idea of Bita's college training and began asking her a lot of questions. He was over two years older than she and was full of anxiety about a career. His uncle Jordan had put him through the elementary school and paid for four years of semi-secondary education. Anty Nommy had thought it would be a distinguished thing for him to become a school-master or a preacher. But Bab was different from most of the emergent literate peasantry and did not warm to the notion of a pedagogic or clerical career. He could stand almost anything in a church except the sermon part, which delighted the peasants when it was flamboyant and which bored him most then. And as under the denominational system of education a schoolmaster was also an assistant parson, he had no hankering for the lowest of professions. Many of the peasant youth had chosen teaching not because they felt especially endowed for instructing children, but because it barely got them onto the rim of the professional class. Yet because of the rigid respectability and the moral strain it involved, some of the best of them were always getting shaken off back upon the mass.

Bab had had an early premonition that he was not one that could carry through. The new iconoclasm in religion and social life had reached even his far-away village and there was much rustic discussion of omnipotence and the Scriptures, man, monkey and missing link, adult franchise, women's suffrage. Bab had found a good friend and mentor in an Englishman who lived near Banana Bottom. A man who knew a great deal more than he, for he had lived and read more, travelled through the world, and was a sceptic about every form of human society and all the solid-seeming nineteenth-century values. This man had a good library to which Bab had access.

While farming with his uncle, Bab was preparing carefully for the local Civil Service examinations. Jordan Plant's desire was that his nephew should stick to the land. The hunger for land was strong in him. He had added by purchase and other means to his mother's lot until now he possessed over a hundred acres in separate lots of the best land in the Banana Bottom region. The finest of all, a piece of twenty-five acres, planted with cocoa and bananas, he had gotten from an aged slave who quarrelled with his family, quit his house and went to Jordan with the title of his property in his hand and asked in exchange for it to be cared for until his death. Jordan took the old man in and nourished him, putting up with all his vagaries. And after six years the old man died and Jordan took the land. The old man's family, represented by three sons, instituted a long lawsuit over it. But Jordan, with the title in his hand and the deed that the old man had signed with a cross to his name, finally won with costs.

Jordan also had his eye on the fine remnant of the Adair property with the crumbling 'State House, going to jungle right against his well-cultivated place. He was proud of his splendid-yielding land and thought it better for Bab to think about than any profession. But he didn't come right out against Bab's ambition, chiefly because his daughter had been given a higher education and he was afraid lest his nephew should think he did not want him to have his chance too in the polite world. The conversation turned upon the difference between Jubilee and Banana Bottom and Bab said: "I envy you living in Jubilee. Even though it's a tiny town, it's a town all the same and one of our nicest."

"I don't know if I'm going to like it this time as I did before," said Bita. "It has changed. Or I have, or Mrs. Craig. Or maybe it's because of being abroad. I don't fancy it'll be congenial there. I think I could like Banana Bottom a lot better."

The night was dark-warm. Not a heavy but a friendly

darkness. The Cane River sounded over its fall below like a light breeze rustling through sugar-canes. The air was full of fireflies shedding their green light and attracted to a neighbouring yard where children waving torches were singing:

"Peeny, peeny, you' house a-burnin',
Peeny, peeny, come stop the fire."

"Oh!" cried Bita, "it seems just yesterday we used to sing that, too, and catch the peenies under the sheet on this barbecue and watch them shine in the dark."

Over the river came the sharp rattling of a kettle-drum. "What's that for?" Bita asked.

"The first tea-meeting for the holiday. Tonight. I'm going with Ned Delgado."

"Wish you a good time."

Bita was suddenly seized with longing to go too. Tea-meetings were the principal indigenous amusements of the peasantry, and yet she had never been to one. And none had ever been held in the Plant home, because Jordan Plant was one of the better class of peasants. And tea-meetings were classed as vulgar amusements and bad company and denounced from the pulpits. The young villagers were often rejected as candidates for church membership because they frequented tea-meetings. And that was hard on the village youth, for there were only two social centers: the rum shop where the men gathered at night to drink and swap stories of work and sex, and the church with its auxiliary affairs where the young girls flaunted their be-ribboned hats and bright print frocks and the young men their new suits and boots.

Bita remembered when she was a child how her schoolmates, those whose families were not deep in the church, could make her envious telling about the "grand tea-meetings" (so they were announced) that were held at their homes.

GRAND TEA-MEETING

in

MISS SALLY PINTO'S YARD

Big drum and kettle-drum

Guitar and Fiddle

THE QUEEN WILL ARRIVE FROM GINGERTOWN

Admission Free

5

houses.

BITA WOKE LATE AND BREAKFASTED ALONE. ANTY
Nommy was already busy laying the basis of the Sunday
dinner, for she was not going to miss church on Anniversary Sunday. Jordan was in the paddock with Jubban,
the drayman, looking over the pony and the mules that
had come in overnight from the far market. Bab was still
sleeping, for he did not get home from the tea-meeting
until daybreak.

After breakfast Bita remarked in the daylight the familiar flowers around the house. The night jasmine before
the back door of her room seemed a mere shrub giving no
sign of the sweet beauty that bloomed from its breath in
the night. But the bellflowers were lovely cream-white and
the coffee roses had spread all over the place. In the breadkind garden there was the old akee tree leaning over the
far corner of the barbecue, and full of fruit, the vermilion
husks opening to view the deep-cream lobes and shiny
black seeds. The cashew tree with the low crooked branch
where she used to swing had not changed at all and the
breadfruit tree that had been planted for her mother on
her wedding day was spread handsomely broad and high
above the garden.

Then she went a little way down the red road where
she always ran or skipped barefoot. At a deep bend below
the house, where almost automatically her feet always

started in running motion, she was overcome by a feeling to capture and live again that moment of her barefooted girlhood. But at the point of deliberating the mood the sound of voices reached her and round the bend came an animated group of Sunday-school children in their anniversary best and the secretary-and-treasurer of the Sunday school who was on his way to see Bita with an armful of Sunday-school literature and music.

Bita returned with him to the house. The secretary was a member of the Banana Bottom Delgados, next to the Adairs the largest clan in the region, who were the pillars and posts and sills and joists and beams and buttresses of the church. He was a man of thirty-nine and had been managing the Sunday school for six years. He had recently been promoted a leader and was the youngest officer of the church. He was middle-sized, tea-complexioned, and had kinky whiskers. He was very happy and enthusiastic about the work he was doing.

He showed Bita the program, written in red and blue ink, choruses, quartettes, quintettes, trios, solos interspersed with pieces of poetry for recitation by the tots. And on the heavy mahogany table of the sitting-room he displayed the sheet music and music books white-covered and blue-covered, thin-covered and thick-covered (Songs for the Home, Sacred Songs and Cantatas, Songs That Never Die from New York and London), out of which the pieces were taken. All easy-running tunes. The secretary left the music and the program with Bita, and she said that she would try some of them out on the organ with Belle Black.

The church was packed that afternoon with village folk coming up from the bottoms and down from the hills. The green and flowering countryside were well within the walls. For it had been decorated Saturday afternoon by the children and young folk with flowers and evergreens, arches of plaited palm fronds over the gate, and within bright with roses and hibiscus, marigolds and buttonflowers, long bamboo branches, ferns and banana suckers, garlands along the walls and crosses around the pulpit and ropes of running fern diagonal and horizontal across the beams.

The choir was ranged upon an improvised stage alongside the pulpit. Below in the front row right were the Reverend and the three Misses Lambert, with Deacon and Mother Delgado. Behind them Jordan Plant and Anty Nommy. The children were massed in the centre aisle and they began the rally rising and shrilling their joy. And behind them their mothers, some with babies in their arms, beaming under their bandannas.

> "Quickly haste and come where happy children meet,
> Hither come and sing the Saviour's praises sweet.
> Rest from your pleasures, rest from your play,
> Come to our meeting, come away."

Touched by their enthusiasm, Bita played with great pleasure. It didn't seem so long ago when she was also down there singing with her Sunday-school mates and wishing she were bigger to sing in the choir above. She wondered now at growing into womanhood so quickly.

The choir sang, "Children Are the Flowers in the Garden of God." Followed in sandwich patterns quartettes and solos and recitations of short verses by the children. The building filled and overflowed with applause when a little sugar-brown girl in flower-printed frock and heavenly blue ribbon to her stump of pigtail recited and scat-

tered first Congo peas and lastly orange blossoms from
a basket:

"Sow the seeds of children's love
So that they may grow
Flowering plants that God above
Blesseth here below.

"Scatter flowers for children's day,
Flowers so pure and bright
That along life's pathway they
E'er may be our light."

At last the performance was over and it was prize-giving
time. Bita left the organ for the platform, where the prize
books were piled upon a table. Separate piles of them.
Prizes! For Good Attendance. Good Conduct. For Memor-
izing Scripture Verses. For Reading. For Spelling. For Oral
Rendering of the Beatitudes. For Palestine History and
Geography. For Tidiness. Many consolation prizes.

Bita glanced at the books waiting to begin. Bright-
coloured cardboard covers with gold-gilded titles set in
flowery frames, holding tales from far foreign and wintry
lands. Little classics and little thrillers. Selections from
Grimm's and from Andersen's fairy tales. The Leather
Stocking Tales. Bible Tales done up into attractive and
innocent forms. The story of Esther, Jacob and Esau,
Joseph and his brethren, John the Baptist and Jesus. Tales
of a quick-witted and fearless Dutch child stopping a hole
in the dykes with his hands all through the night and
saving the whole country from inundation. Of the perils
of fisher-folk life on the Cornish coast. Of Alpine drifts
and Saint Bernard dogs. Tales of all children, except Negro
children, for little black and brown readers.

Yet Bita regarded the little prize books with tenderness, remembering that it was the stimulation of just such literature that had carried her through the novelists on the mission shelves, Louisa Alcott, Mrs. Southworth, Charles M. Sheldon, Mrs. Henry Wood, to *The Old Curiosity Shop, Vanity Fair, Les Misérables, Jane Eyre* (which last Mrs. Craig had disapproved as being too full of strong passions for a young Negro girl) to the latest staid offering of Mrs. Humphrey Ward.

The secretary-treasurer made a speech reviewing the work of the Sunday school and presented Bita. Bita stood up and, saying nothing introductory, she began calling out the names in her firm round creole voice, pronouncing every syllable clearly as she had learned to speak English.

Once she caught her father's eye tear-dimmed, for he was remembering that it was right after Bita had received a Sunday-school prize for good conduct that the rape occurred. And she, intuitively aware, was assaulted by the same thought and the ribald ditty brutally pounding her memory:

> "Crazy Bow was first,
> Crazy Bow was first."

6

children, the nice young men and women of the choir, special students and school monitors down to the rum-shop fellows who ganged together with flasks in their pockets and were a spectacular nuisance to the higgler women vendors of ginger beer and sweet nuts, young-coconut drink and wild orange drink, pineapple beverage, hominy cakes, coconut drops and mangoes.

THE NEXT DAY THERE WAS THE BIG PICNIC AT TABLETOP. So was called the plateau at the top of Banana Bottom from which the mountain folk could sometimes discern the margin of the sea about fifty miles away. It was the village playground, an extensive piece of fine level land covered with soft fox-tail grass with a clump of trees, mostly rose apple, growing down one side, and a brook running under. Three barren mango trees and an ebony provided shade and were used for swinging. The cricket-field was there and there also the range for target-shooting on holidays.

The drumming started early, giving the signal that it was picnic day. Kojo Jeems, the drummer, had a fine set of drums, and he was loved for his wonderful rattling of the kettle-drum. His son beat the big drum. They went playing down the hill, followed by a few ragged kiddies, to the hub of the village. There they were joined by the fiddler and the flute-blower and played and played, with the sun mounting higher and hotter, until there was gathered together a great crowd. And all marched swaying to the music over the hill, and picking up marchers marking time along the wayside, up to the playground.

The Sunday-school picnic brought together all the various elements of the village. The parson's daughters and church members of all grades, proud mothers of happy children, the nice young men and women of the choir, special students and school monitors down to the rum-shop fellows who ganged together with flasks in their pockets and were a spectacular nuisance to the higgler women venders of ginger beer and ginger nuts, young-cocoanut drink and wild orange drink, pineapple beverage, bammy cakes, cocoanut drops and mangoes.

Bita and Belle Black were in a group with the three Misses Lambert and Miss Yoni Legge.

Yoni Legge was the young sewing-mistress of the elementary school. She was the daughter of Lizzie Legge who long ago had worked as a cook on the Sunderland Sugar Estate in the lowlands, and there Yoni was conceived. It was an estate which employed many indentured East Indian coolies, and Lizzie Legge must have had lots of contact with them. Of her child's name Lizzie always boasted that she got it from the Indians. She said she had wanted to give her child a real uncommon name and one of the Indians had told her that if it was a girl she should call it Yoni.

Lizzie had failed to identify a father for Yoni and so when later she came back home to Banana Bottom and got married, the child took the name of her stepfather.

Yoni was deliciously pretty. She was dark with an under-layer of red like a cocoon, and as smooth. Her hair was straight black and firm like horse mane, and her complexion the kind that was most admired and desirable among the Negroes. The village folk called her Coolie Gal when she was small, thus insinuating that they thought her father was really an Indian. But Lizzie Legge always denied that. She maintained that Yoni's complexion and hair were perhaps the result of outside influence. Her

explanation was that when she was a cook at the Sunderland Estate and young with child the Indians coming to
the house for their wages and wrapped only in loin cloth
made such an impression upon her that it had resulted in
the miracle of Yoni.

In some ways the Indian coolies magnetized the Negro
peasantry. The men in their loin cloths which the natives
called coolie wrapper, their keen eyes, and the straight
mane which even when they were darker than some of
the Negroids gave them an entirely different exotic appearance. And their women moving with little steps (compared with the long strides of the Negro women) almost
gliding like serpents, draped in loose flowing garments of
many colours and weighted down with heavy silver rings
and bracelets in nose and ear, on arms and ankles.

The Misses Felicia, Elvira and Lucinda Lambert were the
cashew-brown daughters of the ebony parson. They were
prim of manners, precise and halting of speech as if they
were always thinking while talking that they were the
minister's daughters.

Under the wild tamarind tree, its vermilion blossoms
scattered in the silver-and-brown grass, the musicians made
their stand and played the country jigs while the kettle-
drum rattled away. And the young folks danced two by
two, four by four and in thick groups.

> "Gal, you' virgin is bruken,
> Gal, you' virgin is bruken."

First among the rum-shop fellows was Tack Tally,
proudly wearing his decorations from Panama: gold watch
and chain of three strands, and a foreign gold coin attached to it as large as a florin, a gold stick-pin with a

huge blue stone, and five gold rings flashing from his fingers. He had on a fine bottle-green tweed suit with the well-creased and deep-turned pantaloons called peg-top, the coat of long points and lapels known as American style. And wherever he went he was accompanied by an admiring gang.

For that gang everything that Tack said and did was charged with importance. For he had not only gone to Panama like many, but he had come back with the gold.

Among the older heads of Banana Bottom and other villages there were some who had sold their cows or horses, even their land, to go to Panama during the first Canal Enterprise of the eighteen eighties to try their chance. And with the breaking of the boom they had returned home with the fever, the smallpox—everything but the real thing. But Tack Tally had made good in little time and come back with the stuff all over his person.

Bita and Yoni were in charge of the fishing-pond—a lottery game where a quantity of rubbish was mixed in with a few good things and placed in a huge box, and one paid a sixpence and took his chance fishing up something. Near by Tack Tally and his boys were buying ginger beer from a higgler woman and teasing her by mixing the ginger beer with Jamaica rum and offering her a drink.

"Gwan away wid you drunken self all a you," said the woman, "and doan tempt a weak body. Ise a church member."

"Theyse a lot a chu'ch members drinking likker and doings wohse," said Tack. "There ain't no harm in feeling good and having a good time."

"Parson Lambert sure hard on rum-drinkers. This ginger

beer is good enough foh me. I wi' drink all you treat me to."

"Because you selling it," laughed Tack. "I'll treat you all you want if you let me mix it wid this beauty of a Jamaica Old."

Neither would give in to the other. Looking to the stand where the girls were, Tack, indicating Bita, said: "And tha's a finer piece a beauty than thisere. Man! Man! Oh, how I'd love to get under her thatch."

"Shingles, you mean, man," said Panhead Flamme, Tack's lieutenant. "Her ole man's house is a shingle one so she's outa the thatch class."

"Is that so?" Tack feigned surprise.

"Oh, didn't you know that little thing," said Panhead. "And shingles them harder to get under than thatch." Although Tack's gang admired his success and delighted in the drinks he provided, they were envious of him and secretly resented his Panama ways which were equivalent to bad manners—his bold and forward talk about the finest type of village folk as if everybody could be cooked together in the same Panama pot.

"*You* are right, mi man," said Tack. "Thatch is easier to get than shingles. But sometimes it's better too."

"You ought to know," pursued Panhead. "Theyse one thatch right next to that shingle."

This referred to Yoni, whose stepfather's cottage was thatched. The village knew that Tack was right after her. He had been seen familiarly chatting with her along the road and once he had gone to her house, but Pap Legge had driven him out. Pap Legge had taken Yoni as his own child and had provided the means for her to stay in Jubilee for three years while she was learning the trade of seamstress. He wanted Yoni to be decorous and aloof like the Misses Lamberts. And he was foaming mad that late afternoon when he saw Tack Tally walk into his yard with Yoni. For with all his Panama success, Tack was in peasant parlance, a hurry-come-up. That was the native word for *nouveau riche*, only more inclusive, as it meant not merely a have-nothing who had risen to be a have-something, but also one of bad reputation.

To Tack's, "Good evening, Father Legge," Pap cried, "Get outa mi yard you good-foh-nothin' dirty-trash ob a hurry-come-up. I doan want you' pusson in heah not ef youse covered from head to foot wid Panama gold."

Faintly Yoni protested, "I invited him, Father." But ignoring her, Pap picked up his shining hoe and, uplifting it and approaching Tack, cried, "Get right on back out right now or I'll hoe you down as ef you was a yam-hill." And muttering, "Crazy old man!" Tack without the assumed dignity of a strut unceremoniously hurried through the gate.

But Yoni's head was turned for Tack. And often after the sewing session at the school she would visit Mrs. Fearon, the schoolmaster's wife, until dusk so that she could keep a tryst with Tack down by the roadside. She liked his "panamerican" clothes which were better than the schoolmaster's and anybody's in Banana Bottom, and his Colon strut. And if Tack was too raw-mannered for the village church circle she would go back to Panama with him.

"Tha's all right," said Tack. "Sometimes a thatch house is nicer than a shingle house."

"When the woodpecker cain't bore the lignum-vitæ tree him say it's no good," said Panhead.

The gang laughed loudly at him and Tack repeated the old Crazy Bow story about Bita.

Jubban, Jordan Plant's drayman, was drinking a bottle of ginger beer with his back to the Tack group. Overhearing Tack repeat the old joke, he turned and said, "Jes' say that again."

Jubban's strapping bulk moved threateningly towards the dapper Tack. Tack quailed, but he did not mean to stay cowed before his fellows, and said: " 'Tain't none a you' business what I says. You ain't in our class."

"Ah know I isn't," said Jubban, "but ef you say dat thing again a'd slap it dung you' throat like dat!"

Jubban boxed Tack's mouth with his open palm. Tack backed away a step and, crying: "But youse fast, man. Youse fast to butt in in thisya. An' ah'll break you' big bammy face wid this bottle ef you fools wimme."

Tack raised the bottle, but Jubban caught and wrenched it from him and flung it over the heads of the picknickers into a bed of thick trailing fern. Grabbing Tack by the collar, he hoisted him into the air, slammed him flat to the ground, and kneeling down upon him began kneading his mouth with his fist.

Yoni let out a wild scream and leaving Bita alone with the lottery started running towards the spot, followed by the Misses Lambert (who made a pretence of hiding their excitement by walking instead of running) and a crowd swarming and buzzing around the scene like a host of black bees.

Tack's friends had kept aloof. Three men from the target-shooting broke through and got Jubban up. Superintendent Delgado pushed through and said: "Shame a you, Jubban, foh labouring a man so much littler than you'se'f. Whasimatter with you?"

"Teach him to keep am mongoose mout' offen folkses bettarn him," muttered Jubban as he heaved heavily away.

"If it wasn't foh the law I'd shot him down like a dog," said Tack, trying to fix his torn stiff collar.

"Tack! Tack! What is it? What's the cause of it?" asked Yoni, taking him by the shoulder. "Is you hurt?"

"Ise all right," Tack said, shortly. Like all peasant men, he didn't like a woman making a fuss over him in public. It made him feel more ashamed than taking a beating. And he turned away abruptly and impatiently.

Yoni saw the elder Miss Lambert fix her with a surprised and disapproving stare, and recovering her senses and seeing that she had betrayed her relationship with Tack and remembering that she was the sewing-mistress of the school, now making a public exhibition of herself, she left the spot and walked slowly back to the lottery stand.

It was now mid-afternoon and the bag race and boy-and-girl race and donkey race, the high jump and long jump, the stone-throwing, hand-and-head walking, bamboo-pole balancing and grease-pole climbing—all the prize-giving features were at an end and dancing was the chief attraction.

Under the wild tamarind tree around the fiddle and the flute, the big drum booming, the kettle-drum rattling, the young village jigged, two by two, four by four or many in a ring, girls together and boys opposite, jigging close up together and backing away, then bowing and repeating, the dancers spreading away from the tamarind tree like a flock of frolicking goats.

The dancing was wild and noisy like a bush fire when Bab Plant came on to the picnic ground with Squire Gensir. Squire Gensir was a remarkable personage among the peasants. He had taken up residence near Banana Bottom after Bita had been sent abroad. The peasants were his hobby. He was always among them in the fields, their grass huts, their thatched cottages and shingled houses.

He ate their food and sat with them out upon their barbecues on moonlight nights, listening to their Anancy stories. And he had made a collection of them. Now he was engaged in writing down their songs, jammas, shey-sheys and breakdowns. Songs of the fields, draymen's songs, love songs, satiric ditties of rustic victims of elemental passions. Any new turn of speech, any original manner of turning English to fit peasant ways of thinking and speaking, could make him as happy as a child.

He was about sixty, thin, middle-built, and wore a little goatee. The peasants called him Squire. He lived alone in a little bungalow between Banana Bottom and Breakneck Hill. His suits were made of the cheap cloth the peasants used, Holland drill or khaki, and the only thing about him that hinted of means were his stout broad-toed imported boots.

The peasants liked and took him simply as he took himself. But they knew he wasn't a simple man and that the most eminent people in the colony would be delighted to honour him. Among themselves they said he was a lord.

Bab went straight to the lottery-stand and introduced the squire to his cousin Bita. The squire had heard about this native product cultivated in his own country and wanted naturally to see Bita. He felt a lurking prejudice against her. He couldn't tell why, but it was there, and he was prepared to dislike her even as he did the Misses Lambert and the Reverend Lambert. Not because they were God's servants and he an unbeliever, but because he thought them priggish and depreciated their influence upon the peasant folk.

Bita invited Squire Gensir to try the lottery. He put a sixpence down, dove his hand into the box and came up with a little pillow. They cut it open and imbedded in the fox-tail grass found a *Child's Story of Jesus*. He handed it to Bita and said, "You may give it to one of your little followers."

"Not mine, but his," she replied with a laugh.

"His? Whom?"

"Jesus's."

They laughed together. And he said: "It's great dancing. Don't you feel tempted?"

"Yes. When I was little I used to dance like that. Before I went to Jubilee. I couldn't now. We church folk can't dance like that."

"But at Jubilee you're independent. A Free Church. And nearly all those people dancing so wildly there are church people. They can't punish them for that! Prevent them attending the church?"

"If they did the church would be left empty," said Bita. "But there's a difference. They are all church-goers but not all church members. And those church members who dance are not so closely associated with the church like myself and the Lambert girls."

"Too bad." He remained silent awhile, thinking of the admirable work the Free Churches had accomplished in the struggle for the liberation of the Negro slaves and in educating the freedmen and their children. But as an unbeliever he thought of it only as a great social achievement in which religion had played an active rôle, and felt that now that that job was done the church was merely living on its tradition and more of a shackling than liberating institution to the native spirit.

"Well, it must be all right for you," he said, "as I suppose you learned to forget all about dancing at your college."

"Not at all! We had fine dancing lessons all the time—waltz, schottische, minuet. But such dancing is for indoors."

"I hear there's going to be a big indoors dance tonight."

"Yes? Where?" Bita asked eagerly.

"At Kojo Jeems', the drummer there. He's giving a big tea-meeting tonight."

Bita felt disappointed. It was just another tea-meeting.

"It's going to be the biggest for the holidays," said Bab. "Kojo Jeems' tea-meetings always draw the biggest crowd."

Kojo Jeems was also much in demand for drumming in the villages contiguous to Banana Bottom, and being so popular he always drew a big spending crowd when he gave a tea-meeting. Often he played without charging anything. And so the villagers felt they were just paying him his due when they spent a little freely at his tea-meetings.

"Will you be going?" Squire Gensir asked Bita.

"No, I couldn't go. I've never once been to a tea-meeting. And it's impossible now even if I wanted to."

"Why impossible?"

"Because there are some things you are not always free to do even though you may want to. All depends on your position. And my position is such if I went to a tea-meeting I know Mrs. Craig would be shocked to death."

And this gentleman who had travelled and travelled, contacting with all classes of humanity, high, middle and low, travelled until he was weary and had resigned and retired to this bush hamlet of a remote colony, knew that Bita had simply expressed an eternal truism. There was no absolute freedom anywhere under the sun. One type of person was free this side of the land, and just over the boundary he would be a slave. And the taboos of one group of society were the signposts of progress to another.

"I am going to the tea-meeting with Bab," said Mr. Gensir. "I think they are the finest affairs in this island. You ought to see one. Why don't you go with us tonight?"

Bita promised to go. She thought it would make all the difference if she went like a spectator to a tea-meeting with her cousin and a person like Squire Gensir, who could do as he liked and yet command the respect of the highest and the lowest people.

That night Bita made up a party with Belle Black and Yoni. Belle Black went to tea-meetings all the time and, in spite of Pap Legge's disapproval, Yoni used to go on occasions before the dignity of sewing-mistress of the Banana Bottom Elementary School was bestowed upon her.

Bita told her parents that she was going out with the girls and Yoni informed Ma Legge that she was spending the night with Bita. To that Pap Legge could not object because, as the most cultivated native girl of the region, Bita was just the person he preferred Yoni to be with and he had the highest respect mixed with a little envy for Jordan Plant with his fat acres of banana and cocoa, coffee and sugar-cane and his sugar-mill and dray-and-five-mules and a saddle horse.

Yoni came over to Bita's after supper. Anty Nommy went to bed early. Jordan Plant had gone down to the hub for holiday dinner with the proprietor of the General Provisions shop.

The girls waited in the sitting-room. Bita had changed its look a little, putting up bright cretonnes in place of Anty Nommy's lace curtains, and she had moved the organ from its corner near the door giving into the dining-room, over to the window looking out on the valley which the sun sought first each morning.

A piece of fine wainscoting ran round the room, taking up about one-third the height of the lime-washed wall. This sort of work was much in favour among the more prosperous peasantry, and in some houses the native carpenters had let their fancy go and turned out some lovely carved panelling.

The roofing was bare and from a crossbeam depended a chandelier of conical crystals in which was set a kerosene lamp, which lit up the neat-laid shingles above and flared down below upon the mahogany floor that had been waxed and scrubbed gleaming like laccine with brushes sawed from dry cocoanut husks. The chandelier had been bought in the city by Jordan Plant for Bita's homecoming.

"You no' tell them where we going?" Yoni asked, meaning Bita's parents.

"No, I thought better not. Anty Nommy wouldn't object, but she might think it wasn't wise and that would spoil the pleasure of going. And I want to feel happy going for the first time. They'll know tomorrow."

"I jest love tea-meetings," said Yoni. "It's so chupid

you can't do one thing nor another 'causen you l'arnin' little naygar chits to sew. It's bettah to be able to do what you feel like all the time and don't care nothing about what nobody says, like Belle here."

"I got to follow mi feelings them, honey," said Belle. "I sings in the choir all right, but I'd rather not to sing than no gwine a tea-meetings and dances. Ain't nobody loosing and tying mi pettycoat string them but meself when I get ready."

Yoni giggled. "Ma knows ahm going, but Pap don't know a thing. It's a long time I no been to any. Oh, I feel so good and ticklish all ovah."

It was late when Bab came and got the girls. The first part of the tea-meetings was always taken up for the auction sale of the cakes and Bab did not care to be present to bid cakes for the girls he knew, for he was saving up to buy clothes for town and office wear if he should pass his civil service examination.

But Kojo Jeems seemed to have been aware that Squire Gensir was going to his affair and had shrewdly delayed the bidding of the two most interesting cakes: the gate and the crown. The peasants knew that although the squire lived cheaply he had money—at least much more than they. And although they did not trick in dealing with him (they often allowed him to fix the prices of things he bought—vegetables and chickens) they expected more of him than of the colonial gentry. And invariably he always paid more.

And so when the party arrived in Kojo Jeems' vast yard the bidding for the cakes was still in progress. A tea-meeting was good for lots of fun and the more fun there was the more money it would make for the promoter. For the peasants it was a kind of practical lottery which was often resorted to to replenish an empty coffer or help out in an emergency such as finding the funds for an unfortunate lawsuit. The trousseau of many a village bride and the cost of the wedding feasts had been paid for by means of a tea-meeting.

Money was made from the purveying of rum, orange wine and ginger beer, but the most exciting money-making thing was the auction of the cakes.

The cakes were created in shapes of divers things: flowers and fruits, letters, birds and cats, and the two largest and most elaborate and important cakes were those that represented the gate of the village and the crown for the queen of the tea-meeting. A cake that was worth sixpence could be auctioned for about two shillings and the gate and the crown could make as much as five shillings each at a small tea-meeting. At a big one where there was rivalry the young men of one village banding to buy the gate and crown away from another which was the proud possessor of a pretty queen, the bidding for these would go as high as ten shillings.

Kojo Jeems' yard was a big wide one levelled down to an under surface of soft rock. It was not a paved yard, for Kojo Jeems was not a lover of the soil and did not raise any coffee or cocoa to dry in the sun on a paved barbecue. Behind the house (a two-roomed thatched thing with board floors, occupied by Kojo Jeems, his concubine and his mother) there were a few straggling coffee shrubs and tania plants that had just sprung and flourished by themselves. The land around was left to bush. In a poor season when Kojo made no money from drumming he made bamboo baskets. The little house was dwarfed by the size of the yard, and now with the big palm booth erected for the tea-meeting it could not be seen at all.

The cake representing the gate of Banana Bottom had just been knocked down when Bab entered followed by Squire Gensir and the girls. Kojo Jeems gave a long flourish of the kettle-drum and the fiddler played a few bars of "Lady, Lady."

Then Kojo Jeems mounted the stand where the cakes were auctioned and exhibiting the crown said:

"Ladies and lasses and gentlemens. Look!

"Here right under you' unwordy beholding eyeballs is the crown for the glory a Kojo Jeems' tea-meeting, the most injuicing temptation of the feelings that human hands can fasten togedder to water you' moutses an' ticklish you' eating injun. Here the most wannerful crown in the jewels of Banana Bottom.

"Gents and gentlemens, most specially to you I petition to make thisya tea-meeting a success an' pertake a the interest a this crown until youse exarses. Doan' letam slip too easy outa you' handsem as am pardner, the gate. Show you wordy gentlemen foh the crown of Banana Bottom.

"Wese got here tonight some scrumptious visitas and one dat we all most appreciate causen he's a gen'man who appreciates us too. A big gen'men who showing that though he's a highmighty he can appreciate us ordinaire folkses an' what we doings. Wese proud a him coming here causen we know dat him come among us not to laugh at our fun but to enjoice it. So t'ree cheers foh the crown cake . . . t'ree cheers foh the queen . . . t'ree cheers foh our scrumptious visitas . . . t'ree cheers foh Squire Gensah."

The party took seats at the deep end of the booth facing

the cake-stand and the music. Squire Gensir did not like the open reference to him, but understanding the spirit that prompted it, he didn't mind very much.

The auctioneer was a little tamarind-brown man. He mounted the stand and said:

> "The gate is done gone
> But the fight not yet won
> Till you get to the crown.
> Who will win the crown of Banana Bottom?"

He started the bidding at half a crown instead of a shilling as was the custom. When five shillings was reached, Kojo Jeems looked expectantly at Squire Gensir and the squire said six. Kojo Jeems rattled the drum and the fiddle tuned a bar of "Lady, Lady."

Merrily the bidding continued. Seven and six. Eight shillings. Nine. Squire Gensir said ten. The fiddle played again "Lady, Lady," and Kojo Jeems' face was as jolly as a pot bubbling with Congo peas and a chunk of salted beef. Now the fast set of Banana Bottom boys felt they would not be able to save the crown alone and still be able to spread joy for the rest of the evening, so they banded with others from Breakneck and Roaring River, a village down Gingertown Road, chinking their shillings to save the crown. . . .

Fifteen shillings! "Gracious goodness!" cried an excited young man. "Ole Kojo Jeems will be buying him one cow outa thisya tea-meeting."

Seventeen and six. Nineteen . . . and six. . . . One pound! Kaan' go no moh," cried a Banana Bottomist. Squire Gensir said a guinea. And that was final. Like a swat on the heads of the peasant lads, silencing their tongues. For a guinea was unknown to peasant vocabulary. It was

a gentleman's privilege. Only gentlemen dealt in guineas.
A most exclusive sterling word.

So the bidding ended there. They all thought the squire
would give the crown to Bita, but instead he told Kojo
Jeems to present it to the queen.

Play the music: Crown for the queen. And the parade
of the queen started. She came out of her chamber veiled
and accompanied by four maids. And a grand strutting
started round the booth. And when she reached the spot
where Squire Gensir was sitting she threw back her veil,
displaying the ripe star-apple face that the Banana Bottom
lads had been bidding so hard for, curtsied and danced
a jig.

That was the signal for general dancing.

> "Lady, lady, do mi lady
> Lady, lady, get you ready.
> Lady, lady, do mi lady—
> Curtsy foh lady,
> Bow foh gentleman."

Quadrilles, lancers, mintoes, jig. Round and round the
warm palm booth. Belle Black had jumped into it from
the beginning and didn't miss a one. Now she was rearing
up against Bab. Yoni was fidgety. Afraid of trouble over
her job, she could not dance and she was disappointed
because Tack, his face swollen up, had not been able to
attend. She said she wanted a drink, and pushing through
the dancers and keeping to the sides of the booth, she
arrived at the end against the house, curtained off by a
bed sheet where Kojo Jeems' woman was dispensing the
drinks.

"And what are you going to do?" Squire Gensir asked
Bita.

They felt mutually curious about each other. He because Bita (a peasant girl just like any of those wildly shaking their feet in that booth) had been sent to his own country for higher cultivation and that had made her really different with a different charm of refinement of her own. She wasn't like Belle Black and had nothing of the affectations of the Misses Lambert, who seemed to be wilting like river reeds transplanted to the soil of the mission pen.

And she was curious because he represented in himself by education and by birth the flowering of that culture she had been sent abroad to obtain. In England she had gone on a few short visits to the homes of some of her college friends, where she had met English gentlemen. But none like this man who had come up there to live in the hills among the peasants and enjoyed it, remote from the city where the majority of the European colony congregated.

Squire Gensir had taken a quick mental inventory of Bita. When Bab told him about his cousin he had assumed that he was going to meet a very affected made-to-order young lady indeed. And he had asked her to go to the tea-meeting out of pure mischief. Her ready decision to go and her manners had been a delightful surprise. He had thought that with her background, her training, she would probably be an impossible if not an intolerable person, with mannerisms that would be irritating to him. If there was one thing he detested it was that social quality that has been ridden so hard by moderns and bohemians: middleclass gentility.

The civilized cream of the colony was predominantly middle-class. Once Squire Gensir, against his inclination, was bound to go to an affair in the city among some of the high people. He returned disgusted to Banana Bottom and told Bab that the most intolerable experience to him in the world was to associate with people of your own tribe who talked your language and yet had a different form of manners.

This had sounded strange and harsh to Bab and he asked Squire Gensir how then he was able to tolerate the manners of the peasantry. And he had replied, "easily and with pleasure," because the peasants were like foreigners to him and so he could not measure them by his code of conduct but rather had to study theirs (and it was a diversion doing so) living among them.

"At college," said Bita, "that was the chief question the girls were always putting to one another. 'What are you going to do when you are finished?' And the answer was always, 'Expect to get married.' The girls used to get so excited about the kind of man they wanted to marry and the careers they would like their husbands to have. And sometimes they asked me, 'And what are *you* going to do, Bita?' Of course, I said, 'Get married, too.' And they'd ask, 'But to who?' 'A man, of course, not a monkey!' I would say. 'But what *kind* of a man,' they'd insist. And I replied, 'Suppose I'll find a man among my people back home.' And they were all kind of shocked. You see, none of them ever dreamed of going to a colony excepting a big one like Canada as the wife of a governor or some one just as big. And they couldn't imagine any other kind of man worth while but a white one. So there I was such a puzzle. They thought I'd just been caught right up out of naked savagery to be educated. And when I said I was going back to

marry a man of my people then I was going straight back
to cannibalism to marry a cannibal."

"Well, I hope you don't take me for one of your college
friends," said Squire Gensir.

"Oh no!" protested Bita. "I didn't mean that at all.
Only your question made me remember."

Squire Gensir laughed. "Don't apologise. I really enjoyed
your story."

And now they were performing the famous line-up.
From one end to the other of the booth the men formed a
single line and the women another opposite them.

A young man sitting with the fiddler and flutist sang,
clapping and stamping while they played:

> "Got a gal and de neatest
> Gal I ebah did fin';
> Stucky gal an' the sweetest
> Lak a ripe sugar pine.
> When de nighttime I hug har
> Stars am trimble to fall.
> Gal you sweeter than sugar,
> Boy ahm in a mi saal."

The women chose the partners, calling names formally:
Miss Lamb will take Mister Kidd as partner. Then shuffling
places, changing partners, and the master of ceremonies
calling: "Hold! Let go! March! Right through! Change
back! Line-up!"

Bita was swaying to the measure of the dancing. "Don't
think I'm the devil tempting you," said Squire Gensir,
"but don't you feel like dancing?"

"Yes, I do. And you?"

"I enjoy it, but I don't dance. When I used to dance, or

rather try to, I always stepped on the ladies' skirts. That was very humiliating and so I gave up trying long ago."

"I'm going to join them," Bita said.

"You'd better not if you think it will make trouble for you."

"Oh, I don't care, anyhow."

Her body was warm and willing for that native group dancing. It came more natural to her than the waltzes and minuets, although she liked these too in a more artificial atmosphere.

And Bab was surprised when he came by that Bita grabbed his arm and joined the dance. Now the line-up was merged into a grand altogether breakdown and Bita danced freely released, danced as she had never danced since she was a girl at a picnic at Tabletop, wiggling and swaying and sliding along, the memories of her tomboyish girlhood rushing sparkling over her like water cascading over one bathing upon a hot summer's day.

The crowd rejoiced to see her dance and some girls stood clapping and stamping to her measure and crying: "Dance, Miss Bita, dance you' step! Dance, Miss Bita, dance away!" And she danced forgetting herself, forgetting even Jubilee, dancing down the barrier between high breeding and common pleasures under her light stamping feet until she was one with the crowd.

At last it was over. Bita was tingling with sweet emotion. It was hot and close in the booth. She left Bab talking to Squire Gensir and went to the end of the booth that was sheeted off to serve the refreshments. Kojo Jeems' woman beamed upon her and offered a tumbler of ginger beer. Bita thanked her and drank. A slight breeze wafted up from the gully and stirred the orange blossoms shedding down their scent. She stepped outside and drew long draughts of air.

From the shadow of the house came sounds of low murmuring and she could discern couples a little distance apart, under the long thatched eaves against the wall. The door of the house was ajar and, curious, she approached and looked in. A kerosene tin lamp was burning dimly on a little cross-legged table and young men and women, exhausted dancing, sprawled close together crosswise on the big bamboo bed. Others were lying on mats on the floor.

A young man on the edge of the bed recognizing Bita asked her: "You wanta res' you'se'f, miss?"

She shook her head and at the same time heard Bab calling: "Bita! Bita! Where are you?"

He had followed her to get a drink too. He stepped through the booth entrance and saw Bita turn from the door of the house.

"Why did you go in there?" he asked.

"Oh, I was looking for Yoni. . . . I think I'd better go home now. I'm tired."

But nowhere in the booth nor in the house was Yoni to be found. "I wonder where she can be?" said Bita, almost plaintively.

Belle Black, notorious for her uncontrollable tongue, remarked: "B'lieb she's awright, poah t'ing. Sence she couldn' dance in de bood, her musbe dancing someways in de bush."

Bita glanced at Squire Gensir, and wondered what he was thinking and feeling. Clearly he was enjoying the evening. But was it merely cerebral, she thought. Were the nerves and body cells not touched as hers? Some day she might ask when she knew him better.

As Yoni was not to be found, they started to leave. Kojo Jeems halted them a little and presented Bita with a cake shaped like a little garland. Squire Gensir took the short cut by way of Tabletop to go to his bungalow and Bab accompanied Bita and Belle to the house and returned to the tea-meeting to stay until daybreak.

7

IT WAS THE MANGO SEASON AND BANANA BOTTOM WAS a famous mango country. The spreading bower-like trees grew everywhere. Thick together in groves down by the riverside in fat wormy soil, or singly upon barren hill tops, in gardens or tilled fields, among yams and cassava, pineapple and ginger, and along the roadside. Mangoes of many kinds: the common, the number eleven and the delicious-tinted-and-tasting kidney mango.

Now children attending school at this season could dispense with the midday meal and do with a few mangoes. Now their faces were always touched, their hands sticky and their clothes daubed with the thick yellow juice, and avidly they ate until their little brown bellies were loose.

It was market day and the mango was a staple in the products of the peasants. There were dray-loads of it and whopping women with their broad and long print skirts tucked up short toted huge baskets on their heads; village lads, their brown drill pantaloons turned up high over bare feet, drove hampered donkeys laden with the ripe fruit packed in the scentful fever grass, both mingling and shedding along the road their delicious aroma.

And along that road rocked Sister Phibby Patroll bent on taking a shocking piece of news to Priscilla Craig at Jubilee. On her head she bore a basket of selected number eleven and lovely akees from a tree flourishing in her own yard that she was taking to present to Mrs. Craig.

Nine years before she had been the first to carry the news of the rape of Bita to Mrs. Craig. The result of her mission had been good for Bita. And since then she had been the happy bearer of other bits of Banana Bottom news. But she had never dreamed that Bita would ever again be a subject for evil gossip in Banana Bottom. For when the Craigs adopted her it seemed that she had been lifted too high above Banana Bottom ever to participate in that lowly life again.

Sister Phibby Patroll, as the most excellent midwife of the Banana Bottom region, was credited with knowing more about the troubles and secrets of village families than any other person and what she did not know she conjectured.

Since the death of her husband, who had been the best barbecue-builder of Banana Bottom, she had been read out of church membership exactly three times and her cases had provided the most entertaining members' meeting in the history of Banana Bottom. For among sacred entertainments there was none to challenge that that was held when the members of a church were summoned by the parson to a general meeting to review the lapses of transgressors and backsliders.

Sister Phibby's first trial came when she was surprised in adultery with the village shopkeeper, whose wife she was attending in childbirth. But after adequate suspension she sought redemption and was received back into the fold again. The second shock came five years after her husband's death when, as a redeemed communicant, she presented herself with a fatherless baby. And the third marked the period of her change from being picturesquely sinful to become the chief village gossip of sin. She was cited for bearing false witness against a neighbor, because she had abused her position as midwife to declare that all the signs on the baby of a loose village wench pointed to a respectable married leader of the church as its father.

But with the years of graying hairs Sister Phibby had become more circumspect and, except for a few venial lapses such as when she got drunk over the washing of a dead body, and backslid on such occasions into lecherous language, her manner of self-expression was limited to discreet gossip.

Her aberrations did not create any real difference in her life and her status for, in those Negro communities, it was a commonplace for people to fall from grace and return again and again, as if their native philosophy was that in the enjoyment of life there must be constant sin and repentance.

"Good marnin', Sistah Phibby." A fellow member overtook her, driving a donkey loaded with sugar on his way to the local market.

"Marnin', Breddah Halky, an' how is you dis marnin'?"

"Middling, Sistah, an' thinkin' Gawd. Middling. And dat was a wunnerful Sundy-school rally, wa'n't it, though, Sistah?"

"Mahvellously and a real credit to mi Cousin Dan. Gawd bless him."

"Him surely is the bestest secretary ob the Sundy school we ebber had. But Miss Bita too. The meetin' would nebber a been so grand ef it no was f'her playing so splendifully."

"Ah got to say the trute she did. But, Breddah Halky, ain't it a big shame dat after all the ejucation the Reverend

Craig them give her she gwan disgrace herself dancing a tea-meeting?"

"Say what, Sistah Phibby? I nebber hear a thing. And when did dat take place?"

"Eh, eh, Breddah Halky! Under what bush you burying you head foh no hear the news that de young woman was a Kojo Jeems' tea-meeting?"

"Well, ah didn't hear a wud tell now and I doan' know what to t'ink, 'cep'n' she been mad."

Breddah Halky switched his donkey. "Kui, kui, Quashee. Got to leave you, Sistah. Got to mek fast time."

It was late afternoon when Sister Phibby arrived at Jubilee, and Mrs. Craig was pleased to receive her basket. She had long acquired a taste for fine mangoes. And also the cream-lobed akee—a fruit that was eaten like a vegetable—with its burnished black seeds set in vermilion case, so like an antique flower-shaped brooch fashioned of jet, ivory and coral, and which had seemed so strange to her from her first coming to the colony and after long years still held its strangeness. At first she used to have it cooked and served as a separate dish, but she had succumbed to Rosyanna's way of doing it with salted cod and plenty of butter, for thus she had proved it more delectable.

When Sister Phibby unburdened herself of her message, Priscilla remained silent for a good breath with her hand to her cheek, before she said stonily: "Impossible, impossible!" Then: "She's coming today. She will explain."

Sister Phibby sighed and said: "Maybe it no look possible to you, missus, but is de trute all the same." And she retired to the kitchen to sup and chin with Rosyanna.

That evening Bita returned to Jubilee. And when she spied Sister Phibby with Rosyanna at the kitchen window as the buggy drove up the gravelway, she knew that the story of the tea-meeting had already reached Jubilee, and was prepared for an ordeal.

Mrs. Craig greeted her gravely. And she presided over the dinner table like a piece of sculpture, betraying no sign of the agitation burning within her. But as soon as Malcolm Craig had retired to his study she invited Bita to go for a talk in her dressing-room.

She felt sure that Bita must have been the victim of a stupid error. She did not want to believe that the girl had deliberately participated in a tea-meeting. And she had a sensation of being struck down by a foul hand when Bita admitted that she had attended the tea-meeting voluntarily.

"But certainly, Bitah"—she pronounced the name broadly—"you must have been out of your senses. A tay-meeting! A tay-meeting! I cannot understand it. I will not understand it."

"I went with my cousin and Squire Gensir," said Bita.

At the mention of Squire Gensir's name Mrs. Craig's feeling and her attitude underwent a magical change and Bita's attending the tea-meeting was seen in a happier colour.

For Squire Gensir was held in high esteem everywhere and enjoyed an honourable reputation among all classes, clerical as much as lay people, although he was openly atheistic. For he was not antagonistic to ecclesiastical folk as a social group and sometimes on his long lonely tramps in the country he had taken tea with some of them as well as the gentry. Indeed he was asked more often than he accepted, as he preferred to live his life almost entirely among the peasants.

Certainly it was not just the fact that the squire was a member of the most self-contained remnant of the feudal aristocracy in the world, which made him so generally respected and liked, despite his inconoclastic ideas and ways of life. There were aristocratic estate-owners whom the peasants hated. But he also dominated the mind of the gentry because he was a rare intellectual and the main quality that must have enhanced the value of his reputation, at least among the clerical, was that in a country where concubinage between white men and black and brown women, also exclusively among Negroes and Mulattos themselves, was a common feature of social life, where illegitimate children flourished like mushrooms, he lived aloof from sexual contact, a happy old bachelor with (as Mrs. Craig often remarked) "not the slightest blemish upon his character,"—a character about which nothing was whispered either naturally or otherwise.

Ah, Priscilla sighed unburdened of a cruel pain. She had spent an afternoon in hell wrestling with the devil, who all black and flame-red with lifted tail kept dancing around and darting up to her to whisper satanisms in her ear:

Bita was atavistic as was her race. A branch of the same root and the deceptive lovely flower would wither to seed a similar tree. . . . All the money she had spent would be as wasted, all her planning and thinking and careful cultivation of this girl come to naught. For evidently she lacked the character to stand it. Mrs. Craig thought less of character as something intrinsically individual than as an essential of the development of a people, a nation, a class-flowering in the finest types. And now she wondered if she had not overdone things with Bita, demanding and expecting too much of her, considering the girl against the background of her race and its place in the Occidental idea of the universe.

Suppose under that cultivated crust she was noways better than any of the herd of common black wenches who took religion as a plaything and were often converted in sin and went down to baptism with babies in their bellies.

Mrs. Craig thought of those little notes of progress among the native converts that she had published in the *Mission Field*. And of the pious wealthy who, touched by them and similar effusions by other hands, had donated money and clothes to the semi-savages, and of the fact that the story of many subjects of those notes who had fallen from the Jacob's ladder of grace and back into sweet sin had never been chronicled.

And now she was lost in a fog of doubt, wondering if all that faithful and careful building up of mission work might not some day go the same way as did the solid-seeming façade of the great plantations now abandoned to decay and crumbling in the dust before the huts and fields and the careless living and grin of the blacks, who shouted praises to the Christ God in the church in the daytime and muttered incantations to the Obeah God in the night-time. . . .

"Get hence behind me, Satan!" Mrs. Craig cried, and reproaching herself for permitting wicked thoughts to pollute her mind, impulsively she locked the door of the room, and asking Bita to kneel with her she prayed to God for them both and implored forgiveness for sinful doubts.

When they arose she asked Bita about Squire Gensir, remarking that he was a very, very cultured and learned man and that it was a rare experience to know him even though he did not accept Christ. She had taken tea with him twice, first on the near-by coffee plantation of a creole lady and then she had invited him to the mission. She wished he would come again, but he cared nothing about the social amenities. However, now that he knew Bita and was so interested in the natives, he might be induced to call again.

All the same Priscilla's mind was not altogether tranquil about Bita and that tea-meeting. And that night when she related the incident to Malcolm he also shared her inquietude. They came to the conclusion that it might be a wise step if Bita were married as soon as possible. Within a year Herald Newton Day would be graduated from the theological college and ready for holy orders. And as he was coming that very week on a vacation to Jubilee it was decided to start propaganda at once to get Bita thinking seriously about the happy idea.

After one of those suffocating summer nights when it felt as though the trade winds that always cool the island had died on the motionless breast of the sea, the morning broke languorous and heavy. The city was like a terrible oven and the slabs like radiators under the people's feet.

At the Tabernacle Theological College, situated in the centre of the city, the nine boarding students, black and brown, were breakfasting on bread and butter with jam and coffee. One of them, Herald Newton Day, was in a hurry, for he was going home on a vacation to see his prospective intended and wanted to catch the train. Breakfast was served in a corridor-like room having large low windows on one side only and looking out down on a little garden shaped like a long trough and full of crotons and variegated tanias whose leaves were marly with dust.

After breakfast Herald Newton said good-bye to his fellow students, went up to his room to bring down his bags, and took a cab to the railroad station. The train would take him to within about forty miles of his destination. The rest of the way to Jubilee was usually made by horseback, buggy or omnibus, according to the pecuniary capacity of the traveller.

Herald Newton felt happy. Everything had gone smoothly in the making of his career. He had won a theological scholarship and all the expenses of his college training were free. And as soon as he was graduated there would be a coveted place ready for him as assistant to Malcolm Craig. Malcolm and Priscilla had done well together. But they were growing old and with all the week-day meetings and the choir and little societies pertaining to the church in which they were actively connected and the two outstations of Buxton Hall and Little Gap, which were five and nine miles distant respectively, and above all their determination to have a Negro succeed them at Jubilee, Herald Newton would find himself a much-needed assistant.

Old Deacon Day gave a dinner to celebrate Herald Newton's visit home, inviting the Craigs and Bita, the schoolmaster of Jubilee and his wife and a mulatto schoolmate of Herald Newton's, who was now employed as a clerk in a dry-goods shop, and his sister. The deacon had a good house that had been erected with money loaned by a building society, but unlike many of the peasants, he had not been negligent about the mortgage, and was now the free owner of his home. At the time of the coffee scandal he was a member of the church. His father had been a leader and suffered a big loss and had left the Jubilee church, taking all his family with him to The Ark.

Touched with decent pride about his son, grizzly-bearded, Deacon Day presided like a patriarch at the head of the table, inclined a little forwards with his hands like fine bits of ancient and well-used ebony resting on the white stiff-starched cloth.

Mother Day, as the neighbours familiarly called his wife, had prepared a formidable dinner. There was a great old-fashioned platter of akee and codfish done in butter, boiled ham, a boiled chicken in rich sauce and a selection of the many vegetables that feature the peasants' table: two kinds of yam, the yellow afou and the delicious starchy white; boiled breadfruit; boiled plantains and boiled sweet cassava.

Mother Day did not sit down to table, for she was occupied in making and serving the dinner helped by an able-bodied girl who lived with her. Her face like polished oak was sweet with affection when she leaned over her son. And upon Bita it beamed. For to her the occasion was a preliminary celebration of the engagement of Bita and Herald. Seated beside the dry-goods clerk Bita had a sensation as if they were all conspiring against her.

Mrs. Craig sat next to the schoolmaster and she and her husband between them kept the conversation going with little pleasant items about the mission, the immigration of the Negro workers to Panama and South America, the agitation to prevent East Indian coolies and Chinese entering the colony and the controversial articles in the daily newspapers about the extention of the railroad, which would surely benefit Jubilee as the centre of a flourishing fruit and grain trade and as an attractive little town for tourists. Conversation without any bite or object, trivial as conversation is apt to be wherever more than four are gathered together to eat and drink politely, but it saved the meal from degenerating into a piggish feed, for peasants are prone to devour in grim silence when good victuals are set before them, delaying to talk until afterwards when the stuff is settling inside and giving them a contented feeling and they can lean back somewhere under a tree or a barbecue to make digestion easy.

That Sunday, Herald Newton preached at the little outstation of Buxton Hall. He was offered the use of the mission gig and, Mrs. Craig suggesting it, Bita accompanied him.

Wearing clerical clothes, a black coat reaching to his knee and a round felt hat, Herald Newton was a clean-cut type of the new generation of Negro students of theology. Bita was dressed simply as a church organist in indigo skirt and a rose-apple-cream blouse.

An eager and friendly congregation turned out to welcome the young student and his intended. Bita played the baby organ. Herald Newton preached from the text in Ecclesiastes: Remember thy creator in the days of thy youth. . . .

He possessed a good clear voice and used it effectively, for the people listened eagerly, apparently satisfied with his deliverance, but to the critical ear there was a sound of too much oil on his tongue like a person who was full of self-satisfaction and, considering his youth, on too intimate terms with God.

The sermon was adorned with many congregational "amens" pronounced by the older heads, who always felt very exalted whenever the preaching was especially directed at youth. And in this instance the feeling was emphasized because the preacher was himself a youth. Thus spake Herald: " 'Youth is the time to serve the Lord!'

"Many there are who say: Today we are young and because we are young we can forget God—give ourselves up to the sinful flesh now without restraint, and thinking that there is plenty of time later to repent and be saved . . . [Amen.]

"But I say unto you, my young brothers and sisters, there is danger in delay—the danger of sudden death in sin. [Amen! Amen!] Do not be eleventh-hour seekers of salvation. [Amen.] How sad it must be for a person who has given his whole life to unrighteous living to be calling upon God for forgiveness in the last hour of affliction! [Amen.] And for us who are young, my brothers and sisters, beware of waiting until it is late. For the angel of destruction may strike suddenly, cutting you down even as a machete shears through a banana sucker. [Amen! Amen! Amen!] . . .

"I am only a young watchman of God. And my voice speaking to you is not my own, but his trumpet. And when I hear his voice saying to me: Watchman, what of the night? I shall be able to answer: Lord, I did watch and warn the people in Thy name. [Amen.] . . .

"From the pleasures of the grog shop and the racecourse and tea-meetings I warn you, my young brothers and sisters, to cease and come to Him." [Amen! Amen!]

Driving back to Jubilee with Bita, Herald Newton took the opportunity of letting her know his thoughts.

"I think the sermon made a good impression," he said. "I did my best."

"The people liked it," said Bita.

"Oh yes, the way they crowned it. I poured all I had into it although it was only a bush village. I kept imagining all the time that it was a bigger and a better audience. That's the way, to practise in the small places, so that when you come to the big you won't feel intimidated."

"Yes," said Bita.

"I haven't had the chance yet of anything at Jubilee but evening services and such. But the day when I mount that pulpit will be a day. I want to beat the Rev. Craig at his best."

Bita said nothing.

"Of course you know I expect to succeed Mr. Craig some day. I'll be the first Negro to take charge of Jubilee. Won't that be a grand thing?"

Bita said, "Yes," but it was a doubtful yes. She had a deep affection for Malcolm Craig and rapidly appraising Herald Newton could not visualize his measuring up to the gaunt and ascetic figure of the present incumbent in the pulpit of Jubilee.

"Yes, it will be fine for you and me, Miss Bita. You know I wasn't thinking of Jubilee without you. For we were both trained to think of Jubilee—I might just as well say it—for the two of us together. I don't know if you feel about it as much as I do. If it will appeal to you as much as it does to me. But I know my father will be very happy. And Mrs. Craig too. Everybody would be happy if we both got married."

Bita made no reply and after an interval Herald Newton said: "Well, what do you think of it, Miss Bita?"

"I suppose we might as well do it and please everybody," she said.

Herald Newton slackened the reins and took Bita's hand.

"What a nice way you've put it, Miss Bita. Or may I say Bita now? I didn't think of phrasing it as neatly as that."

"But I just borrowed that from you," she protested.

"Well, that's an indication already of how we'll be helping each other, our minds working together. You know at first when I began studying for the ministry and thinking of the great work before me, I thought that perhaps only a white woman could help me. One having a pure mind and lofty ideals like Mrs. Craig. For purity is my ideal of the married state. With clean hearts thinking and living purely and bearing children under the benediction of God.

"I know you will understand,"—Herald squeezed Bita's hand, but she felt that it was not she herself that inspired the impulse, but perhaps his thought—"just as Mrs. Craig would. For you have been trained like a pure-minded white lady."

"I don't know about that," said Bita. "But whatever I was trained like or to be, I know one thing. And that is that I am myself."

"And yourself is the best," he said.

Bita broke a pretty laugh and Herald Newton caught up the reins and shook the pony into a trot.

It was while Herald Newton was preaching his sermon that Bita saw that she could not love him. But if she could just like him even, she thought, since it would please the Craigs for them to marry. And no doubt the families on both sides. But principally because it would please the Craigs she was inclined to do it, for they had made her what she was. After all she would have to marry. That was the proper thing, the main objective for a nice young girl.

And what could a cultivated Negro girl from the country hope for better than a parson. Marrying a good parson was a step higher than marrying a schoolmaster. If she had happened to be born a light-brown or yellow girl, she might, with her training, easily get away with a man of a similar complexion—a local functionary of the law courts, revenue or some other department or a manager of a business worth while in the city. But she was in the black and dark-brown group and there were no prospects of her breaking into the intimate social circles of the smart light-brown and yellow groups.

And the vision of climbing and pushing and trying to crash the barred gates was not inspiring to her. She had been educated to the point where she was able to look down and see how futile and mind-racking was such a manner of existence. She remembered at college how girls would spend their time cold-shouldering some who they thought were socially unimportant, and calculating and scheming to get invitations from those whose families were, and how ugly was the game—the heartburnings and cynical reflections from disappointments, setbacks and barren achievements.

She thought it would be just as well for her after all to marry the heir-presumptive to the Jubilee Free Church. As a ward of the Craigs she would no doubt have a substantial dowry (from Mrs. Craig at least) if she married a man of whom they approved. And that was something to reckon on.

After breakfast on Monday Herald Newton called at the mission and was received by Mrs. Craig on the dining-room side of the veranda. There they engaged in a long confidential conversation until they were interrupted by Patou appearing creeping and blinking upon them. Mrs. Craig asked Herald to go into the study to the Reverend Malcolm, leaving her to humour Patou a little. Later she joined them there and the conversation was continued between the three.

Meanwhile Bita was at the piano in the sitting-room practising Mendelssohn's, "Hear My Prayer." The choirmaster had asked her to find a new anthem for the choir and she had chosen that instead of one of the stereotyped ones out of the big blue-covered anthem-book.

There, after Herald Newton's departure, Mrs. Craig came and kissed her on the forehead and said: "I'm so glad, dear child, and so is Mr. Craig. I'm sure you will both do well together and be happy in the work of the Lord."

She sat close against Bita on the piano stool and scanned the music. "It's a fine piece, but don't you think it's a little too steep for them, eh?" she said, meaning the choristers.

"They have the voices. All they need is plenty of good training," said Bita.

"I think you're right," said Mrs. Craig. "The soprano part is lovely and will be a magnificent vehicle for Belle Black's voice."

She withdrew, closing the door. And went back to the study to talk some more about Bita and Herald Newton and chiefly about a house for them to live in.

"I don't think they should stay at Deacon Day's," Priscilla said, "although his house is large enough, with room to spare."

"No," agreed Malcolm, "I think they would be more

comfortable and contented together in their own little house."

But for a house in Jubilee they would have to pay rent. And as Herald Newton would be starting his career only as an assistant, it would be better if he were not burdened with rent as well as marriage at the beginning.

Mrs. Craig suggested that the couple could stay at the outstation of Buxton Hall, which was just five miles from Jubilee. It was a pleasing little village with a macadamized road going straight through to the busy banana port. And it possessed a cottage of two comfortable rooms for the visiting preacher. Mrs. Craig thought that the church folk there would exert themselves to build an additional room to the cottage, when they knew they were going to have a resident minister.

8

A MERRY-GO-ROUND HAD COME TO JUBILEE. A NICE little painted one with box seats and horses and pigs and cows to ride upon and lively music zooming out of its belly. It was set upon a level stretch of green not far from the Ark, the famous church of Jacob Brown's. And afternoon and evening the townsfolk of lowly tastes went to the grass plot to joyride. Strapped to painted ponies and pigs the little tots shrieked and whirled around, the lads stood up in the stirrups and the girls sat side-saddle and whipped their steeds.

Many nice young folk went to the merry-go-round to watch the common folk, but couldn't take a ride themselves even though their hearts craved it and their skins were itching for the sensation. Nice choirgirls and neat shopgirls, just two generations removed from the state of slavery and concubinage, could not afford to merry-go-round under the watchful eyes of benign uplifters who were pointing them the way to go straight on, their eyes fixed upon a star.

One girl there was, Gracie Hall, who had recently returned from the city, where she had been learning the trade of seamstress. In the city she had had much more liberty than her parents in Jubilee imagined. For she had gone to house dances that were not so refined. And she had gone alone of an evening to the seaside garden where they gave the monkey show and the fireworks and she had certainly ridden round a circle before, even if it were no more than when she took the belt line to see the city by tramway.

Contrary to her parents' expectations the little city of Kingston had had the effect of destroying the prim reserve of her Jubilee upbringing and made Gracie a little free. And so while the other damsels of Jubilee were contented to look on and be amused at the common peasant girls mounting and riding, Gracie was not. She paid her coppers and went riding too.

Her father, upon hearing that she was riding, hurried to the place. He arrived just as she was finishing and slapped her off the horse and would have smashed the merry-go-round if restraining hands had not been laid upon him.

Out of the incident a local ballad-monger created a new ditty similar to the many that always spring like mushrooms out of the tragic and comic phases of native life, and the draymen and coachmen, the donkey boys and all the rough lads of the town, were soon sweetening their tongues to it:

> "Oh, Breddah Hall, an' where was you
> When Gracie went a-ridin'?
> Good Breddah Hall, we know is true
> Dat Gracie went a-ridin'.
>
> "Merry-go-roun' is come to town
> An' naygurs ridin' ebery way.
> Oh, Breddah Hall, you' gal gone roun'.
> Today is Gracie ridin' day.

"Oh, Breddah Hall, doan' be so cross
   'Cause Gracie went a-ridin'.
Knock off you' gal, but not de hoss
   Dat Gracie went a-ridin'. . . .

"Merry-go-roun' is come to town. . . ."

At the grog shop near the Jubilee market there was a gang deep in drinking and discussion and one of the boys sitting on top of a cracker barrel was drumming the staves and whistling:

"Gracie went a-ridin' . . ."

"Well, dat was one to fall down," said a little-sized brown drinker. "Wonder who be the next?"

"De nex' is you," said the barkeeper. "You habent call fer a roun' yet."

"Set him up, set him up deah," said the little one. "Dis is one way a falling, but de way Gracie fall is anodder dat I wasn't bohn to be."

"To fin' out de nex' you mus' ask Hopping Dick," said a tall black.

"Hopping Dick ain't nuttin'," said the little one contemptuously.

"Him get a look in on the miss in de mission, though," said the tall one, "an', dat's somet'ing. None a we heah ain't get dat chance, neider anybody like us in Jubilee, 'cep'n' Hopping Dick."

"Dat was jes' a fluke. You t'ink a gal like dat could fall fer Hopping Dick! Not fer all him fancy stepping."

"You jealous a him," said the tall one.

"Jealous a what? Jealous a somet'ing dat's nuttin'?" asked the little one. "I ain't jealous a no naygur or malatta in Jubilee."

"But you jealous a Hopping Dick."

"You t'ink so because youse him big tool."

"Ah ain't nobody's tool but mi own. But listen to me, all a you. I hab a point to make."

"Gwan an' mek it so long as it not mine," said the little one.

The grog shop filled with deep belly-shaking laughter and the little one put his thumb in his braces and nodded approvingly.

"Well," said the tall one, "Gawd made man an' then woman from man, accordin' to the Bible. An' Gawd put a O in woman. But dere's no O in man. Now dere's an O in the reading and the figuring a life and woman is in both a them an' both ways. So you nebber can tell about a woman whedder her is in de readin' or figurin' side a life an' when you come to any man an' a woman, well, you jes' cyant tell nuthin' at all. An' when a man tell you him is gwine mek a woman doan' you start a-cryin' him down an' say him cyant, becausen de woman is high up an' stylish an' nice-speakin' an all. Fer de leetlest thing can mek a woman fall, when a man can get away wid 'most anyt'ing an' still stand 'pon his feet."

There were rummy h'ms and other murmurs of appreciation and understanding and the tall one called for a bottle of rum.

But the little one said: "Das all right in a general way, but dere's a big differance between talking an' doing. Doing is one thing an' talking is anodder and talk is the cheapest thing dere is. I doan' belieb in shooting mi mouth off about life because it's better than youse."

"Das sound talkin'," said the proprietor, "an' thas de

best way to tek life. We hab to be respectin' our bettahs. De lower mus' look up to the higher an' de higher to the highest. That's de way life is plan' an' we hab to fallaw de plan, or dere wouldn' be any kind a life to speak of."

"Sure thing dat," said the little one. "Now dis Miss Bita she one of our own people and we ought to feel proud a har gwine abroad an' gettin' ejucated widouten collect har wid a pusson like a Hopping Dick."

At that hour Bita with Herald Newton, and Malcolm and Priscilla Craig, were attending a roadside salvation meeting a little way out of the town. It was on the way to Buxton Hall at a crossroads. About a dozen church members had accompanied them from Jubilee. And a few dozen more came out of the straggling huts and houses around the crossroads.

Stationed by the wayside under the laden mango trees against a bank overgrown with thick guinea grass they sang:

"In the harvest field there is work to do."

Malcolm Craig spoke in his familiar persuasive manner to the villagers, reminding them to think of the Lord always and not to neglect going to church.

At the finish he knelt down in the dust to pray and Priscilla and Herald Newton did likewise, also some of the villagers. But Bita only leaned against the bank and closed her eyes.

After prayer Herald Newton delivered a little sermon on the sufficiency of God's love. It was in the same tone as his sermon at Buxton Hall. And the impression was the same—that he was exalted by the pleasure of his own delivery (which was good) and exposition of his theme without much thought of the audience.

Bita was occupied all the time now devising means to be as little as possible alone in the company of her intended. Herald Newton was so gravely serious about it all that he became funny to her. She just couldn't think about him seriously. Yet she was aware that marriage was a subject to think about seriously. Aware too that she had assented to his proposal of marriage merely to fit into a plan—something thrust upon her that she had not felt even a reaction to refuse, because, like her training, it was designed to serve a purpose that was more than herself—the crowning of her education.

There was a perceptible change in the life of the mission now since the engagement. Mrs. Craig was benevolently sweeter. And even in the voice of Mr. Craig, whom she loved and who to her was a paragon of fatherly correctness, there seemed to have crept just a nuance of affectionate approval.

It had never been lost upon her, from the time that the Craigs adopted her after the rape, that she was the subject of an experiment, and as she grew in understanding she had voluntarily conceded herself as one does to a mesmerist. Neither had she ever been blind to the advantages of it as compared with her peasant heritage. She had never had any anxiety, never had to think about the future. And now to prolong that state indefinitely and for ever she had simply to go straight through the motions of compliance with automatic gestures in harmony with the decorous righteousness of the mission life. Her little essays at independence and the resultant passages with Priscilla Craig had indicated clearly the way she would have to go if she were to reap the ripe benefits of that experiment.

But a moment of contact with Herald Newton and her physical self recoiled from, as much as the spiritual rebelled against, him. Hopping Dick was by far more desirable, even if he were not educated and refined. He had a way about him of approaching a woman that was tantalizing and he inspired at least a little physical interest. But between her and Herald there was a block of ice. She longed to be free from the irritation of his presence, so that she could push the eventuality of their union far out of her mind and then play without effort at the make-believe of being engaged.

But he was so inevitable. Always intrusive and entirely lacking in intuition. She felt that if she had to bear always that constant contact she might just break out one day with something that would destroy irreparably the whole fabric of the plan that had been so carefully charted for her.

She found a happy way of escape by a telegram recalling her to Banana Bottom, for her Anty Nommy had had one of her periodic attacks of illness and was in a dangerous state.

9

ANTY NOMMY WAS A CONSTANT SUFFERER FROM UTERINE troubles. They said that when she was giving birth to Bab she had had an incompetent midwife who had injured her womb. Since then all her conceptions had been abortive and she had given up hope of having another child.

Nearly every year and always at the same time the illness recurred: excruciating pains in her womb. At times the attacks were so severe it seemed as though she would pass out, but sometimes they were also slight. Jordan had called in doctors from Gingertown and Jubilee and he had taken Anty Nommy to consult well-known doctors in the city. But she had never found a cure and so the sickness had become chronic.

Sister Phibby Patroll had come to the house and installed herself as nurse as soon as she heard of Anty Nommy's illness. She always did that and was well rewarded for her services by Jordan. But Jordan was very relieved to have Bita come. For he was in the midst of yam-planting. And Bab was not there to help him, having recently left for the city to begin his examination for the Civil Service and Anty Nommy had preferred that he should not be sent for. On the day that Anty Nommy took ill Jordan had given a yam "match." That is, with hundreds of yam-heads on his hands sprouting vine quicker than he could plant them (even with the help of Jubban and another hired man) he had proclaimed a day for yam-planting. He prepared a feast: great boilers of yam "tail"—one of the most prized parts of the yam, a piece that is sometimes cut from the head at the time of planting—yampies and pink cocoes, with a pig killed for the occasion. And a host of young villagers came with hoes upon their shoulders to feed and to work.

Digging yam banks and singing sweating in the sun. The holes were dug wide enough to take three yam-heads in a row, with space enough for the young yams to bulge and swell and grow down into the soil. From two to three feet deep. And then the earth was broken finely and heaped into a mound. Twenty-five of these for one man were not a bad showing for a day's work.

It was a great digging-day. The soil was the rich dark loam splendid for nigger-yams. Rarely was there a stone to turn the blade of the hoe. Only the dull thud of the hoes as they were sunk to their necks and a village ballad-monger leading the men singing "jammas":

> "Dis a day is working-day,
> Dis a day is feasting-day,
> Dig away, dig away, dig away.
> Mouth an' hand mus' go togedder,
> Lak a sistah and a bredder,
> Dig away, dig away, dig away."

And after working without letting up all day, superintending the feeding of the diggers, Anty Nommy had been seized with the pains in the middle of the night. Yet so brave and strong-willed she was, she had objected to Jordan's going to telegraph Bita. And she had begged him not to interrupt his work in the field. For, said she, the crisis would pass in its own time just like the others before. She had come to resign herself to her illness as chronic and incurable. In fact she was so concerned about the smooth running of the house-field-and-market work that she even blamed herself for becoming ill at that season. For after the big digging-day there were so many yam-heads that were just crying out to get planted with their long vines trailing along the ground in search of some-thing to climb. The yield was better if the first vines were not destroyed. And the planting would not even be over before there would have to begin the cutting of the long bamboo poles and driving them fixed in the earth for the vines to climb.

Bita had betrayed such a joyous eagerness to return again to Banana Bottom that Mrs. Craig had remarked: "Well, one would think you did not realize that it was your aunt who is lying dangerously ill." But Bita could not hide her delight. Inwardly she thanked Anty Nommy for being in-strumental in getting her away, although she felt sorry for her.

When she arrived, the doctor from Gingertown was there. He was a member of one of the old landed mulatto families. And he had been attending to Anty Nommy for many years. Anty Nommy exhibited no new symptoms that could give the key to the source of her trouble and all he could do was to apply the old remedy: the douche within and poultice without.

Bita prepared the doctor a light lunch: soft boiled eggs, bread and chocolate. And he delayed his departure, stay-ing longer than he usually did on a backwoods visit to a peasant home, except when that was imperatively profes-sional. Bita's education made it possible for him to approach her easily as he would a woman of his own set. They chatted a little. Years before he had graduated from a famous British medical college. But since his graduation and return to the colony he had never gone back to Britain. They talked about the tourists' sights in London: Trafalgar Square, St. Paul's from the Tower Bridge, Hyde Park, The Crystal Palace. . . .

That week-end Jubban the drayman went alone with the dray to the far market. The cutting of the yam-heads for the planting had given Jordan a mighty heap of lovely "toes." These he and Jubban had painted with white lime and they were splendid for marketing. The littler "toes" were kept for home consumption. Some of the men who had worked in the field had helped themselves to a number of "toes." For no part of the yam was more valued than a fresh "toe" rich in starch. Such a "toe" well roasted and eaten hot (sometimes with butter or a piece of meat or fish) with the morning's coffee was manna to a peasant.

The yam "toes" made up half a dray-load. And two women were putting in tins of sugar and hampers of sugar-heads (sugar-heads are sugar hardened into bell-like forms in bowls or frames and weighing about two pounds each), and a lad some fine bunches of plantains. This was the way of loading a dray—all together making a full dray piling up as high as the stanchions.

Jordan usually accompanied his dray to the far market and sometimes Anty Nommy or Bab substituted for him. Bita had suggested to him that he could go this time for she with Sister Phibby was capable of nursing Anty Nommy and looking after the household. And in the big canopied carved mahogany four-poster, that had belonged to her mother, Anty Nommy joined urging Jordan to go— as much as saying she was not going to get worse or die.

But Jordan said he had confidence in Jubban to take care of the market. Jubban had drifted into Jordan's home from a neighbouring parish that always suffered from lack of water during the dry season. There were hundreds of poor kids like him about the country, who always try to find a home among the better-off peasants. When Jubban came to Jordan's he was a weak kind of a boy, evidently because of malnutrition. And he couldn't tell his own age. That was a few years before the rape of Bita. But his development was a marvel and now he was one of the best and most reliable of the husky draymen of the region.

That evening when Jubban came to the house to check up on the goods for the market and take orders from Jordan, Bita became conscious of the existence of her father's drayman for the first time, remarked his frank, broad, blue-black and solid jaws, and thought that it was all right for her father to have confidence in him.

By Monday Anty Nommy was in an improved state. Sister Phibby said: "I t'ink in spite a all them sudden seijures you gwine lib longer than 'most a us in Banana Bottom."

"Gawd knows de best," said Anty Nommy.

Next to the experience of officiating at a successful birth, Sister Phibby loved to relate how she had piously closed the eyes of a dear dying Christian. But one should not unkindly construe that because of her religious feeling for such a melancholy ceremony she did not sincerely wish Anty Nommy better.

It was a very sultry day. Too hot for staying in the house. And even on the honeysuckle-shielded veranda.

After the one-o'clock recess bell had rung calling the children back in to school, Bita went into the garden. The lot was large, lying between the main parochial road and a neglected back path that was sometimes used as a short cut to the market.

Crossing this track she waded through a deep bed of trailing fern down to the bank of the Cane River. She skirted the bank, continuing up towards the direction of the school. She knew the scene well when as a girl she used to play down the slope and along the river bank.

At last she stood under a mammee tree high over the Blue Hole where the schoolboys bathed. And looking down she saw a group of five, truants from school, standing naked upon a ledge, remarking their armpits and groins for signs of hair and arguing how much more time it would take for them to be full-fledged men.

A twig broke under Bita's foot and glancing up sharply one of the boys shouted and dived into the water followed by the others and all together beating up white heaps of water.

Bita continued on through the fern, wondering if they had seen her and were scared of her telling the schoolmaster. She hoped they hadn't, because it was such a close hot day it was just what she would have done if she were in their place.

A little higher up, straight down under the schoolhouse from a direct line, but a good distance away, was Martha's Basin, where the girls used to bathe. The long stout trunk of a fallen mangrove tree separated Bita from it. She took off her shoes and climbing upon the trunk walked along it, balancing herself until she reached the pool and jumped down.

All of her body was tingling sweet with affectionate feeling for the place. For here she had lived some of the happiest moments of her girlhood, with her schoolmates and alone. Here she had learned to swim, beginning in the shallow water at the lower end with a stout length of bamboo. She remembered now how she screamed with delight with her schoolmates cheering and clapping their hands that day when she swam from one bank to the other.

She slipped off her slight clothes and plunged into the water and swam round and round the hole. Then she turned on her back to enjoy the water cooling on her breasts. Now she could bear the sun above burning down. How delicious was the feeling of floating! To feel that one can suspend oneself upon a yawning depth and drift, drifting in perfect confidence without the slightest intruding thought of danger.

And thoughts flitted across her mind like cinema scenes. Of her college days and what some of those white girls she had grown to like were occupied with now. Of a moment in the dining-room of the pension at Munich with Mrs. Craig when it seemed that all the guests were observing her and commenting, but not offensively. Of the brother of one of her college friends that she had liked a little in England. Of Jubilee and Herald Newton Day.

She had no idea how long she floated dreaming there between fancy and reality before she turned over and swam back, clambering up the bank to find that her clothes had disappeared. She thought it was one of the kids who had mischievously followed her from the Blue Hole, and was not angry. So she plucked a handful of the furry trailing ferns, wrapped them around her loins and started towards the mangrove trunk to see if the kids had hidden her clothes there.

Suddenly she heard a slight sound like the shearing of a limb and from the smaller end of the mangrove trunk she saw the face of Tack Tally grinning at her through a rose-apple branch.

"You ugly monkey!" Bita cried. "I'll have you arrested, I will." And she started towards him. But Tack plunged through the guinea grass. Bita climbed over the mangrove trunk and found her clothes at the root of the rose-apple tree. Snatching them up and returning to the river bank she dressed herself.

10

SQUIRE GENSIR WAS AMONG THE MANY SYMPATHIZERS who had called during Anty Nommy's crises. And as soon as her aunt was feeling better Bita went to visit him in his bungalow at Breakneck. The squire had a piano and had invited her to use it while she was staying at Banana Bottom.

The squire referred to his bungalow as the "Hut." It was a spacious place. A little barrack, forty by twenty feet, screened in two. One part contained the piano, a cot, a table, two deck-chairs and some cane chairs, and a book-shelf was built against the entire short side. In the other part there was a clothes-closet, an extra cot, a large rough broadleaf table. And right outside against it was a small covered portico that was used as a washroom. There was no veranda, but in front the roof sloped off about five feet to form a piazza. The house opened with large French windows on a level with the sills looking over the Banana Bottom valley to the mountain chains beyond.

Squire Gensir lived modestly. Once a visitor remarking how simple was his way of living, the squire replied that it had been a difficult thing to achieve.

"Difficult? Why there's no difficulty in living like this. You have nothing to worry about. It's so primitive."

The squire replied that primitive living was more complex than his visitor imagined. That it was the art of knowing how to eliminate the non-essentials that militate against plastic living and preventing accumulations, valuable or worthless. It was easy for hampering things to heap up in the homes of all classes of people, because it is traditional in human nature to cling tenaciously to things that have no more place in material or spiritual living than manure, and as the home is cluttered up so is the mind.

The piano was the only luxury in the place. The squire was a lover of music and a fairly good pianist. And the piano was indispensable to him to record the native airs he wrote down. He would devote a great deal of time to fix a single nuance in the recording of a melody while it was sung in turns by different natives. And that was no easy task, for the singers often varied the tunes according to their whim.

Bita's favourite playing was Chopin and second favourite were the spirituals, which were known in the island as Jubilee Songs. Of the many remembered images of her college days the dearest was that of her piano-teacher—a frail stalk of a person but possessed with a powerful enthusiasm for Chopin—an enthusiasm that she had also imparted to Bita.

Squire Gensir's first question was to ask Bita if anything had happened because of her going to the tea-meeting. Bita replied that if it hadn't been for him the consequences might have been disastrous.

"Me!" he exclaimed. "What do you mean?"

"I mean that your reputation saved me," said Bita. "Mrs. Craig was going to have a fit or die. Her face was white and cold as ice. Then I mentioned your name—that I went with you. And you should have seen her face. Like an angel's.

It made me think she was sorry she was not there too—in your company."

Squire Gensir laughed. "Well, it's good to hear that. I thought I was a no-rep."

"No, you don't really," said Bita. "You're so certain of yourself. And besides, you have your class and your colour —open sesames for you everywhere. It's grand. You're a thousand times freer than we."

"I may be freer than you," he said. "Because you passed through the same system of education as myself. Something to fit you into a rigid pattern. But I don't think I am as free as the peasants here in their daily life—I'm not as naturally free as they are. So free that they don't have any idea of words like freedom and restraint."

"I don't agree," she said. "What freedom have they? Plodding and digging and digging all day. And never going anywhere except to market. And never any fun but tea-meetings. And you—you have had the run of the world. Even here, you can go anywhere from the governor's house to the lowest peasant's hut."

"But I never meant that kind of artificial educated freedom. The peasants' mind couldn't grasp that. Your cousin Bab, yes. For he's educating himself up from the peasantry. I like him very much in a personal way. Even more than I do the peasants in a general way. But I think he is restless and unhappy. And he'll be worse when he wins his desire and gets into that Civil Service jacket. But when I speak of the freedom of your peasants, I mean that unconscious freedom in their common existence, their natural instincts. They don't know what repression is."

"But that is so animal," said Bita. "Don't you think

it would be better if they had a chance for finer living and education? You believe in education, don't you?"

"Yes, I do in the intrinsic sense. Education as a thing for individual cultural development. But I don't believe in the system of modern education. It grinds out certain fixed types on different grades to fit into a preconceived plan. And there is no room in it for one who would like to think and to act independently. I know what I am talking about, for I went through the machine. And my freedom that you admire—well, you don't know how hard I had to fight for it. All of my relatives and friends had some better idea than myself of how I should live. What purpose I should live for. Wanted to dispose of my life for some noble ideal of service: a class, a cause, a loyalty. They were horrified because I thought it was the best thing for a man to devote himself first to the understanding and adjusting of his own life to life. I was an eccentric, egoist, hedonist. However, I did. I went my own way. And they followed the traditional. I've never been sorry I didn't go their way. And I am very happy in my way."

When he stopped Bita said, "I wish you'd go on and tell me some more about yourself. If you don't mind me asking?"

He was willing to talk about himself. . . . At his university, he said, he had been a member of a small serious group which had set as its aim the achievement of something for each member different from that which was obtainable in the channels that were ordinarily open to them. What was ordinary to them of course might have seemed very extraordinary to a proletarian, peasant or clerk and well worth striving for.

But the ideal of achievement was one thing, the reality

quite different. . . . Of the four principal members of the group the one who had been the most sensitive had chosen a career that seemed altogether incompatible with his delicate spirit. And among the high distinctions he won was to become famous to the world as "The Butcher." . . . A second had become an imperial fire-eating orator, winning great plaudits for his dialectical skill and sophism. While a third had achieved eminence as a courtier. He himself had travelled and drifted away from everything until he had reached and stopped in that warm isolated little island.

But it was all an enigma to Bita. She could not quite believe that he who had grown up a favoured child at the hub of mundane life could be satisfied with existence there in that remote place. With her it was very different. She was born to that rude and lonely mountain life. She was attached to it by family and scenes and unconscious childhood habits. And she had been educated with the purpose of returning to it. Yet sometimes she was overwhelmed with the feeling of it being an empty lonely life. She wondered if Squire Gensir was not sometimes agitated by that feeling also and therefore dissatisfied. But it was doubtful, when he could take such a child's joy in little things. And his face, like ancient worn marble, was as tranquil as the Buddha.

The Squire showed Bita a native tune that he had written down, music and words. It was a tune that had been known up there in the heart of the hill country for years and which was fiddled and sometimes sung to a dance called the minto, perhaps a native name for the minuet. But what had excited the squire was his discovery that with a little variation of measure the melody was original Mozart.

They went to the piano to look at both versions together. There was no doubt about the resemblance. Bita sat down and touched off both. As a little girl she had swayed and jigged to the lively measure and thought it just a lovely trifle, purely native. Identifying it now with Mozart made her romantic and filled her with a pretty fancy of a wistful slave mistress on one of the lonely plantations of that region conjuring that savage and tragic scene with the magic of Mozart, while a slave listening near by stole the performance to recreate it for the blacks gathered together in their barracks for singing and dancing after the day's work was done.

"But maybe there are other native tunes like this that aren't original," said Bita.

"Some are; some aren't. I don't think it matters. Everybody borrows or steals and recreates in art. Next to enjoying it, the exciting thing is tracking down sources and resemblances and influences. That is one reason it's so interesting to go to the tea-meetings and to listen to the Anancy stories. I think some of our famous European fables have their origin in Africa. Even the mumbo-jumbo of the Obeahmen fascinates me."

"But Obeah is not the same," said Bita, "it is an awful crime."

"Oh, it's just our civilization that makes it a crime. Obeah is only a form of primitive superstition. As Christianity is a form of civilized superstition. That's why it can't be rooted out by long prison terms and the unspeakable brutality of the cat."

"But it is a low practice," said Bita. "Father hates it.

And I think we're the only family in Banana Bottom that don't believe in it. You know many of the people dislike Father because they think he's too prosperous. And they go to the Obeahman and pay him a lot of money to make him unlucky. Father said it would be better if they saved their money and bought land to make themselves prosperous, for he never would have come to anything if he had spent his earnings with the Obeahman to make himself prosperous."

"I don't mean that it is good to practise Obeah. But the peasants waste a lot of money on Christianity also. Money that might have done them more material good. One must be tolerant. When you read in your studies about the Druids, the Greek and Roman gods and demi-gods, and the Nordic Odin, you felt tolerant about them. Didn't you? Then why should you be so intolerant about Obi and Obeahmen?"

"I don't know. It doesn't seem the same."

"But it is, though. You're intolerant because of your education. Obeah is a part of your folklore, like your Anancy tales and your digging jammas. And your folklore is the spiritual link between you and your ancestral origin. You ought to learn to appreciate it as I do mine. My mind is richer because I know your folklore. I am sure you believe the fables of La Fontaine and of Æsop fine and literary and the Anancy stories common and vulgar. Yet many of the Anancy stories are superior. It's because of misdirected education. But Mrs. Craig could never see that——"

"She would be horrified to hear you say that," said Bita.

"Because she sees you with the eyes of a good Christian— like a little heathen to be brought up in the doctrine of salvation. You know I believe it might be worth while for Negroes in America to know more of folklore Africa and less of slave-trade Africa."

"Somebody should tell that to the missionaries."

"Humbugs!" exclaimed Squire Gensir. "They are mainly responsible for the wreck and ruin of folk art throughout the world. It is easy to understand why Mrs. Craig was so upset about your going to a tea-meeting."

"I shall never go again. Pretty soon I must settle down to be a good minister's wife." Bita exhibited the ring that had been given to her by Herald Newton.

She thought the squire would have said something against that and was surprised that he didn't. On the contrary, he thought she might be just as happy being a parson's as any other professional person's wife.

"But I'm not enthusiastic about it," she said. "It was just an arranged thing."

But to her amazement he answered: "Lots of marriages are arranged and turn out all right. Perhaps better than the falling-in-love ones. Nearly all marriages are arranged among Eastern peoples. That is, for the greater majority of mankind."

"Were you ever married?" Bita asked him abruptly.

"No, not ever."

"Never in love?"

"Yes, once, but the woman married my friend. But I soon found out that I was really not a marrying man. So it was no irreparable loss—no sacrifice," he laughed dryly.

He told Bita that the friend was the son of a famous poet, and she was astonished to learn that it was the poet whose lyrics she admired more than any. Even though she had been to school in England, her first childhood reaction to the poet had remained unchanged. And his world had always appeared to her like a dream country with carefully cultivated flowers, lovely and wistful, that were his poems. She had never imagined that she would have any knowledge other than out of books of the reality of him. Yet here in her obscure island home conversing with her was a man who had known him in the flesh. Right then a change took place in her idea of the squire. There was a transfiguration and a romantic cloud seemed to descend and envelope him before her eyes.

She began practising a minuet from Mozart that he had open on the piano. But all the time her head was full of the thought: How strange he is! How strange he is! No white person had ever touched her with such a feeling of otherworldliness as this man. The way she felt about him was no doubt what Mrs. Craig would have liked her to feel about herself and for which she had educated her. But what Mrs. Craig could not achieve in years of education this man had in one hour.

After taking tea, Bita said good-bye and the squire accompanied her to the gate. And as she walked away Busha Glengley of Gingertown rode up. Busha Glengley, besides owning half of Gingertown, also owned the property that lay between Banana Bottom and Breakneck. It was he that had condescended to sell Squire Gensir his lot just to humour the whim of the strange Englishman, whom he held in high respect, although he could not understand him. For Busha Glengley believed in large properties and never sold little pieces of them. Whenever he visited the mountainside he would drop in to see the squire.

When Busha Glengley came out to the island a young man, his only capital was his prepossessing appearance and a fair line of speech. He had read some fine literature about the colony and decided to take a chance there. He had not troubled to find out anything about it and so he did not know that the island had been a colony for some two hundred and fifty years and as such, according to Western standards, was no attraction for white men who were poor, but suitable only for those with some capital.

But Busha Glengley was not the type to be daunted because he had mistaken Jamaica for a tiny Australia or thought there were still pieces of eight and doubloons to be picked up in the land of sugar-cane and rum, like diamonds in South Africa. He had come out to make his way. The ordinary channels having been used up, he had chosen one that squeamish souls might be inclined to disapprove as "immoral," especially when it is exploited by plebeian people, although with just a slight change in procedure the same thing has managed to pass very honourably. . . . But the story of Busha Glengley is not a Banana Bottom but a Gingertown tale. It is enough to say that Busha Glengley's chosen way carried him to success and made him in time the boss of Gingertown. . . .

Busha Glengley looked after Bita and said with a leer: "Nice girl, eh?"

There was the greatest contrast between the two men. The thin squire and his pensive delicate face and the gross hearty Busha astride his horse, his white hair straggling from under the white helmet, his streaky cheeks red like ham.

If a native had made the remark about Bita, the squire might have thought it funny, but he was repelled by the robust and purely animal sexuality of Busha Glengley with his many concubines, from black to near-white, and his array of children in Gingertown.

"She's a very cultivated young woman," said the squire, "and came here to practise on the piano."

"Oh yes, I heard about her," said Busha Glengley. "Too bad she should have been taken and educated above her station."

Squire Gensir was annoyed: "*Above her station!* One cannot be educated above one's station. Real education is an intrinsic thing and not the monopoly of any class."

"I mean her education has put her out of touch with her own people. She has no one to associate with here."

"She can associate with me. And I feel honoured by her company."

"But that doesn't answer my argument. You're just an accident here. I know this country and these people better than you. A girl like her is bound to be unhappy in the long run."

"You may not be right. She may be happy just as I am happy here. But I was unhappy among the people of my so-called class. Among these people I am not."

"But don't you ever feel you're wasting yourself among them? And I'll tell you Negroes are ungrateful."

To this the squire did not reply. Surely he thought Busha Glengley should have more practical experience of wasting oneself and the ungratefulness of Negroes with his Joseph-coat army of children, some of which did not recognize one another when they met in the street, because they had been whelped on different beds. And as it was with the children so was it with the mothers, whose hatred of one another was a standing talk of Gingertown. He ought to know—this man who had all his life been so absorbed in the bodies of Negroes that he had never had any time to find out anything about their souls.

"Anyway, look out about teaching them wrong ideas," said Busha Glengley. "They may use them against us some day."

"Us?"

"Yes, us—we of the white race. Our national poet, Kipling, has warned us: 'East is East and West is West and never the twain shall meet.'"

The squire laughed his dry laugh. "That is more a warning for you than for me. And you did not heed it. However, I don't believe in any race. I take my ideas from the experience of the whole world. And if ideas are good they should be universal and useful to all humanity without any artificial discrimination."

Saying that, he invited Busha Glengley up to the Hut for a drink of whisky. He did not drink himself but always kept a supply of liquor on hand for just such occasions.

11

A FEW DAYS AFTER HER FUNNY ENCOUNTER WITH TACK Tally, Bita received this letter from him:

Honard miss

I beg to apolojoys for trying to mek a little plesantry wid you as a genelman and you not a lady as big to apreachiate it. I not jest a fool country naygur not know nothing, but I is a pusson travelled far abroad jest lak yousef an I is acquented wid all the etykwets. Thas why I wait until you was all alone by yousef to get a good introduction to you. I is sorry you did tek it in sech a bad way and insult me lak a dawg but I is willing to forgive you and even be a frien to you ef you will tek that back. And ef you apreachiate freinship between female and male I doan want to praise mesef too much but I doan tink you can fine a finer pusson than me in Banana Bottom. I nebber tek an insult lying down from nobody not eben a woman, but you is one lady a man will tek almost anyting from. But ef it will pleas you to say I was sorry and tink better of me I can feget eberyting an as I put my pen down after writing this apolojoys I hope you feel lak taking your pen up in response to send an apolojoys to Yours Afeckshunly

Tack Tally

Bita was still going off into intermittent fits of laughter from the effects of Tack's letter when she heard a knock at the front door. It was Yoni Legge who had come seeking a sympathetic ear for her troubles. It was proving overwhelmingly difficult for Yoni to hold to a middle course, to control her passion for Tack and maintain her nice place as a sewing-mistress. The secret trysts were having a bad effect upon her, for she was a simple, affectionate girl and preferred to be open about what she did. And she was romantic and would like to receive the fellow she admired the way it was done: genteelly sitting upon a couch and pressing hands and more. All the refined touches in her home were her handiwork: the frilled muslin curtains over the jalousies, and, in the front room, the drawnthread covers over the chair backs, the crocheted doilies on the centre table and the patchwork of primary colours, worked by the schoolgirls from gaudy remnants and bordered with blue.

But Pap Legge was implacable against Tack coming to the house. And he had set his only little daughter by Ma Legge like a kind of watch-dog to guard the place. And Yoni could not meet Tack anywhere else (indoors) for he was shunned by all the young women of her set. Tack had been urging her to throw up the sewing job and run off with him to Panama or Cuba and she rather inclined towards the idea.

As soon as she was seated Yoni said: "Tell me, Bita, do you believe in Evil?"

"What do you mean? I prefer to believe in Good."

"But don't you believe in Evil too—in nigger Evil?"

"You mean ——?"

"Obeah. Don't you believe it can work harm or good?"

"No!" Bita spoke harshly. "I don't believe in Obeah. It is stupid. Beastly."

"But the Bible says there *are* evil and good spirits, Bita. And Obeah is black people's evil god."

"I don't have to swallow everything the Bible says. And

I could never believe in a foolish thing like Obeah, Yoni, and I hope you don't, either."

"Oh, Bita, I can't say like you. I believe it's the Evil against me. And that's why Pap and everybody's against Tack."

"Tack Tally, Yoni! Everybody's against him because he's a dirty disgusting bully and beast."

"Don't, Bita. I love him. I love him. Everybody hates him, but I love him with all my heart."

"Well, if you do I can't understand how you could love such a type of person."

"I love him, though, Bita. I don't know what I'll do about it, but I love him. I thought maybe you'd understand me . . . help me. But you only hurt me instead."

"But Tack Tally is no good for you. Yoni!" cried Bita. "Just look at this silly letter he has just written to me." And Bita told Yoni about Tack Tally swiping her clothes when she went to bathe in Martha's Basin.

Upon reading the letter, a feeling of jealousy against Bita took possession of Yoni. The man she loved was being seduced by her friend. It didn't matter that Bita disliked Tack and was indifferent to his gallantry. It was enough that Tack was enamoured of Bita.

Yoni dropped the letter on the table and coldly said good-bye. She had come for consolation from a girl friend and that was what she had received. She returned home in a hysterical state and, sobbing, poured her heart out to Ma Legge. There was no peace in her life, no joy, and she felt no interest in her work, for the love of Tack Tally was eating her inside out.

Ma Legge was a firm believer in Obi, the Evil Spirit, and

she decided at once to take Yoni to consult Wumba, the Obeahman of Banana Bottom.

That night, carefully wrapped from head to foot in large fringed Indian shawls, Yoni and her mother set out for the Obeahman's cave. If they had gone a few nights earlier they might have encountered Tack coming from *his* rendezvous with the Obeahman. For Tack had just that week feed the Obeahman nicely for a charm against Evil and to turn Yoni's head so that she should consent to run away with him.

However, they met others who were engaged upon the same errand. A man when they were going, and whom Ma Legge was certain she could identify as a leader in the church; a woman upon returning, whose way of walking very much resembled that of Sister Phibby Patroll, who had that day been rewarded with a sum of money from Jordan Plant for her services in helping to nurse Anty Nommy.

And that particular and purely midnight mission was not typical of Banana Bottom only. Of the thousands of native families, illiterate and literate, in that lovely hot island there were few indeed that did not worship and pay tribute to Obi—the god of Evil that the Africans brought over with them when they were sold to the New World.

In Banana Bottom there were three families only of which it was positively known that they did not practise nor believe in Obeah: the Plants, the native shopkeeper's at the Crossroads, and the schoolmaster's.

Of the Reverend Lambert it could be said that he was honest and sincere in the denunciation of the practice of Obeah, but he believed in its potency, quoting the Scriptures as authority. And that percentage was about evenly distributed in all the villages and little towns of the island. The people worshipped the Christian God-of-Good-and-Evil on Sunday, and in the shadow of night they went to invoke the power of the African God of Evil by the magic of the sorcerer. Obi was resorted to in sickness and feuds, love and elemental disasters.

And often families that had been friendly for years, the different children growing up together like brothers and sisters, suddenly would be rived apart with deep hatred by the Obeahman's maliciously imputing that one family had invoked the Evil Power against the other.

The colonial government had used every means to stamp out Obeah—long terms of imprisonment and the cat—but it flourished as strong as ever and the demand for the sorcerer seemed greater than the supply.

To reach the Obeahman of Banana Bottom one had to travel out of the village on the main road in the direction of Gingertown. Then along a track turning sharply to the left where jutted out above, like tents upon tents, a group of hills; follow an unfrequented course of the Cane River, then up a deep ravine half hid by a jungle growth of ferns, tree and trailing. At the top of the ravine a pair of twin rocks formed an arch. It was overgrown with cutting grass, wild fig trees and orchids. And under was the large long cave that the Obeahman had preëmpted for his Art. And in front of the cave and almost concealing it, a broad cashew tree.

There was a dog there who had been trained to announce arrivals, not by barking, but by standing in the entrance and growling. Wumba, the Obeahman, waited under the cashew tree to receive Yoni and Ma Legge, holding a candlewood torch that lit up the length of the ravine, revealing the towering tree ferns like sentinels under the starry night. Enormous rat-bats whirled around him, circling in and out of the cave, which was thick with them and their cockroachy odour.

He was a stout junk of a man, opaque and heavy as ebony. Two goat skins were strapped around his loins and from the waist up he was naked except for a necklace of hogs' teeth and birds' beaks. His hands and forehead were stained with mangrove dye and his hair was an enormous knotty growth.

Yoni was very timid, but Ma Legge was not afraid of that apparition, for it had the power to combat Evil. So Wumba led the women into the cave and to the magic corner where a tallow candle flickered faintly in a lantern. The women sat down upon kerosene boxes against the wall hung with animal trophies: among which were buzzards' wings, hawks' feet, dried lizards and snake skins.

Wumba squatted on the ground upon a piece of tarpaulin, and set in a circle around him were a jackass's skull and a human too, the brush of a stallion's tail, two suncured owls, a large glass jar of rum containing an afterbirth, two calabashes (one containing water and the other the blood of a cock), a dragon's-blood freshly rooted up and a number of closed boxes of varying sizes. A pot of broth was brewing in the fireplace. The cave was hot, Wumba's torso beady with perspiration, and the women constantly mopped their faces.

Wumba seized a strand of supple-jacks twisted into a rod and traced confused figures in the dust, stuttering incantations. Then without warning, with a sharp thrust he touched Yoni's navel with the rod. Taken unawares Yoni shrank back with a little shriek. . . . But her mother put her arm around her shoulder, patted her and whispered in her ear not to be afraid and hold herself back, but to put her trust completely in the Obeahman so that the magic could do its work without encountering resistance.

Again Wumba took the rod and traced a ring of three circles in the dust, made three times a diagonal cross in the air, and tapped three times upon a little box near him, bent over and whistled against the box, then opened it and a black snake crawled out and coiled itself around his left wrist.

Yoni uttered a low "Oh" of wonder and fear. The practice of Obeah was a more awesome thing than she had imagined. It was hard for her to believe that many of her neighbours were always resorting under cover of darkness to séances like these and carrying their secrets buried in their bosoms during the day, full of neighbourly laughter and harmless gossip on the surface.

Yet the snake that so horrified her was merely one of the harmless Jamaica species that all Obeahmen keep as pets. To Yoni, however, whose head was big with fear of the supernatural powers of the snake, from the Bible story and African magic tales, the reptile was the Creeping Symbol of Evil.

The Obeahman seized Yoni's hand with his right and made her touch the snake. And he chanted:

"Obi, Obi tek you' sowl,
Tu'n you inside out,
Tu'n you upside do'n.
Obi find you' enemy
Dough him hidin' in de sea.
Obi tell you' secret now
Draw you' secret out you' haht."

He let the snake slide back into the box. He opened the pot. The cave was filled with a pungent odour. He made slow motions with his hands over the pot and finally rested them over the calabash of water. When he removed them there was a salamander in the calabash.

No Obeahman's stock could be complete without a salamander. The legend ran that it was the principal animal that the Obeahman used to put the Evil upon a victim. When it was discovered in a neighbour's yard it was taken as a sure sign of the Obeahman at work. And if one was bitten by it it was another sign that the Obeahman meant death for the victim. And the only cure was for the victim to make quickly for water and wash himself. But it was a race between the victim and the salamander (who also ran for water right after biting anyone so that it might beat its victim and escape death). For the one that failed to reach the water first would surely die.

Wumba opened the pot again and looked fixedly at the escaping steam. After a time he said to Yoni: "De rebelation a come. I seen all a you' troubles. You hab a wicked enemy."

Yoni said: "I don't know."

"But I know 'causen I has seen. Them is jealous a you. I seen you' enemy. You was de fust young miss in Banana Bottom. Them wanta tek away you' pohsition from you. Deah's anodder young lady dat wanta be de fust in Banana Bottom. Ah seen it."

"Ah! Ah tink ah know," exclaimed Ma Legge. "Ah know, ah know." And she whispered to Yoni.

With her mother's prompting and the Obeahman insinuating, the fact was revealed to Yoni. Her enemy could be no other than Bita. Yoni thought how unsympathetic and unundersanding Bita had been about her trouble. And Ma Legge recalled that Jordan Plant was a man who was all for himself. The way he had bought up all the spare lots he could in Banana Bottom. And bamboozled the backra folk into educating his daughter abroad. And now his nephew Bab was off to the city to study. . . . The Plant family could pretend all right to laugh at Obeah. But only strong-working Obeah could have given them all that prosperity.

The Obeahman gave Yoni a flask filled with some of the broth from the pot, with instructions to sprinkle it in all the doorways of her house and also in that of the little annex of the schoolhouse that she used as a rest-room and to keep articles that were needed in her work. He also produced a wisdom-tooth, dipped it in the broth, wrapped it in a piece of rag and gave it to Yoni. This she was to sew in a little bag and keep upon her person always. And finally he made her gaze into a piece of looking-glass and as she gazed he smashed it in his hand and said: "Aie! Now ah ketch you' ebil shadow an' nubbody can use it fer harm you. Youse safe from all ebil."

Ma Legge dipped into her thread-bag to find the sum Wumba asked for his fee, which was two pounds: Yoni's salary for two months.

12

BITA SAT IN THE SHADE OF THE VERANDA OF HER HOUSE, turning pausingly the leaves of a wine-coloured leather-bound volume. It contained the collected lyrics of the poet who was the subject of the conversation between her and Squire Gensir.

Among them were some of those verses that had been prescribed during her elementary-school days as "recitations to develop the love of poetry in children." Also the "memory gems" that did service as "little moral lessons in short poetic flights."

For a while she was shut entirely off from her surroundings and was back in school again, absorbed in the blue-covered reader and the poems (how she did love to prattle them!) sandwiched between the prose: descriptive passages from great writers and little stories of famous men and women such as "Michelangelo and his Faun," "Florence Nightingale and her Lamp."

And there in the back of the textbook was a nice lot of them with marks as in French script, denoting the syllabic accent. Now the poems took on a new glamour and the poet a lovelier halo, his personality more interesting because of her talk with Squire Gensir. And it was with a new delight she turned from the pathetic "memory gems" of her Banana Bottom girlhood to those liquid verses whose movement was like the passive perpetual motion of the lake beyond Breakneck: words drowned in music, music dripping with honey, perfect for brief tasting.

The veranda took in a vista of the road for about fifty yards where it curved. Looking up from her reading, Bita spied Yoni as she made the bend, followed by her small sister toting a basket of sewing and knitting materials on her head. Yoni was on her way to the school for the afternoon sewing-session.

Bita kept lookout until Yoni came within view of the house, and she ho-hoed to her, waving her hand. But though her little sister, hearing, pulled at her frock, Yoni feigned not to hear and never did speak at all, but kept straight on, her head firmly turned the other way, walking sideways and resembling thus, and strikingly, a painting of an ancient Egyptian beauty.

Bita wondered what thing under that tropic heaven could make Yoni angry with her. Was it because she had been tactless about Tack?

The schoolhouse was situated on the church property, between the mission house and the teacher's cottage. And the annex for the sewing-mistress's private use had an independent outside entrance.

Yoni kept the sewing-class at one end of the schoolroom. She had about half-a-dozen bigger girls, between twelve and fourteen who were in charge of the tots, teaching them to thread their needles and to baste and hem and stitch. These bigger girls Yoni taught to mend and darn, crochet, knit and cut a little. For the girls the two sewing-sessions a week with Yoni were like a holiday away from the schoolmaster. For many of them had a real aptitude for the needle, when figures and letters bounced off of their little tight-rolled kinks and could not get into their heads at all.

That afternoon when the sewing-session was ended Yoni sent her sister home with the work-basket, saying she had an appointment with one of the Misses Lambert. But she did not go across the lawn to the mission nor to the teacher's cottage to chat with the schoolmaster's wife, as she sometimes did. But lingered instead in the annex, for she had made a rendezvous with Tack there.

Tired of the trysts in the green pastures, soft and lovely though they were, Yoni's feelings had so overpowered her that she had invited Tack to the annex, where she hoped they would be able to hold sweet communion in civilized fashion.

Tack arrived at the rendezvous in a roundabout way. Taking a track from down the village, he went up a path by the other side of the Cane River, where his movements might not appear suspicious, cut across Tabletop, and entered the mission property by the gate of the teacher's cottage. Keeping under the cover of the mimosas that grew thick and high along the road, making a natural fence for the church property, he arrived at the annex confident that he had not been seen.

But he had reckoned without the ever alert Sister Phibby Patroll. Now Sister Phibby's cottage was straight across the way from the teacher's cottage. She was standing peeping at the landscape through her jalousie window when Tack entered the scene, and she was astonished and puzzled to see him pass through the gate and at once sniffed an intrigue.

But who was it and what? Impossible to think of Mrs. Fearon, the schoolmaster's wife, in connection with that.

Hastily Sister Phibby slipped out of her house. Peering through the mimosa trunks, she saw Tack making quickly and stealthily for the annex. She broke into a little run and was just in time to see Yoni let Tack in.

"Ah ketcham!" she ejaculated to herself. "So dat's what. Jes' a twat like any udder in de fox grass wid all har preening and primping an' fanning har 'long de road like a high lady. Widouten shame fer de mission and de school! Teachin' children fer sew. She oughta be l'arnin' to sew up har ownase'f. Needle an' t'read an' wo'sted balls. So much a dem dat's gone to har head.

"S'help me Gawd!" said Sister Phibby. "Ah got to stop har dis time befo'm dessicat de mission."

So she hurried to the mission and called out the Reverend Lambert: "Oh, Rivrind Lambut, dere's a t'ief in de primisses."

"A thief!" exclaimed the minister. "Where is the rodent?"

"Right heah," said Sister Phibby, leading him on to the annex, "dis way. Dere in de nest," she said, levelling her forefinger. "We mus' git him out befoh him bruk de eggs."

"But that is Miss Legge's rest-room," said the minister in an astonished tone.

"Dat doan' mek no diffarance, Rivrin', dere's a man in deah all de same."

And Sister Phibby battered with both fists upon the door.

"Who's it?" answered Yoni tremolando.

"Open the door and come out of that," the minister sternly commanded.

"Oh God!" Yoni clutched at her throat. And she remembered then that she had forgotten at home the little bag with the tooth that Wumba the Obeahman had given to her.

"Open the door, I say," repeated the minister, "or I'll break it down."

At last the door was opened and Yoni stood sullenly back by the little table.

"Sister Patroll said she saw a man go in here a minute ago. Where is he?" demanded the minister.

"If you don't see any man, then Mrs. Patroll must be lying," said Yoni.

"You daring me, you low an' wut'less wench," retorted Sister Phibby, and down she went on her knees and swinging her hand under the couch she caught a man's leg.

"Him's heah, right heah," she cried triumphantly. And Tack Tally was pulled out from under the couch where he had doubled himself up.

"Pudenda!" he ejaculated, looking down and from right to left like a trapped dog.

"Stop your Spanish obscenity, you licentious Panama bed-presser," said the minister. "Don't think I don't understand. Remember that you're in the presence of an educated man. Your superior. Now get off the lot."

Tack cleared out.

"Well, well, ef de young people hab no respect fer Gawd," said Sister Phibby, "wha's to hinder dem gwine to do dat t'ing in de pulpit next?"

Curious when Sister Phibby called out the minister, the three Misses Lambert, the mission cook and the coachman had followed. And the schoolmaster (scenting the scandal in the air) had joined them with two monitors who were doing special lessons late after the letting out of school. The minister waved his daughters away. And taking one look at Yoni and without saying another word to anyone, he strode from the scene.

Sister Phibby, with a sanctimonious look at the schoolmaster, held her withered breasts and wailed: "Oh what a shame! What a shame! What a big disgrace fer Banana Bottom! What is dis wul' comin' to?"

. . . .

When Pap Legge heard of the affair and that Yoni had lost her job, his anger blazed up like a bush fire. All the trouble and expense he had been put to to bring up Yoni a decent girl—the differences with Ma Legge, who had always been inclined to take life a little too loose and easy—all had ended in this.

He had taken the little bastard coolie pickney for his own child. Sent her to sewing-school in Gingertown. Paid willingly for her tuition, labouring like an ox in the field to do it. Made her a little lady of the village. But she was an obstinate wrong-headed girl. She had refused to listen to his warning against Tack Tally and stop keeping company with him——

Pap Legge turned Yoni out of his house. She would have gone to ask Bita for temporary shelter if the Obeahman had not made Bita her enemy. She even thought that Bita's evil influence had been responsible for her forgetting the charm and being caught with Tack. So she went to beg a little shelter from the sister of Crazy Bow who lived with her slatternly brood of children in the remnant of the crumbling 'State House.

The following day Pap Legge marched to the place where Tack Tally lived. It was a dirt hut situated on a lot back in from the Crossroads. There Tack lived with his mother Emmelina and a little brother who worshipped the bigger and his adventurous life, and in emulation was already a bully among the kids that frolicked down by the Crossroads.

In spite of all the cash he was reputed to have and his many fine Panama suits and jewellery, Tack had never thought of building a decent home. He was very particular that his collars should be starched stiff like cardboard and that his mother should press his pants with creases that looked as if they were pasted fixed. Yet he had no place to keep them but the tin trunk in the dirt of the hut. But Tack was content with that. After all, his main pride was to show himself dandy in the street, the rum shop and tea-meeting booth. He was no home-loving lad.

The moment Tack appeared in the entrance of the hut, Pap Legge lifted up his hands with clenched fists and cried: "Didn' ah tell you to lef' me darter 'lone, you blarsted, low-dung, stinkin', prawncin', tarpole, dutty good-fer-nuttin' dawg ob a nigger?"

Pap Legge was frothing at the mouth and gasping for breath. He wanted to go on for ever, but his throat was full of saliva that welled up to his mouth, spewing forth in jets.

Tack was fuller of anger than repentance for the frustration of his assignation in the annex and he wasted no regards on Pap Legge, who thought Yoni was too good for him.

He cried: "Owl man, you come slap into mi yard fer fass wid me? You bettah get outa mi yard befoh ah ferget meself."

"Me 'fraid a you, you facey dutty nigger? Ah know you when you was de biggest piss-a-bed in Banana Bottom an' now you 'magin you'sef strong enough fer fass wid mi darter!"

Tack rushed up to Pap Legge and collared him: "Lawd Gawd, owl man, I'd kill you like a hog ef it wasn't fer de law. 'Pon mi sowl I'd shoot you' heart out. . . ." And Tack meant it. He boasted two notches in his stick for two hearts that he had shot out in Panama.

Pap Legge roared out fearfully: "Oh, you low-dung dawg fer defile me wid you' bloody dutty hands. Tek you' han' them offen me. . . . Tek you' han' . . ." Foaming at the mouth, he collapsed in Tack's hands and fell to the ground, dead.

"Mamma! Mamma!" cried Tack. And he stared pop-eyed at the corpse at his feet, wondering if it was not a fit. Surely he hadn't collared Pap hard enough to choke him to death.

Emmelina Tally rushed out and lifted Pap Legge's head. "Him dead, oh, him dead!" she wailed.

13

THE DISTRICT CONSTABLE WENT TO TACK'S YARD AND took charge of Pap Legge's body. He sent a message to Bull's Hoof, a tiny town between Banana Bottom and Gingertown, and a regular constable was detailed from there to help him.

The body could not be touched until the doctor came. It was covered with a sheet there where it fell in the yard and all that day and night the district constable and the regular took turns watching.

All night the villagers came in groups to view the sheeted thing and to comfort Mrs. Tally and whisper about the scandal and the trouble. The village was accustomed to periodic tribulations. But they were chiefly elemental: hurricanes, floods, earthquakes. Or (like the cholera epidemic that had swept through the country, killing off hundreds three years before) God-sent. But now this was a calamity of human passion enacted out of their own daily living. It was nine years since there had been anything like to it. That time when a poor fellow returned from Colon a little off his head, and one day murdered an old cripple in his cabin.

Oh, the villagers were terror-stricken under the shadow of Pap Legge's murder. It came home to them more terrible than the destructive hurricane—this single death—more than the cholera dealing death to hundreds.

In the morning the doctor arrived. And after the post-mortem he announced that Pap Legge had succumbed to long-standing heart disease. But nobody could find Tack to tell him the happy tidings. For he had disappeared from the moment he knew Pap Legge was really dead. Evidently he was already on his way back to Panama.

Yoni had returned to the house of death and lay prostrate, mourning, not for her stepfather, but for Tack. She could not understand his deserting her without leaving a word. It was like a betrayal. How could he expect her to bear it alone. She lay like a wounded bird, baffled and frustrated.

The young cocks of the village had just been getting ready to crow in song over the first event when the second came like a thunder-clap, scattering rhyme and music from their heads.

•　•　•　•　•　•　•　•　•

Two days later, Wumba the Obeahman, who had been away magic-making in the neighbouring parish, returned to Banana Bottom. He returned, as was usual (whenever he went abroad upon his occult missions), in the dead of a dark night. As he picked his way home through the trailing ferns up the ravine, a monstrous bald-headed white buzzard flew down at him and, sorcerer though he was, he trembled with fear as the bird swept past. For a white buzzard is a sign of black Evil.

Wumba quickened his pace towards the cave, where he would at least have some feeling of safety among his creeping companions and charms against Evil. But as he passed under the cashew tree to enter he felt something like a soft hugging around the neck.

Wumba stood stiff still in his tracks without looking up and said: "Yes, Lawd, ahm coming. Yes, Lawd ah know dat de sins ob de wicked will find 'em out. Oh Lawd ah knows ahm a sinner, a wretched, wicked, lying, t'iefing an' murderin' black sinner. But, Oh Lawd, lemme go!"

He dropped upon his knees praying to God to forgive him. Then he thanked God for letting him go. . . . And when at last he summoned up courage enough to glance upwards he saw the shape of a man suspended above his head. He jumped up with a blood-curdling yell, leaping long and high like a madman down the ravine and bawling: "Lawd Jesas judgment come! Lawd Jesas judgment come!"

Over rocks and gullies, through the deadly cutting-grass across the Cane River: "Lawd Jesas judgment come!" On through the village. The astonished churchgoers opened their doors to see. Those who could not see heard the voice of their High Priest of Obeah roaring: "Lawd Jesas judgment come!" And they trembled with fear.

And Wumba, high-jumping and shouting, continued to the church steps, where he fell down: "Lawd Jesas judgment come!" The Reverend Lambert wrapped himself in his dressing-gown and went forth to see what the roaring racket was all about. He found Wumba kneeling on the church steps trembling and gibbering. But no word of understanding could he extract from that jargon. He touched him upon the shoulder and Wumba leaped up, prancing and running: "Lawd Jesas judgment come . . ." The magic man had gone quite mad.

It was the gathering and flapping of the buzzards above the twin rocks that brought about the discovery of Tack's body hanging from the cashew tree in front of the cave.

The buzzards had picked the balls of his eyes out and were struggling to strip him of his clothes.

For convinced that he had murdered Pap Legge, Tack remembered that he had recently paid Wumba well to protect him from Evil. And with wrath and hate in his heart he had gone straight to challenge Wumba. Not finding him at the cave he had hanged himself there.

14

YONI FINALLY FOUND HER WAY TO BITA AND, CONFESSING that she had harboured unkind thoughts against her, related her midnight visit to Wumba. But it was about Tack mostly she wanted to ease her mind.

"Ah, Bita, I can't tell you how I did love him. Now I can only think of all the sweet times we used to spend together. He was sharp like pimenta an' sweeter than sugar. I remember one day when he was kissing and squeezing me he said, 'Yoni is the sweetest name in the wul' and I felt I was all a piece a honeycomb. . . .

"I used to have such marvellous dreams about him. I remember the last thing we talked about was a dream. I had had a bad dream, but sweet. It was about a death and it was all so sad at first with everybody mourning. Then suddenly there was the most curious change. I was the open grave and Tack he fallen down into me. . . . And when I told him about it he took it for a joke and said that he wouldn't mind being buried for ever in such a sweet grave.

"Ah, Bita, he laughed all right, but it was really his death that was revealed to me. . . . But I am cured now, Bita. I am cured. Honest to God I am. He cured me when he committed suicide. It was such a coward thing to do. And I couldn't love a coward. For all his big and brazen talking and acting, he was nothing but a coward at bottom.

Afraid of standing trial, of facing a judge and a jury . . . a coward, a coward——"

"But I don't know if he was, Yoni; it takes lots of courage to commit suicide."

"What kind of courage? It wasn't courage with Tack. It was fear. And I had thought he was really daring, not caring a snap for anybody. I was ready to throw up my job and go to Panama or Cuba with him. It's better it happened like that. That he didn't know he was innocent. He was nothing but a big bully—a coward underneath."

"I can't agree with you, Yoni. I never could like Tack Tally. But now I think better of him. I think he was a born killer and no coward. If I knew I had to lose my life I'd rather kill myself than be executed. That seems to me really courageous."

But Yoni was not convinced.

Tack was buried on a Saturday. And that Sunday the Reverend Lambert took for the text of his sermon the Story of the Witch of Endor. It was a long sermon denouncing Obeah, its worship and its work. And the minister showed that even as God had confounded Saul with Samuel and then slain him by the hands of the Unbeliever, so likewise had he slain Tack by his own hand and confounded the Obeahman with his body.

The minister faced that solemn congregation of humble black and brown folk, who by their demeanour and countenances seemed to be, of all the worshippers of Jesus, the most childlike and pure in heart, and shouted at them the native truth: that he knew that most of them were secret and diabolic worshippers of Obi, spending their hard-earned money with the sorcerer to keep one another down and to set the Evil under their neighbours' door-sill.

Said he in part: "From the beginning of creation there has been war between Satan and God. Satan is Evil. God is Good. And from the beginning Satan has been scheming in hell without let to compass man with Evil. The power to conjure Evil is of Satan and not of God.

"The Bible has warned us against sorcery. The Bible has told us that there are millions of evil spirits roaming the world and ready to serve the wicked ways of men. Remember that when our Saviour cast the demons out the possessed he allowed them to find a refuge in the bodies of the Gaderene swine.

"Oh, my benighted brothers and sisters! You who are communing with such evil spirits today are putting yourselves on a lower level than swine. For all your nice Sunday suits and crying boots, your frills and flounces, ribbons in your hair and feathers in your hats, your sweet soaps and perfumes, you belong in the pig pen!

"From the beginning of the world there have been wicked people indulging in idolatry and sorcery. Just about a hundred years ago they were burning witches in the mother country. Today our witches are the Obeahmen. And lucky they are that their only punishment is prison and the cat-o'-nine tails. I say their punishment should be the pillory and the rack.

"There are no people so addicted to sorcery as we Negroes. The continent we came from is cursed and abandoned of God because of magic. We brought along the curse with us from over there. It is sapping our strength. Making for disunity. Setting friend against friend and family against family. All the profit you wring from hard toiling is sunk in the Obeahman's bottomless pit.

"Yet we need money for good clothing to cover our

black nakedness. Some of you would rather wear rags or a coolie wrapper so that you can pay the Obeahman. But we can't go back to the days when a little straw apron eight inches long was enough.

"We need money for times of sickness. We let our relations die when they might have lived, because we pass our good doctors over and go to the Obeahman. I see some of our little children poorly fed. If it wasn't for mangoes and star-apples I don't know what they would do. Yet I know you parents are spending that money with the Obeahman.

"We need money to build and repair our churches and schools. The Obeahman is robbing the churches of their dues. The preachers can hardly make a living. Take my own case. Half of you church members don't pay your dues. You'd rather support the minister of Satan than the minister of God. Yet you expect me to live decently and support a family and wear good clothes without patching the seat of my pants.

"You can't serve Jesus-God and Obi-God. To do so is blasphemy. You've got to choose between the two. Or God Almighty will blast you even as he did Tack Tally and Wumba the Obeahman. Oh, my God! I wouldn't trust myself to put this congregation to the test about Obeah. I dare not say: Those who do *not* deal in Obeah put up your hands. I do not want you to perjure yourselves in God's house. But I warn you all to stop here and now. I warn you to flee from the wrath to come. Give up the God of Obeah and put your trust in Christ God. You can't worship both at the same time. Do even as I do. Choose the God of Light and live by him. Give up our ancient God of darkness. Throw the jungle out of your hearts and forget Africa.

"The Evil One is strong, but God is stronger. The Evil One is wrestling with God for our souls. And we must do as Job to overcome. God is long-suffering. But he is a jealous God. He won't stand for your serving him with half a heart and Obi with the other. He is a revengeful God. And if you do not change your ways, when he strikes again it will be even more terrible for you than it was for Tack Tally and Wumba the Obeahman."

15

THE CHRISTMAS HOLIDAYS HAD PASSED. UNEVENTFULLY for Bita, who on account of Anty Nommy's condition could not participate in any of the village amusements. And so she had not been tempted by tea-meetings this time.

Now at last Anty Nommy was convalescent enough to sit out on the veranda to take the morning sun. It did not seem to her she had been ill so long, from the beginning of the coffee-picking season all through the hot December holidays until now the time of the annual Harvest Festival.

Of all the celebrations that Christian observance had established among the people there was none that seemed so significantly and simply beautiful (as if it were a spontaneous outgrowth of their own social instincts) as the Harvest Festival. Certainly it was not such a formal affair as the annual missionary meeting, when many preachers were brought together to orate over the virtues and the necessity of subscribing to foreign and domestic missions; when the Negroes, praising God for their redemption from savagery, brought in their envelopes to the Salvation Fund for the conversion of heathen souls who had not had their good fortune to escape from pagan and savage lands.

The Harvest Festival possessed something of the spirit that prompted the peasants to lend working-days to one another for the clearing of ground and the planting of crops and also for the time of heavy reaping. The only difference was that the church was the centre of the Festival. And it was for the benefit of the resident minister—all the people bringing their gifts together into the church to make a glorious love offering.

It seemed fitting that the Harvest Festival should come in the early year after the heavy gathering and sale of grain, mainly coffee and cocoa, and at the time of full fruit. The Banana Bottom Harvest Festival was akin to an agricultural show except that no prizes were given for the exhibitions. Yet how keen was the rivalry between the village folk to give of the best of their first fruits.

The entire village participated in it, church members and non-church members bringing in gifts, little and big. From the evening preceding the Festival and the early morning before, the girls and boys of the elementary and of the Sunday school went out on the hunt for flowers and evergreens to decorate the church. Besides stripping the village gardens they brought in wild flowers from the fields, orchids from the rocks and moss and wild pines from the trees.

The cocoanut palm was the base of the decorative scheme. The grand and graceful fronds reigned everywhere. They formed the high arch of welcome over the wooden gate. Placed vertical against the doors, they covered them full length and breadth. Some were cut in pieces to fit along the railing of the platform. And all dexterously plaited by the young men so that the girls could fix the flowers into them deftly as into a buttonhole.

The imagination of one little boy, the son of Sunday-school Superintendent and Leader Dan Delgado, had been so struck by the effect of the decoration that he was seized by a desire to add something unique to all that had already been done. And so, his father having in his garden a young cocoanut palm in full bloom, the boy climbed up into the bower and cut out the whole long heart bunched with beautiful blossoms. Superintendent Leader Dan was so vexed he was speechless. He wanted to spank the kid, but seeing how crestfallen he was and understanding the feeling that had prompted him to the act, he forgave him. After all, it was Harvest Festival. He accompanied the boy to the church to present the stalk of delicate scented and creamy flowers to the decorators. It was suspended from the centre of the arch and easily came first as the most strikingly beautiful decoration of the Harvest Festival.

Running close to the palms were the ferns. Giant tree ferns were dug up by the roots and planted along the aisles of the church and before the palm booths outside where the sales would take place. The trailing ferns were twisted into ropes running around the walls and into garlands to hang from the ropes and from the rail-heads. Bamboos went branching up to the roof, and from the beams were hung many fine bunches of ripe and green bananas.

The people brought their offerings, as individuals and by families, straight into the church. White yams a yard long, preserved at the cut ends with lime wash, dried in the sun and put away for this day of giving; the yellow afou yams and the staple nigger yams; hampers of yampies, mauve-coloured; cassava tubers longer than corns on the cob; pineapples whose honey odour, radiating from a pyramid heap, could set a thousand rats madly frolicking; custard apples as delicious as the name; naseberries as emollient to the throat as marshmallows.

Great green balls of breadfruit, the peasants' bread that was made high up in the air. Large tins of unrefined sugar.

Little bags of the purest picked coffee beans; cocoa; pimento; ginger. From the pens goats, chickens and rabbits and the little chubby pigs called Chinese.

Choicest of first-fruit offerings. They stirred the feelings of the people giving them, precisely as a person of limited means might, after long saving and careful choosing, be stirred upon giving a gift to his most dearly beloved. For the peasants had been thinking of this event and preparing for a year, talking over and comparing their gifts, and many a person had made up his mind beforehand to buy that pig or that goat of his neighbour's.

As the Banana Bottom region was the most fertile of any that supplied breadkind to Jubilee and Gingertown, there was naturally a cultural link between the hill country and the little towns. Boys and girls served their apprenticeship as tailors, carpenters and seamstresses in the towns and there the smart light-skinned ones found places as clerks and salesgirls. Because of that a Banana Bottom celebration always drew a few visitors from the town.

For the Harvest Festival Belle Black had written to Bita that she was coming from Jubilee. And Hopping Dick had gallantly offered to accompany her in the dray. He was one of the far-flung branches of the Delgado family (first cousin to Superintendent Leader Dan) but he had not visited the roots of his family up in the mountain district since he accompanied his father there once when he was a little boy.

Herald Newton had also notified Bita that he was coming down from the Theological College. He had regretted very much the postponement, on account of Anty Nommy's illness, of the long discourses on courtship and marriage that he had had in preparation for her. He wished, as he said in his letter to Bita, to "get our minds working as one together to explore the field of our future noble work."

"Oh God, will I be able to stand that again!" she had exclaimed. She had been thankful that Anty Nommy's illness was protracted after the acute pains were assuaged and the crisis past, happy to have an excuse to stay away from Jubilee as long as she could. It was so much pleasanter and freer at Banana Bottom. With a fine piano at her disposal it was as good to her as any place in the world could be. And it charmed her to talk to Squire Gensir and have the run of his library. From long conversations with him and from reading she had become almost an unbeliever. For exercise there was her father's pony and the long walks over the savannah.

The savannah was part of Busha Glengley's property, but it was a kind of barren land. Level enough and broken by gullies and little mounds covered with quartz that were lovely in the sun from a distance. The only vegetation was stunted palm thatch and clumps of shrubby coco-plums. It was not fit for any kind of planting and ever since the village was a village the folk had used it to pasture stock, mainly donkeys and goats, and as a back way to the local market.

The Wednesday on which the Harvest Festival was held was a bright, hot and glad "D. V." day. The notices had read, Wednesday, "D. V." And everything about the day proclaimed that the Almighty had condescended to be very willing. No rain had fallen to muddy the roads. The sky was blue, blue with clouds upgathered high like bleached and tattered sheets bellying on the air. And the high blazing sun dazzling the world.

All the goodly things for the big Banana Bottom Benefit were brought into the church and gathered in a large space in the back. . . . The musical program was arranged by Teacher Fearon, Bita playing the organ and Belle Black the leading treble.

"Give unto the Lord. . . ."

The Rev. Lambert repeated a prayer after the anthem. The Senior Deacon, Father Delgado, his skin like dried banana leaf framed in frizzly white beard, representing the people, spoke very shortly about the joy of giving and presenting the people's annual gift. Rev. Lambert had invited a neighbouring minister to read the psalm of praise, and Herald Newton was asked to say something. But there was no demonstration of oratorical talent as on "Missionary Day."

The ceremony was limited to the essential only, so that the best of the day should be given over to buying and selling, bargaining and bartering, for the realization of the Harvest Festival Sum.

The offerings were arranged in the stalls, all similar things ranged together: white yams in one stall, afou in another, all down through the line of breadkind, and fruit to grain, with the most trusted church sisters in charge, while brothers supervised the disposal of pigs and goats.

Even the higgler women who sold refreshments had brought their offering: ginger beer, sorrel drink, pineapple drink, cocoa-nut drops, bammy cakes, pindar wafers, banana pone, gingernuts. The two stalls with the drinks and sweetmeats were presided over by the Misses Lambert, helped by two stout bandanna-kerchiefed sisters, who did the rough work, bringing water from the spring and washing and wiping the glasses.

Although there was no dancing, the young folk celebrated the day as joyously as they would a tea-meeting. It was just changing the church for one day into a glorious market. And what joy is more common and precious to a village as a whole than the joy of a market day?

The only shadow was a reminder of the suicide of Tack. That event had brought Banana Bottom (which was not even marked on the local map) before the public eye. A ballad-maker of Jubilee had put the incident in verse and printed leaflets of it, which he was selling, making a tour of the island, and he had arrived at Jubilee just at the time of the Harvest Festival. His ballad sold for three pennies and was a long complaint of many verses like these:

"Young men of Jamaica now going abroad,*
Take warning from this and forget not the Lord,
For if you forget him your future may be
Even like to Tack Tally hanging from the tree.

"Our young girls are freely indulging in sin,
Not out of the womb come before they begin,
Their breasts hardly grown there are babes on their knees,
And all over the country the bastards increase.

"Jamaica is ruined and drifting to hell,
The Obeahman king where Jehovah should dwell,
The people make show of church-going but all
In secret bow down to the throne of Baal.

"But God in his anger will blast us again
With cholera, fever, and fierce hurricane,
Bananas and yams will be blown to the ground,
And not enough food in the land to go round."

* With apologies to the unknown balladist for freely paraphrasing the original.

The people bought the ballad and remembered Tack and poor Yoni, who was never seen at church and other places now. But that did not affect the general fun of the festival.

It was the first local affair that Bita had attended since Anty Nommy's illness. She and the eldest Miss Lambert had the job of running the Harvest Festival post office. It was most profitable and infectious fun. The selling of lozenges, that cost about a penny a dozen by the gross, for a penny each. One was given a slip of paper and an envelope. On the slip was written only the name of the sender. The letter was a lozenge enclosed in the envelope.

The lozenges of different colours were all printed with pretty charming love-making phrases, questions and answers, affirmations and denials:

Are you engaged?	Should I say it?
Do you love me?	You make me blush.
I admire your blue eyes.	You appeal to my fancy.
I adore your cherry lips.	I am delighted, sir.
May I touch your little ivory hand?	You make my heart throb.
Will you give me a tress of your golden hair?	With pleasure, Prince Charming.
Will you give me a kiss?	My intended would be angry.

The belles collected in a giggling crowd to compare lozenges and many an ebony hand trembled with pleasure holding its lozenge: "May I touch your little ivory hand?" Miss Chocolate Lips shrilled with unfeigned delight over: "I adore your cherry lips" and pretty Miss Browneyes was deliciously wide-eyed over, "I admire your blue eyes," while Miss Tressie fingered her stubborn unruly kinklets, wondering if she might as she read: "Will you give me a tress of your golden hair?"

And of all the Prince Charmings there was none so dandy as Hopping Dick, most of whose letters were returned to the post office since they were directed to Bita. Enjoying the fun, Bita replied to everyone of them. But Miss Lambert, watching her enthusiastic participation in the game, did not quite approve and remarked:

"Take care, Bita, that man don't forget himself and think it is more than a piece of pleasantry. He's not of our class, you know."

"But we can't discriminate in a place like this where all are enjoying themselves together," said Bita. "If the people want to enjoy themselves with us, so much the better. If we are not too proud to take their money we shouldn't be too proud to play with them. . . . And besides, the more pennies we can make the bigger will be the benefit for the mission," she added slyly.

Bita had a lurking admiration for Hopping Dick ever since she had met him that day at the market in Jubilee. She was impressionable to gallantry and a little flirting fascinated her.

Herald Newton Day, after appraising the festival offerings with the Rev. Lambert and the visiting preacher, had separated from them and came up to the post office with a copy of the "Ballad of the Death of Tack Tally" in his hand. He began to talk about the beauty of such innocent country amusements in his usual rhetorical phrases which were much more agreeable to Miss Lambert than Bita.

Before long Herald Newton became aware of the game that was carrying on between Bita and Hopping Dick. Herald Newton's personal acquaintance with his fellow townsman was slight. He had not come into speaking contact with Hopping Dick since he began his training at the theological college four years before. But he knew him thoroughly by reputation and entirely shared Mrs. Craig's opinion of him.

It was not long before Hopping Dick, intoxicated by the sweet-letters, strutted up and presented Bita with a tumbler of sorrel than which there is no more delicious drink on a hot tropical day. Thanking Hopping Dick, Bita mischievously seized the opportunity to introduce him to Herald Newton.

"I don't know if you're acquainted with Mr. Delgado," she said; "he is also from Jubilee."

Herald Newton admitted a little stiffly that he was. And suddenly pulling the "Ballad of the Death of Tack Tally" on Hopping Dick, demanded: "Have you seen that?"

"Oh, I seen the man singin' it down a' Crossroads yesti-day to some jigger-foots and liver-lips," said Hopping Dick, "but I didn't pay him no mind."

"You should, though," said Herald Newton, putting on a sermon face, "and I hope you'll take the warning and change your ways."

"Yes, your reverend," replied Hopping Dick. Bita could not suppress a giggle and so shocked Miss Lambert. But to Herald there was nothing funny in it at all. He enjoyed being addressed as reverend; the country people often ad-dressed a theological student that way. And after all in the interval of a few months he would be that by formal ordination.

At that moment Bita and Miss Lambert were busy with the post office, for a group of girls and lads had rushed up demanding lozenges and envelopes. Belle Black also came along with some girls and grabbed Hopping Dick: "Come on an' treat all of us. Whe' you been hidin' you' stingy se'f. We want ginger nuts and ginger beer and everything."

16

BELLE BLACK AND A DISTANT COUSIN OF ANTY NOMMY'S from Gingertown were staying at the Plants' and so the schoolmaster had been asked to put up Herald Newton. To avoid being much alone with Herald Newton during his visit Bita depended heavily on Belle Black and they were inseparable on this occasion.

Rather than bluntly show Herald Newton that he was intolerable Bita preferred the politer way of evasion. She could be forthright and stinging when the occasion demanded it. But ordinarily she preferred to follow the sweet-tempered way. Belle Black was soon aware of Bita's real feelings toward Herald Newton and became a very willing obstructionist.

So she was always with Bita, at home, walking down to the village hub, or over the savannah. And as Hopping Dick was a great one with Belle he was always in their company. Bita could bear his presence and understand Belle Black's liking him. He was a dandy all right, but not a little ratty sort like Tally.

Herald Newton was troubled that whenever he wanted to expatiate about the serious side of life to Bita she was always with such lightweights as Belle Black and Hopping Dick. And it irritated him that whenever he was fortunate enough to find Bita alone and began ministerially clearing his throat in anticipation of settling down to serious palavering, Belle Black would put in her appearance with all the signs of making it permanent. And sometimes she even contrived to carry off Bita away from Herald Newton.

There was one thing, however, that Bita could not escape and that was going with Herald Newton to see the squire. When Herald Newton heard about the friendship between Bita and the squire he was charmed with the idea of a big backra, other than a missionary, who accepted a Negro as an equal without any reservations. He felt about the squire precisely as Priscilla Craig, only for reasons that might be considered racial or social (take it as you will according to your particular prejudice) his admiration was more utter.

What after all did it matter if it was *rumoured* that the squire was an *Unbeliever*! When he was a shining example of a man—a gentleman, a rare one without necessity of the trimmings of class, decorations of pomp, and the symbols of power to convince fools of its realness. In the eyes of Herald Newton he was very much more a Christian than many a planter who guzzled Jamaica rum with kippers and wenched with the Negresses but employed Indian coolie labor (because they would not pay the Negroes more than starvation wages) and belonged to the Church of England.

And so when Bita suggested that Herald Newton might find the squire's company uncongenial because of his religious opinion he waved away the objection in the finest Christian spirit of toleration.

"Oh, that is all right with me. I don't mind at all. I know all about those over-educated persons who don't take the Bible literally. The Higher Criticism, you know. Too much erudition. A disease of scholarship. But at bottom you will find them good Christians. I am broadminded and can talk to the squire without mentioning his weakness."

"But supposing I should have the same weakness from too much contact with Squire Gensir?" said Bita.

"You're joking, Bita, talking that way. You're not a white person to go crazy from education."

"Mr. Day!" cried Bita. "This is not the first time you've used that 'white person' phrase to me in that invidious sense. Let me tell you right now that a white person is just like any other human being to me. I thank God that although I was brought up and educated among white people, I have never wanted to be anything but myself. I take pride in being coloured and different, just as an intelligent white person does in being white. I can't imagine anything more tragic than people torturing themselves to be different from their natural unchangeable selves. I think that all the white friends I ever made liked me precisely because I was myself. I hope I shall never hear any more of that nauseating white-and-black talk from you."

"Oh, I didn't mean any harm, Bita," said Herald Newton. "I am sorry you take what I say as an offence. I didn't mean to make an unfavourable comparison between white and black. I meant we are just beginning to learn from the whites as they are all ahead of us, more modern and progressive and everything, you understand——"

But in spite of his lack of penetration it was possible for Herald Newton to perceive that there was no understanding in Bita's eyes and so he stopped. He was badly eager to take that tea at the squire's and was able to realize that he might be spoiling the party beforehand.

Bita had invited Belle Black to go along to offset Herald Newton. But Belle, after having agreed to oblige Bita out of friendship, pulled out at the last moment: "Me no gwine noways, honey," she said. "T'ink I gwinea mek a poppy-show a mese'f a-settin' up an' drinkin' tea wid a backra man an' not knowin' what ter do wid mi mouth when it no full whilesen unno all talking away like outa books. 'Sawright fer you, sistah, for you done l'arn backra ways. You an' Marse Herald. But me, me no gwine noways."

The squire had prepared a high tea for his guests: cold fowl, hot roasted plantains with butter and jam, cassava wafers and cocoanut cakes, all prepared and served by his servant, a little black woman squat and hardened and inured to the tropical climate like a shrubby ebony tree.

From under his craggy protruding eyebrows the squire scrutinized Herald Newton taking tea, and for all his intellectual freedom and hatred of snobbery he was nevertheless engaged in appraising the young student by the severe and supreme standard of manners.

Herald Newton was also engaged in an appraisal of his own. Surveying the large sparsely and simply furnished room and wondering why the squire should live so modestly and not upon a large scale like the planters with plenty of servants. And he believed the reason could be found in the fact that the squire was a congenital miser masquerading as a simple liver.

At last Herald Newton said: "I'm glad you find our common mountain people interesting enough to live among them. They are so rough and coarse. But of course it's far from the towns up here and they haven't had the chance for real refinement and progress like us townspeople."

"I can get on without refinement," said the squire, "and I don't care anything about progress."

"Really, sir! But life without progress is stagnation. Look at us Negroes, for example. The savage brutish state we were in both in Africa and in America before Civilization aroused us. We owe all we are today to progress."

"That's a fact," said the squire. "After all, progress is a grand fact. It doesn't really matter whether one believes in it or not."

Turning to Bita, the squire said to her that Jubban, the drayman, had told him about a lovely flower that he had noticed in the armpit of a tree while he was bird-shooting two days before in the rocky woods beyond the savannah. Jubban had not removed the flower because the squire, who collected orchids and other plants, liked to remove them from the soil or the trees and rocks himself, as the villagers were careless doing it. The squire thought it might be a rare specimen and had spent a great part of the previous day hunting for it, but without success.

The squire had plenty of flowers, garden and wild, around the Hut. As the Banana Bottom region was rather inaccessible to travellers, its woods and forests and ravines were quite virgin and unexplored. And whenever the men of the village, engaged in cutting timber in the wood hills or bird-shooting, saw any unusual flower, they informed the squire of it.

"I think I'll try again tomorrow," the squire said.

"By God's help you'll succeed in finding it, sir," said Herald Newton.

Bita was shaking from suppressed laughter and Herald Newton, remarking a humorous expression on the squire's face, wondered what he might have done. Surely he had not made a mistake and stuck the knife with the jam in his mouth.

"I wish I could be sure God will help me to find that flower," said the squire, his eyes twinkling. "Do you think He could help me, really?"

"I am sure He will if you ask Him in faith," replied Herald Newton.

"Let us play," said Bita, turning to the piano.

"I suppose you are a virtuoso," Herald Newton said to the squire. "I adore music. I never feel so uplifted—so sure of the divine purpose of human nature as when the pipe organ of the City Tabernacle fills the church with the grand notes of the 'Te Deum.'"

"Some of the greatest music is sacred," said the squire.

"I should say *all* great music is sacred," responded Herald Newton. "I don't care about popular music. It doesn't stir me. I think it is a shame that such a noble thing as music should be put to such degrading purposes as dancing."

"Let us play," said Bita again, and standing by the piano she touched the keys at random with her left hand.

17

THAT WEEK HERALD NEWTON WAS ENDING HIS VISIT TO Banana Bottom and as valedictory was taking the service on Sunday. He was scheduled to leave in the evening after the service so that he should be ready for the opening of college on Monday. He was returning to the city full of selfness and confidence to go through the necessary gestures of finishing the last term. It was almost over, after all, except for the formal handing out of a piece of parchment. He was well satisfied with his visit to Banana Bottom. The villagers had been so deferential, proud of his accomplishments as a son of the black folk, and addressing him as reverend. And above all he was proud of meeting and conversing with such a great scholar as Squire Gensir.

Frequently during that week, Teacher Fearon and his wife overheard him rehearsing his sermon, the text of which he had taken from the Psalms.

"Wherewithal shall a young man cleanse his ways . . .
By taking heed according to thy words . . .
With my whole heart. . . .
Oh, let me not wander from thy commandments . . . ."

The schoolmaster was sometimes disturbed and annoyed as Herald paced his room emphasizing the subheadings of his sermon:

"How youth should go cleansed before the Lord . . .
Avoiding the pitfalls of youth . . .
The personal purity of the body . . .
     of the soul . . .
     of the spirit . . .
     of the mind . . .
The attainment of purity
 by daily meditation . . .
 by constant prayer . . .
 by thinking purely . . .
 by watchful vigilance against corrupting influences.
 by wrestling with God for the Beauty of Holiness."

Herald Newton worked carefully over his words, elaborating his sentences, rolling them along his tongue, fixing them in paragraphs, pulling them out and rearranging, going over each again and again until he had the whole thing by heart. Until at last he felt that he had not only found a perfect sermon but that he had found The Perfect Way.

It was one of those pleasant Sunday mornings. And from over the hill and up from the valley the country folk had preened itself stiff and starched to hear the young preacher of Jubilee. Broad-frilled petticoats treading the air like kites supporting brocaded gowns smelling of camphor balls just taken out of cedar trunks for the occasion. Gorgeous plumes of all colours. Hard shining standing collars that would soon be sagging like wet rags from the profuse tropical perspiration of black skins. White and brown drill suits and tweed and serge cut-aways.

Bita had preceded Herald to the Sunday school and was now waiting at the church and playing the organ for the interval that comes before the service. That week she had been practising with Belle Black and the village choir the anthem, "Wherewithal Shall a Young Man Cleanse His Ways." Herald Newton had specially requested her to render it during the service.

But while the great congregation waited and waited with Spanish and palm fans flapping, the preacher did not appear. For in the interval between morning and sermon time there had occurred one of those strange, unaccountable phenomena that sometimes startle with impish ingenuity even the most perfect Utopia: Herald Newton Day had descended from the dizzy heights of holiness to the very bottom of the beast.

The rumour ran through the region that Herald Newton had suddenly turned crazy and defiled himself with a nanny goat. Consternation fell upon that sweet rustic scene like a lightning ball of destruction. And there was confusion among those hill folk, which no ray of understanding could penetrate. They were of one accord that only the mighty African Power of Evil could have spirited Herald Newton Day away from his sermon and his God, by the back premises of the teacher's cottage, through the sweet-scented rose-apples and down to the deep ferny gully to the tethered goat that was feeding in the garden of Sister Kanah Christy.

Sister Christy was getting ready for church when the bleating attracted her attention, and casually going to her garden down under the hill thinking perhaps that the creature had gotten entangled in the rope, she was horrified to discover Herald Newton.

Teacher Fearon immediately took the matter in his hands. And before it reached the knowledge of the local authorities, Herald Newton was hurried off to the city, from where, as soon as he obtained the necessary funds and clothing from his father, he embarked for Panama.

The animal was destroyed. There was no doubt left in the people's minds after the awesome events of two seasons that in some occult struggle between the unseen spirits Obi had triumphed and was supreme in Banana Bottom. God was using Obi to chastise them for their sins and Herald Newton had been doomed to abomination and sacrificed as a victim to Obi.

God and Obi. Simply believing in life and magic, they could reconcile any destiny of man with the world of nature: destructive hurricanes, earthquakes, drought and devastating floods. Grimly they bowed under the inevitable and after the passing of the dire episode or the cruel calamity, they bent themselves again with dark tenacity to the everlasting tilling of the soil.

But for Squire Gensir the thing was not so simple to accept and understand. Being an enthusiast of the simple life, he was like many enthusiasts, apt to underestimate the underlying contradictions that may inhere in his more preferable way of life. In spite of the broad bases of his high erudition it was easy for him to be puzzled by singular deviations from the common and regular procession of daily living around him, where an ignorant person (but who was nevertheless in whole contact with life) might have been aware.

The squire thought that such a thing might be manifest among a different kind of peasantry—a kind that had been stunted and worn out by civilization, but not the forthright and primitive, albeit strangely unfathomable, black peasantry among whom he had elected to live. After many years among them it was the first experience of its kind that had been thrust upon his observation and his theory was that the case of Herald Newton might be attributed to temporary amnesia, the result of too much exclusive concentration on sacred textbooks and holy communion. If he had suggested this to Bita she might have informed him that Herald Newton himself had thought that only white people went off the head from too much book learning. . . .

"Paul, too much learning hath made thee mad. . . ."

But the squire preferred instead to speak of such things to Teacher Fearon. And Teacher Fearon did not agree with him at all. "But, Squire," he said, "it's an ugly affair all right, but there's nothing mysterious about it in spite of the stupid talk of Obeah among these bush people. Not long ago there was a canine exhibition that was pedalled down."

"But I never had the slightest knowledge of any such proclivity among your people before," said the squire.

"Oh, Squire! What you talking about now?" said Teacher Fearon. "It's all in nature. If I should tell you about my experience with the kids. The curious little aberrations that crop out among them with all kinds of things. Playing with themselves just like toys in their hands. But I never bother them when I surprise them, for they are kids. When they grow up they will throw away the toys quite naturally. I think that's a better way than horrifying their little immature minds about sin-and-health talk. The only thing strange about this is that one of Herald

Day's toys may have remained with him and he growing up with it without being aware."

At Jubilee, Priscilla Craig was unapproachably austere in her grief or wrath. Neither a little theory of Obeah or amnesia, sin-eating, all-in-nature or destiny could propitiate her. Malcolm Craig, great reconciliator, endeavoured to visualize the thing as a momentary triumph of Satan when the archangel was nodding, and to take comfort from the motto framed over his desk: "Man proposes, God disposes."

But Priscilla Craig could see nothing but the deed. "Shocking! Shocking!" She reiterated aloud and to herself, striding straightly through the mission like a person distrait.

"I feel that our work here is wasted," she said, huskily, from vexation of the spirit. "All our giving freely of our money and ourselves. Spending, planning, building—all broken down and buried in the mire. I shall not do any more. I have lost faith."

Malcolm Craig directed her attention to the large framed photographs of preachers' conferences upon the walls of his study. Coloured men, black and brown, with white men. Outstanding among them was the pastor of the City Tabernacle, a solid hearty-faced black man who was publicly adored as the golden-tongued preacher and the most exquisitely discriminating speaker of the "King's English" in the island. And others. Justices of the Peace. Members of Parochial Boards. Members of the Legislature. All law-abiding men and respectable heads of families enough to more than justify the result of any Missionary Work, clerical and civil.

But Priscilla Craig, not possessed with her husband's objective outlook, was unconsoled. Herald Newton was, after all, a part of her personal contribution to the Work. And he had failed. It was as if she herself had failed making a failure of the Work.

Malcolm Craig's disappointment also cut deep. But his feelings were a different colour from his wife's. He remembered his father and his wish. That wish that had become his hope. He had been enamoured of the idea of training the son of Deacon Day to succeed him at Jubilee. But the defeat of his plans and the disappointment he felt were as nothing compared with his thought of the old man's sorrow.

Mrs. Craig turned from the study with a firm vertical march on to the veranda, where she stood erect and gazed steadily beyond the market over the town. How beautiful it was! More than a village yet hardly even a town with the wilding vegetation so dense in the heart of it, almost hiding the little white houses everywhere. Around them growing natural fences, hibiscus red and white and pink, six-months, dagger palms, pingwings. And over these fee-fees running and climbing, spilling their delicate scent and the kids raping the pretty blossoms to blow whistles. The black thatch upon the slope rearing on its slender stalk way up into the sky like an umbrella reversed. And the giant bamboos moving in the bottoms.

"Beautiful!" Priscilla whispered. But the sounds of the market came humming up to her and she repeated a line from the famous missionary hymn:

"Every prospect pleases and only man is vile."

18

UPON BITA'S RETURN TO JUBILEE, PRISCILLA AND MAL-colm had been discreetly silent about Herald Newton Day. No word, no hint, nothing. As if he had never existed, never been known to them. Only Bita noticed that the signed photograph of himself that he had presented to her (it was taken standing before a rostrum with the Bible in his hand) had been removed from its place on her dressing-table. By way of discretion she also made no comment, but resumed her old way of living at the mission as if there had never been any talking or planning about an early marriage for her.

The strange mishap of Herald Newton Day was the most moving event of her experience. She had accepted the idea of marrying and allowed herself to be affianced to him even though her spirit and her body were resistant. And ever since the engagement she had been trying to evade the reality of it, pushing it off into a vague future. And now without ever facing the thing, without any struggle, without the least effort on her part, she was re-leased from the dreaded thing. As if a mysterious agent in nature had acted for her, but by a means so unusual, so terrible.

She thought of Herald's mother, good old Mother Day, and that moment she felt she could have sacrificed herself to the marriage if that might have saved Mother Day from the pain and shame.

The day after her arrival from Banana Bottom, Bita went to visit Deacon and Mother Day. Mother Day had been expecting the visit and thinking she would have to console Bita. But when they met it was to Bita that fell the rôle of consolatrix. Bita had cut a bouquet of delicate pink-and-white roses from the mission garden, and when she arrived at the Day's house, it was the deacon who opened the front door and let her in, fatherly fashion, but his voice and manner had lost that fine pride that Bita had remarked when he welcomed her on the day of the dinner, and he appeared as if he had suddenly shrivelled up.

Mother Day entered and gathered Bita in her arms. "Mi poah pickney, mi poah pickney! Ah beg you pardon. Ise so sorry."

Then all at once she crumpled up and was clinging to Bita. "Oh mi pickney, mi pickney! What a blow! What a blow! A wha' mek Massa Gawd a bring dat upon we—we always lovin' and sarvin' Massa Jesas."

Deacon Day went quietly out of the room. And Bita led Mother Day to the sofa, hugging her and repeating any soothing phrases that rose to her lips. "Don't cry, Mother. Please don't. Don't take it so to heart, Mother. Never mind. Hold up, Mother. Don't break your heart."

Although Mrs. Craig never spoke to Bita about the shattered plan, so that the girl had no inkling of what was going on in her mind, she nevertheless indicated by her attitude that she was even more austere in her ways, more haughtily uncompromising than ever in walking with God.

For on the very week of Bita's return Mrs. Craig came

to lunch one noon with a letter in her hand. The letter was from a parson's widow announcing that she would soon be married again to the overseer of a coffee plantation near Little Gap. The widow was a light-skinned coloured woman, belonging to one of the old Spanish mixed-blood families. But her people were poor. Her first husband, also a Eurafrican, had been accidentally drowned while on a mission to one of the Turks Islands. His widow had returned to Jamaica and after a difficult time had found a situation as mistress of one of the post and telegraph offices —which provided a sort of haven of employment for poor light-coloured women of gentle breeding.

"Fancy her marrying again!" exclaimed Mrs. Craig. "I never thought she was capable of that and I am finished with her." And fixing her eyes on Mr. Craig, "Imagine you or I thinking of marrying again if one of us died."

"Perhaps, dear, she may have yielded to the temptation because of loneliness."

"Jesus is the Great Companion," said Mrs. Craig. "As a minister's wife, Mrs. Delavanti should be setting another example to the parishioners. Dear Queen Victoria did set an example for all noble-hearted women to follow. She never took a second husband, although she had nine children to bring up and a kingdom to rule. She was never tempted aside from the strait path of living her life as a model for Christian women for all time. Mother . . . wife . . . and Queen."

Emphasizing the last word, Priscilla Craig straightened herself in her chair and although she was rather rigid, with her golden-white hair upgathered into a crown, she was undeniably queenly.

19

AMONG THE UNGODLY LOWLY OF JUBILEE THE TALK OF the town was the spectacle of Hopping Dick going to church and sitting through a sermon. This had coincided with the return of Bita from Banana Bottom.

Hopping Dick, although nothing of an infidel, had never worked up any enthusiasm for church-going. And his interest in the churches had been limited to the semi-secular affairs that were given by the various choirs.

The ungodly set agreed that Hopping Dick must have gotten religion in Banana Bottom. But there was no outward change in his demeanour, such as one might expect from a converted person. His dandified air was still with him, even a little more pronounced. After the service he was often seen in conversation with Belle Black and Bita. . . . And the shrewdest of the ungodly set guessed, of course, to what influence was due Hopping Dick's going to church.

He went further than church-going and assisted at choir rehearsals, especially when Bita accompanied the Choristers at the piano and, notorious rum-tanker though he was, had even sat in during an afternoon session of the Band of Hope. His pious manifestations brought him into closer contact than ever with Bita.

He went so far as to take part in what the ungodly set had voted the dullest local thing. He had accompanied

Belle Black and Bita to an open-air salvation meeting. Malcolm and Priscilla Craig were there, and it was such a compact little gathering that Hopping Dick could not escape an introduction to them and for the first time in his life he touched Mrs. Craig's hand. Priscilla had been remarking for some time the sudden interest of Hopping Dick in religious things, and although she disapproved of his familiarity with Bita she refrained from saying anything that might have been considered detrimental to the saving of a soul. But in her heart she nourished a hostile feeling against him.

One Sunday, Andrew Lakin, a young leader of the church (not a young man in years but young in comparison with other leaders) invited Bita to his home in the country a little north of Jubilee. He possessed a fine pimento orchard, and as it was pimento-picking time he had invited Bita up to see it before the trees were stripped. He knew that Jordan Plant was an industrious and prosperous cultivator and desired his daughter to see his own place of which he was very proud. Mrs. Craig was informed of the invitation and seemed rather pleased that Bita should go. So the following day, after breakfast, Bita started off with Belle Black.

The place was just three-quarters of a mile out of Jubilee. A difference in water supply and land formation had given the Jubilee district a red colour remarkably dissimilar to that of the Banana Bottom country. The Banana Bottom land with its heavy growth of thicket was a fat slate colour with bubbling springs and rivers abundant and a heavy rainfall which imparted a luxuriant green and a rich ripeness to the staples: bananas, breadfruit, pears, coffee, cocoa and sugar-cane. Although the region had been under cultivation for generations, it still preserved its pristine aspect of virgin backwoods. Anything that was cultivatable in that island could be grown in Banana Bottom.

But in the Jubilee district there were no streams and springs. The people drank rain water collected in tanks during the rainy season. And the rainfall was light. The colour of the soil gave a ruddy touch to everything, even the black peasants who lived by it. It was no good for banana, cocoa, breadfruit and other fat-soil plants, but perfect for pimento and coffee.

Of all the fair trees flourishing in that ruddy-warm earth there was none that combined more delightfully a decorative and utilitarian purpose than the pimento. The plants grew straight and high on the little properties as well as the big, along the wayside, their silver-russet bark gleaming as if lighting the way from the main roads to the backwoods.

When Bita arrived at Leader Lakin's the pimento-picking-and-gathering match had already begun. The place consisted of twenty-one acres of land on a slope ending in a valley. The pimentoes grew well spaced apart from the top of the property down to the gully. And in between were custard apples bearing soft-ripe velvet-brown fruits, coffee trees and guinea grass. John-tuhits and blue quits were rioting in the tree tops over the pungent ripened blue-black berries.

It was a big picking match. Leader Lakin had five lads to climb the trees and break off the little branches laden with the full-green and blue-black berries and over a dozen women to strip them off. There were some peasants who spread banana fronds under the pimento trees upon which the climbers threw down the berries. Others used sheets. That way no berries were lost, for many fell off the tiny stalks when they were thrown down.

Leader Lakin showed Bita over the buildings and barbecues. From an external angle the peasants of the Jubilee district showed a higher level of living than those of the Banana Bottom region. In the Jubilee highlands fine timber trees grew easily thick like reeds in swampy soil. And so the poor peasants did not use thatch for their homes. And stones were used everywhere in building—even fences were made of loose stone piled upon stone without mortar and which were very striking, dividing the peasant's lots along the roadside. So also the barbecues for the drying of produce were more numerous and elaborate than those of Banana Bottom.

For good limestone was as common in Jubilee as banana trash in Banana Bottom. Whereas Banana Bottom had to import stone or dynamite it with great difficulty out of the river areas, it had an abundance of the thatch palm and thatch grass. And so the houses of the poorer peasants were almost all thatched and wattled.

However, the stony soil of Jubilee, though splendid for coffee and pimento, did not grow bananas and yams, breadfruit, mangoes and all the staple tubers and fruits that went to the making of the peasants' diet. And so the peasants of the mountain country were heftier and hardier than those of Jubilee.

Leader Lakin took Bita over his five fine barbecues and the coffee-mill which separated the pulp from the grain and the grain from the chaff, the outhouses for the storing of grain and fruit and for his helping hands to sleep. For, like other prosperous peasants, Leader Lakin always had about five people, men and women, toiling for him for their feed and scanty clothing and a little small change.

The dwelling-house, just two rooms and an enclosed piazza, was dwarfed by the barbecues and outbuildings. But it was quite enough for the Lakins, who had no children. Between it and the barbecues were the three large tanks for catching rain water, the gutters around the buildings leading into them.

Leader Lakin mentioned the dry weather and wondered if it were going to be prolonged. The last rainy season had passed almost rainless and the tanks were low. There were native prophets who warned that the island was getting drier and drier every year and that some day it would dry up, and there were superior ones who, basing their prophecy upon science, said that the increased dryness was a result of the destruction of the forests and predicted calamity. But after the longest drought the rains would come tropical, lashing with hurricanes and floods, raising roofs, capsizing houses, breaking bridges, ruining crops and confounding the prophets.

Leader Lakin's anxiety revived sharply in Bita's memory the first great drought she had experienced when she was a little girl, when even in Banana Bottom, land of abundant waters, many springs and brooks dried up, rivers sank under their beds and from the distant Dry Hills and other arid sections, even that very Jubilee district where the tanks had given out, the people came miles upon miles with donkeys and mules and carts in search of water.

The kitchen being too small, one of the barbecues was used by Mrs. Leader Lakin, helped by two other women, for the preparation of the food by the match workers. Down in the field the boys were breaking off the little bunches of pimento and tossing them down to the women, who, squatting in groups on the grass, stripped the berries into the broad bamboo baskets.

A man was leading a jamma, improvising verses to a little refrain in which everybody joined.

"Picking pimento, oh, picking, picking,
Gal and boy sweet picking time, oh picking."

Belle Black, swaying to the singing, took up a basket and went shaking her hips down to the valley to join a couple of girls. She was expert at that kind of work: the gathering of pimento, coffee and ginger, sun-drying and preparing them for the home and for the market. She was born on a little farm patch at Little Gap and had lived there until she was a grown girl, when she discovered her fine voice and left for Jubilee to establish herself as a leading treble and higgler girl.

Leader Lakin after showing Bita the whole place thought that she would like to go back up to the house until lunch-time, but she preferred to stay with Belle Black picking pimento, even though her fingers were not used to the work.

When it was eating-time the leader of the jamma, puckering up his mouth against a large pinky white cowrie shell, trumpeted a long note, and everybody went up from the field to the barbecue. There were two heaps of food upon two barbecues, one for the men and one for the women. Lakin had killed a goat and the meat was stewed and spiced with green pepper and annatto and served in broad pans. And there were other pans of dried cod, boiled, shredded and served in cocoanut oil. And yet bigger pans were heaped up with boiled yams and breadfruit, while there were twenty-quart tins of sangaree concocted of plain sugar and bitter oranges, ginger and chewstick.

Leader Lakin ate with his helpers, but Bita had luncheon served on crockery with Belle Black in the piazza. While they were eating Bita noticed a shadow pass and afterwards she was surprised to find that it was none other than Hopping Dick's. She saw him squatting on the men's barbecue, where he had been invited by Leader Lakin upon his arrival, and eating with them. He was very outstanding with his town clothes and boots among the labourers in Holland-drill shirts and blue-jeans rolled up to their knees and all barefooted, except those who wore sandplatters to save the soles of their feet from thorns and sharp stones. Belle Black was not surprised to see Hopping Dick because he had promised her that he might come up.

The liaison between Belle Black and Hopping Dick was a little strange. Belle liked to have Hopping Dick accompany her to picnics and parties because he was dandy. But she hadn't the slightest inclination to go farther with him and settle down as a concubine or wife, as such friendships always end. Because she said that Hopping Dick lived more precariously than herself in spite of being always well-suited out. Good horse-dealing money came largely from running into luck and one was not lucky every week. Besides, Hopping Dick did not even take seriously his one means of making a living. He was clever and personable and his father admired his brains and wished that he would use them more to help him in his business. Hopping Dick had a flair for picking promising horses and mules and clinching good bargains beside which his father was merely plodding. But he was interested to use it only when he was in need of ready money.

One day when Bita questioned Belle about Hopping Dick she replied: "Him is good company, sister, and awright fer a good time, but him no good fer nummo. As a homemaker he no wut' nutten at all."

After the lunch Bita and Belle went out on to the barbecue and were saluted by Hopping Dick. Bita left them together and went to chin with Mrs. Lakin, who was resting in the shade of a pig-plum tree, fanning herself with the end of her blue apron, while her helpers were gathering up the dishes.

A long blast from the shell was the signal to recommence work and soon the sounds of the jamma came up from the valley telling that it had begun. Bita went back down to the field but Belle Black was not among the pickers. Not feeling like picking then, Bita went along the gully, brushing through the guinea grass towards the other side of the slope where there was a fine patch of young Congo peas. Midway there reared itself a glorious giant cotton tree shedding upon the air its fleecy down, some of which alighted delicately on the long blades of the guinea grass curved like bended bows, while some rested motionless on the invisible rays of space.

Bita gathered a handful of the down and climbed up on one of the great outside roots of the cotton tree. There was a deep hollow in the belly of the cotton tree large enough to build a hut in. And presently a little murmuring inside sounded upon Bita's ears. She remembered when she was a little girl how she always romped with her playmates around the cotton tree down by the river bank. And it was hollow, too, but they were afraid of exploring its belly, saying that a duppy lived in it.

The murmuring grew clearer and Bita recognized the voices. Belle's and Hopping Dick's. And a little panic rushed upon her as she thought that they might emerge and find her there and perhaps think that she had followed them. And so hastily she clambered down from the root, and entering the patch of Congo peas she passed out on the other side and continued up the slope.

When she glanced down that way again from the hill, Belle Black and Hopping Dick were strolling insouciantly along the gully towards the pickers. Her body was glowing and tingling. Ah, she sighed sweetly. She could easily understand the pungent perfume of the pimento exciting love with the pickers up to their necks in it, squatting upon the leaves with stems and berries in their hands, which dominated the atmosphere with their odour. Desire was a radiant thing, more precious than gratification. Her thoughts raced away and brought back a sharp fleeting reminder of a brief holiday in England and a sentimental encounter with a relative of one of her college mates. But only a memory. For her emotional thoughts even were finely framed in that realm of the practical, which her higher training had always emphasized.

From the top of the peas patch and through the caressing guinea grass she walked back down to the gully and to the pimento tree under which Hopping Dick with Belle Black and two other girls were sitting. Belle was furiously picking to finish her nearly-filled basket, for it was about time for them to get ready to walk back to Jubilee.

20

When Hopping Dick told Bita about the house party to which he had been invited, she was not at first interested. But one evening Hopping Dick walked with Belle Black to the schoolroom where the Coloured Choristers were rehearsing and stayed to listen. This was not unusual. The Choristers had a reputation for fine singing and there never was an evening of rehearsal when visitors from the town did not casually drop in at the schoolroom to hear them.

That evening Bita was late coming down to the schoolroom, and when she arrived the schoolmaster was acting as accompanist. Seeing Hopping Dick sitting in the back, she went to shake hands with him. And ever alertly polite, Hopping Dick stood up and refused to take his seat until Bita consented to sit down awhile.

He began teasing Bita about going to the forthcoming house party and proposing that she might do wrong for once and go with him. Bita replied playfully, saying that she was not a novice at wrong-doing.

And with the days the temptation to go grew upon her. She had never had a chance at smart dancing since she left college. Her dancing-teacher always praised her movement and said she was a natural dancer. And this house party might give her an opportunity to excel in the thing she loved.

The occasion of the party was the opening of a new house by a Jubilee shopkeeper. Most of the young invited guests were his clients and could be placed among the Negroes who made up the artisan, small-shopkeeping and trading groups of the town, and also they were for the greater part members of the Anglican Church because it was the smart church and gave them, too, more freedom of social enjoyment than the nonconformist churches.

The Negroes loved their dances and carousals, and because as a people they still possess more of primitive positiveness than formal hypocrisy it was comprehensible that they should ease from under the rigid discipline of the nonconformist churches that had laboured for their emancipation to that church which in the eyes of their slave fathers had appeared to be the exclusive spiritual defender and mainstay of their masters.

Bita turned over the idea of the dance in her mind until it was finally made up to go. But to tell Mrs. Craig about it—she knew she couldn't. Mentally she made tentative steps, but they were impossible of realization. At last the desire to dance—to plunge into an altogether secular atmosphere, won over prudence and she decided to go.

Came the evening of the dance. The only difficulty in Bita's leaving without being detected was that her room was at the farther end of that side of the veranda facing the wood hills, and to get out of the house by her outside door she had to go past Malcolm Craig's and Priscilla's room both. But her native prowess as a country wilding served her well and she got away by climbing down a wild tamarind tree that grew stretching a strong limb over the veranda towards her room.

She met Hopping Dick down by the schoolroom as

agreed and he escorted her to the party as his lady. It was a much more formal affair than Bita had imagined. The invitations were by individual cards each bearing the following: "N. B. Each gentleman allowed to bring a lady. Each lady permitted a gentleman escort."

These people lived in a world that was unknown and strange to Bita. Petty shopkeepers, little speculators in fruit and grain and stock, school teachers and monitors, young tradesfolk, tailors, carpenters, cabinet-makers, masons, seamstresses, milliners—grandchildren and great-grandchildren of ancestors three-quarters of a century removed from slavery, cohering into the building of a middle class that was unknown and impossible to West Indian life under the *ancien régime*.

The new house stood out a pretty painted thing upon a hill above a group of tradesfolk houses beyond the premises of the courthouse. There was a little flower garden in front and roses, scarlet, cream, pink and white, variegated wild tanias, painted-ladies standing flamingo fashion upon their legs, crotons and the piercingly sweet night jasmine.

At the moment when Bita and Hopping Dick passed through the garden gate a little piece was in process of being enacted at the front door. An unescorted young lady, modishly dressed in the latest Kingston fashion and wearing a large feathered Italian-straw hat and a Spanish shawl showing a little of her custard-apple-brown shoulders, had been stopped at the door by a gentleman and lady (evidently the credentials committee) and asked to show her card of invitation.

The young lady lost her perfect aplomb, seemed distressed and, hesitating, said she had no card.

"But were you invited?" asked the lady of the door.

"Yes," said the distressed one.

"Who invited you?"

To this she could give no answer and the door was shut in her face. As the rejected thing hurried down the garden walk, hiding her face with her shawl, Hopping Dick saw that it was Gracie Hall, and said: "Poor gal."

"Do you know her?" Bita asked.

Hopping Dick said yes and told her about the incident of the merry-go-round.

"It's a shame they should turn her away like that," said Bita.

"It's because a dat merry-go-round business," said Hopping Dick, "and they make a sing about her, you know."

Hopping Dick was never such a social success as he was that evening. Many of the young men had told one another what girl they intended to bring to the party and it had been surmised that Mr. Delgado would bring Miss Belle Black. They all gasped when Mr. Delgado entered the reception-room with Miss Bita Plant of the Free Church mission.

All attention was centred on Bita. Most of them there had seen and admired her for her beauty and her accomplishments, but none had had the opportunity of an introduction. And so Bita took the place of guest of honour and Hopping Dick was prancingly pleased with himself.

The assemblage was basically black, but charmingly variegated with the tints of some of the finest flowers of miscegenation. The girls were picturesque in those striking prints that are seen mainly in Southern Spain and tropical countries as if they were specially designed and sold to such places. They giggled and chattered like parrots over little local trifles, and Bita felt a surge of pleasurable relief to be in the midst of them away from the staid atmosphere of the mission.

She was asked to lead the grand march with the owner of the house and there were disappointed dandies for every number she danced afterwards. It was the first time since she left college that she had done the dances practised there for physical and esthetic training. Now it was for the sheer joy of dancing. Not in physical-culture uniform, but in a pretty frock among men and girls who were happy in their fun and who made up in spontaneous warmth for the lack of that cultivated refinement to which she had been trained.

Waltzes, mazurkas, schottisches, lancers and all the decorous ballroom dances that could never do for a fiddle-and-drum carousal on the grass at Tabletop nor in the dust of a crowded palm booth. But there on the waxed mahogany floor how delightful they were! And as Bita stood up to Hopping Dick (who perfectly acted the rôle of his nickname that night), hands poised in the air and she pirouetting around him to the fiddling of the native translation of the minuet, she felt it was indeed a happy choice when the native tongue turned that name to mintoe.

21

PRISCILLA CRAIG WAS VISITING AN ENGLISH MISSIONARY
and his wife, who, after ten years of holy work in West
Africa, had been transferred to the West Indies.

The missionary couple had brought over with them a
striking collection of savage craftsmanship, which they
were exhibiting as heathen idols with lectures on "The
Customs and Superstitions of the Primitive African."

The native Negroes had been flocking in hundreds and
paying to see and hear how their African cousins still lived
in savagery and by fetishism. The idols were mostly fashioned out of wood: men, women and children in strange
provocative attitudes carrying things, bearing babies, playing instruments or reposing. Carved and figured chairs,
staffs for patriarchs, household utensils. Feathered head-
dresses, aprons and loin cloths of straw, necklaces, and
bracelets fashioned of beads of which the perfect juxta-
position of colour powerfully touched one's mind like
delicate chords of music.

Yet few if any of the crowds who paid to see those
strange objects thought that they were created to serve
any other purpose beside a missionary lecture against
idolatry and that they of themselves were more eloquent
of the soul of their obscure creators and their people than
a thousand missionary lectures.

Priscilla Craig had never been to any part of the African

Sudan, and these objects took her to a Negro world that was disturbingly different from that to which she was accustomed. For those small statues with important points exaggerated and others minimized the word that came to her lips was "grotesque." She could find no significance in them, so far were they removed from the classic Greek and Roman tradition with which she was familiar. These objects seemed mere caricatures of a poor and miserably fallen humanity abandoned of God.

But as she gazed fixedly at them they seemed to take on a forbidden actuality and potency, as if they were immortal, of a state of being existing beyond the saving grace of salvation. And vaguely she thought she discerned something of their spirit in the decadent practices of the Obi-worshippers of Jamaica. And as she was the kind of person who is always seeking (and is unhappy if she find not) an obvious explanation of everything, she arrived at the conclusion that those objects were unholy—those statues nothing if not immoral, and all that those masks on the wall, hideous things, contributed to the purpose of life was an eternal obscene grinning.

There she stood in contemplation, convinced that she understood more about them than the missionary exhibitors. There was much more behind their exhibition than they thought. The objects were so positively real. Surely they possessed some elemental force representing more than mere idle idol-making. She was troubled to think that they might have their origin in some genuine belief, troubled to think that such a belief should have prompted magic-workers to celebrate and preserve its potency. That the night-wrapped creatures of Africa might also have had there in the dim jungles their own vision of life.

And puzzled, she even wondered why the Almighty had decreed such a thing and doomed the black heathen to pervert his skill to the fashioning of objects to glorify the cult of Ugliness. For with her sweet-and-severe standards of esthetics, beauty for her was an unthought-of thing in such misshapen and terror-evoking works. All that she saw in them was a satanic power, and Satan was ugly.

Priscilla fell back upon the poetic thought, "God moves in a mysterious way his wonders to perform." He had fashioned the world to his liking, distributing the peoples according to his will, apportioning to them different degrees of belief so that the One True Religion should glow with greater effulgence and, with the Sacred Heart filled with more and more pity for the heathen, scatter its Angels to all the regions of the earth to bear and uphold the Light until the Great Judgement Day.

So Priscilla Craig was able to reduce and reconcile the unfamiliar. But gazing again at the masks, they all seemed to be hideously grinning, and impelled to the wall by a magnetic power she attempted to touch one of them to test the reality of her eyes, when the mocking thing suddenly detached itself and began dancing around her. Others followed the first and Priscilla found herself surrounded by a grinning, dancing fury.

Priscilla remained transfixed, deprived of voice to shriek her utter terror among those bodiless barbaric faces circling and darting towards her and bobbing up and down with that mad grinning. And now it seemed that Patou was among them, Patou shrunken to a grinning face, and suddenly she too was in motion and madly whirling round and round with the weird dancing masks.

.   .   .   .

Meanwhile the night had changed; some persons began leaving the party and Bita intimated that she too must go. In the excitement of dancing and the resultant heat she had drunk plenty of sangaree, and the sweet orange wine, innocent-tasting though it was, had, in its total effect, a pernicious quality.

When she put on her hat and light cape, the house owner and other guests ringed round her, insisting that she stay longer. But Hopping Dick intervened and, realizing Bita's situation, they did not press their demand, but let her go, hoping that soon there would be an opportunity for her to be among them again.

The party was a very enjoyable affair for Bita. The coloured Anglicans had better fun than the Jubilee non-conformists. Elated by the events of the evening, Hopping Dick took Bita's arm and pranced down the garden walk to the road. But in the distance he saw the mission frowning down, and now that the deed had been done, the party ended, he felt a little afraid for her. But the party crowd being a different colour from the prayer-meeting loose-lips —they having no contact nor interest in the mission—he also felt reassured that Bita's escapade might not get to Mrs. Craig's ears. Hopping Dick communicated his reaction to Bita. But she said she had had a nice time and that nothing in the world could spoil it now or make her regret it.

Hopping Dick said it was fine to hear her talk that way, only he wouldn't like her to get into trouble at the mission on account of him. Bita replied that if anything untoward should occur she could always return to Banana Bottom.

"An' leabe we-all! An' what would Jubilee be widouten you, Miss Bita?"

She laughed and said she could always come back to visit. And now they were right under the west side of the mission in the shadow of the lime trees growing thick and high, their balls gleaming like gold in the moonlight.

As Hopping Dick whispered good-bye to Bita, the sign of a lingering warmth in her hand communicated to him something of that sweet sensation experienced when a wary or timid or hesitant spirit reacts favourably to a positive one; and the air full of feeling, the heavy-scented shadows closing upon them, he drew her to him and planted a sharp kiss upon her neck. Bita yielded up herself entirely for a moment, limber in his arms. Then brusquely she disengaged herself and ran through the limes leading up the back way to the mission.

Hopping Dick, happily excited, began humming a jigging ditty, started to return to the party, treading the sweet air, reviewing the pleasures of the night and hoping, with rhyme and reason, to pick up a piece of luck.

As Bita tiptoed in her stockings past Mr. Craig's bedroom, Priscilla's eyes blinked open and she had a dim, unpleasant, confused impression of a dark nymph and African masks and Patou gyrating around her. She opened her mouth wide and cried: "Oh Lord!" and was relieved to find her voice. She rubbed her eyes vigorously, collecting her far-wandering senses, and looking out of the folded Venetian window saw nothing but the long scones of the scentful bellflowers lipping the veranda railing, a gorgeous cream white in the moonlight.

She got up and, wrapping a light dressing-gown around her, opened the door and passed down the corridor to

Patou's room. Patou was fast asleep. When she returned Mr. Craig was awake.

"What was it, dear?" he asked.

"Oh, I've had a horrible, horrible dream!" she said. And she related how she had gone in her sleep to the missionary lecture-hall.

22

THAT MORNING ROSYANNA'S EASY NATURE HAD BEEN irritated, her humility challenged and her honour outraged by a master stroke of morality of the sort that sometimes almost snatches the breath away from the servant in the house.

Mrs. Craig, feeling a little tired, had not joined Malcolm and Bita at breakfast, but ordered hers to be brought to her boudoir. And after breakfast was over Rosyanna began making the beds, commencing as usual with Mr. Craig's room. But as soon as she had started, Mrs. Craig in her dressing-gown of lacy muslin floated down the corridor and into the room, ostensibly to give Rosyanna some perfectly needless information about torn sheets. But when she thought Rosyanna was not looking she dived under the bed and, snatching up something, went quickly from the room. Her action did not escape Rosyanna's wide-open eyes—and which were especially wide open when she scented camouflage.

Rosyanna was determined to find out just what duck was in that diving. So she opened the door and called down the corridor: "Missis! Missis!" Mrs. Craig stopped and Rosyanna shuffled up to her with a long rigmarole about the wearing out of the mattresses which seemed very irrelevant to anything. And as she talked, Mrs. Craig plainly showing her impatience and even annoyance, Rosyanna became restless, shuffling up and down, and appeared to be trying to edge around Mrs. Craig, who was all the time occupied in concealing something behind her.

At last Rosyanna amazed Mrs. Craig by saying: "Ef you no mind, missis, ah we tek them shoes you got in you' han' an' puttem wid de udders fer clean."

"Certainly, Rosyanna, you may," and Mrs. Craig handed over the shoes with sweet dignity. Rosyanna waddle-rocked back to her room in righteous black indignation.

What could the gentle lady mean by such a performance? she thought. Because her eyes had never seen Mrs. Craig in her husband's bed, did the lady want her to think she did not sleep with her husband? She, Rosyanna, who had been making beds so long that she could almost shut her eyes and tell whether two slept in a bed instead of one, and even if they had slept warmly together or coldly apart.

Did she not know the rare monthly occasions, when Mrs. Craig slept in her own room—she who morning after morning had entered it to find a work-basket and balls of silk and wool and knitting-needles and even magazines scattered on the counterpane. Did Mrs. Craig take her for a precocious child from whom all suggestions of wife-and-husband relationship should be kept? She, Rosyanna, with one son in the grave, another in Panama and a daughter going to school?

She a good Christian honestly united in holy wedlock (after her conversion when her first son was five years old) and afterwards baptized in the baptismal tank of the Jubilee Free Church. Rosyanna was amazed at Mrs. Craig's exhibition of holiness. She recalled how often Malcolm Craig had preached against the flourishing state of fornication and quoted St. Paul: "It is better to marry more than to burn." Clear biblical language. And if one was married according to God, Nature and the Church, why practise dissimulation?

Waddling from room to room, shaking the sheets and slapping the pillows, the more Rosyanna pondered the matter the more disgusted she was. Her breast was boiling with indignation. She just had to get it off on somebody and although Bita was not usually a sympathetic listener, Rosyanna was determined to tell her about the incident.

At that time Bita was reviewing the high moments of the party, and feeling that it was the most enjoyable event at which she had assisted in Jubilee since her return from abroad. But with her exaltation was mingled a sense of humiliation that she had participated in it illicitly, stealing away and returning furtively like a cat.

It made her feel uncomfortably little and cheap. It was ugly. Not her idea of living. To do things of which she was ashamed. Her native pride rose against that. And also her education. There was a great pride of tradition behind that education. It was a code that an imperial proud nation had prepared and authorized for her selectest and most favoured sons and daughters. And by a strange fate she, an alien child of enslaved people, had been trained in its principles.

One thing that it had emphasized was independence of spirit, and another was "the correct thing." When first she went to live at Jubilee Mrs. Craig had a fixed way of correcting her mistakes and setting her right. No vulgar remonstrating and upbraiding.

"*This* is the way *we* do it," she said, whether it was the manner of eating buttered toast and treacle with coffee or of pronouncing a doubtful word. And also at college. Once when a girl (not a colonial) from a foreign country had been found with another girl's precious trifle which she declared she had borrowed, the teacher had told her quietly but firmly: "Among us that is stealing."

So Bita was thinking now that if she had to live at the mission she would have to be able to do so in such a manner as to participate in things that made life enjoyable without fear, secrecy and shame—even though such things were not to the tastes of the Craigs.

She turned the matter different ways and almost convinced herself that the right step to take was to do the proper thing and tell Mrs. Craig that she had gone to the party, when Rosyanna entered her room.

"We gwine a market thisya marnin', Miss Bita?" asked Rosyanna.

"Yes, as soon as you are ready."

Quite nakedly Rosyanna showed that she had something to say, but she was hesitant, not certain that she would find a willing listener in Bita. At last she began:

"Well, I nebber did heah 'bouten sich a t'ing in all mi life. Nebber did come up ag'inst anyt'ing so deadickylous. Lak a if dat woman done want me fer t'ink she not jesen a woman lak mese'f."

Bita showed no disapproval of Rosyanna's outburst, but regarded her expectantly. She had an idea that "dat woman" was Mrs. Craig and was surprised, as she had never heard Rosyanna refer to her except respectfully as "de missis."

"Ah could'n' be'n treated wussen in mi life, Miss Bita, not ef ah was a t'ief an' a liard."

"Well, what is it?" Bita asked.

Rosyanna spread herself over a low stool and related her experience of that morning.

"Ise a married woman mese'f," she said. "An' I hab de right fer sleep wid mi husban' all de tim' cepen' when him not at home. Ah doan' shame a nuttin'. Ah doan' blieb in no sintiminious primsin' an' actin' lak I was an angel when Gawd knows Ise a woman. An' de Bible says plain dat Gawd made woman as a hopmeet fer man."

As Bita listened she was able to understand quite easily what Rosyanna, in spite of her years of experience, could not understand. And now all thoughts of her idea of being honest to herself and frank with Mrs. Craig was banished from her mind. She knew that she could not do it and stay at the mission.

. . . . . .

It may be that Bita would never have thought she was passionately in love with Hopping Dick if Mrs. Craig had not come between them and forbidden Hopping Dick to visit the mission-house and warned Bita against keeping company with him. Ever since Hopping Dick had been converted to church-going, Mrs. Craig had silently disapproved of his associating so much with Bita. But for certain evangelical reasons she had refrained from coming out squarely against it until now.

It happened that a Miss Knibbling was giving an At Home one afternoon to announce her engagement to a young man she had been keeping company with for a number of years. The young man was a friend of Hopping Dick's. And Hopping Dick had asked Miss Knibbling to send an invitation to Bita, promising he would get her to

208

come and perhaps play the baby organ that Miss Knibbling
had recently bought.

MISS KNIBBLING
presents her compliments
and invites you to an
AT HOME
at her residence on the
occasion of her betrothal to
MR. EDWIN GRANTHAM

Bita showed the invitation to Mrs. Craig, who had no
objection. But on the Wednesday afternoon of the At
Home, while Bita was in her room dressing and Priscilla
Craig was seated on the veranda gravely talking nonsense
to her handsome parrot, she was petrified to see Hopping
Dick stepping princely across the lawn, so elegant in cream-
flannel pantaloons and a blue-grey tweed cutaway with tan
gloves and a gold-headed cane. Hopping Dick went straight
towards the veranda, doffed his hat smartly, and bowed
and respectfully inquired for Bita.

His dandified air irritated Mrs. Craig and she thought:
How like a dressed-up monkey. But she said: "May I ask
what is it you require of Miss Plant?"

"She axe me to be her hescort to de Atome," said Hopping Dick.

"Did she ask you to come *here* for her?" said Mrs. Craig.

"Yes, she axe me fer come hyah to de mission-house an'
fetch her."

For a moment only Mrs. Craig hesitated as if she were
deliberating whether she should call Bita or not. Then she
said decisively: "I am sorry, but she is *not* going, after all."

"Ef you please tell har I was hyah," said Hopping Dick and he turned to go.

"Just a moment," said Mrs. Craig.

Hopping Dick stopped.

"I think it would be better for everybody concerned that your acquaintanceship with Miss Plant should come to an end," said Mrs. Craig.

"Ah wouldn' a come hyah ef she didn't invite me," said Hopping Dick. And he went, but not so elegantly as he had come.

Hopping Dick had hardly passed through the mission gate and out of sight when Bita came out on to the veranda, wearing a corn-yellow summer frock and a broad-brimmed jippi-jappa hat.

Her face as fixed and lofty as a cliff, Mrs. Craig inquired of Bita if she had really invited Hopping Dick to call for her at the mission. Bita said she had and explained that she had received the invitation through him as a friend of Miss Knibbling. Mrs. Craig told her that she had sent him away. Bita said nothing.

Mrs. Craig spoke after a silence: "Bitah, I think I told you long ago that that man Delgado was a notorious character and that it was better for you to avoid his company. It reflects not only upon you but upon me and Mr. Craig —the mission and our work."

"I have not found Mr. Delgado in any way objectionable. He has always been very decent to me."

"But he is a man of bad reputation, Bitah. Won't you understand?"

"People may say so; but I have found nothing bad about him."

"But you're spoiling your chances and ruining yourself

with him. Have you forgotten *why* your father sent you here to be trained? And all that I have done to make a lady of you?"

"No, but I always thought you were too much of a lady to mention it. Especially as I was too young to make any choice one way or the other."

Mrs. Craig bit her lip and reddened all over down to the nape of her neck, conscious that in her anger she had erred and for the first time compromised her prestige before Bita. But she did not apologize.

"Well, you're a young woman now," said Mrs. Craig, "and capable of thinking for yourself. And since you're obstinate about being friendly to this man, what do you intend to do? Would you marry him?"

"If Mr. Delgado asked me to marry him I would," replied Bita.

"You WOULD!" exclaimed Mrs. Craig.

"Yes, I like him, and I want to get married, anyway."

"But do you *love* him?"

"I could love him."

"How could you love such a type of person?"

The last phrase returned to Bita like a boomerang, reminding her that she had used exactly the same words to Yoni, and bringing to her face a faint ironical smile.

"A low peacock," said Mrs. Craig, "who murders his h's and altogether speaks in such a vile manner—and you an educated girl—highly educated."

"My parents also speak broken English," said Bita.

Anger again swept Mrs. Craig and a sharp rebuke came to her lips, but it was checked when her eyes noted Bita toying enigmatically and ostentatiously with Herald Newton's engagement ring on her finger.

That symbol was embarrassing to Mrs. Craig and made her feel confused and even a little ashamed.

In a low voice she said: "I thought you had thrown *that* thing away," for the first time referring indirectly to Herald Newton since Bita's return from Banana Bottom.

"I thought I'd wait until I heard from him—he may write," said Bita, "or until I am engaged to some one else."

"He will *never* write," said Mrs. Craig. "How *could* he?" And divining that Bita was inclined to discuss the prohibited subject she finished the conversation saying: "If I were you I would throw it away." And she went to her room to pray.

Bita was certain now that the time had arrived for her to face the fact of leaving Jubilee. It would be impossible for her to stay when she felt not only resentment, but a natural opposition against Mrs. Craig. A latent hostility would make her always want to do anything of which Mrs. Craig disapproved. Bita could not quite explain this strong feeling to herself. It was just there, going much deeper than the Hopping Dick affair. Maybe it was an old unconscious thing now manifesting itself, because it was to Mrs. Craig, a woman whose attitude of life was alien to hers, and not to her parents, she owed the entire shaping of her career. And retracing the memorable stages in her growth it came clear to Bita now that although Mrs. Craig had never referred directly to it before that unhappy day there had always been some thing about the woman proclaiming: You are my pet experiment! . . . But perhaps there was no means of the truth about herself being revealed to such an engrained self-confident person as Priscilla Craig.

Bita knew that she was going to go. She could not truthfully say that she was interested in the work of the mission. The profession of religion left her indifferent. She was sceptical about it—this religion that had been imposed upon and planted in her young mind.

She became contemptuous of everything—the plan of her education and the way of existence at the mission, and her eye wandering to the photograph of her English college over her bed, she suddenly took and ripped it from its frame, tore the thing up and trampled the pieces under her feet. . . .

23

HOPPING DICK DID NOT GO TO CHURCH THE FOLLOWING Sunday. But Bita saw him during the week when she went marketing, and apologized for Mrs. Craig's behaviour. She begged Hopping Dick not to mind and assured him that she had no intention of ending their friendship because of Mrs. Craig. But she was determined to be open about it, and although he could not visit her at the mission-house, they could certainly see each other as heretofore. So eloquent was Bita in her desire to go against the will of Mrs. Craig, her ardour so convincing, that Hopping Dick was certain she was in love with him and felt that the real affection had been sprung the night of the house party.

Thereafter Bita seemed determined to demonstrate to Mrs. Craig that she was of age to choose the friend she wanted. She was with Hopping Dick after church service. He met her at the choir practice, at the market and always accompanied her openly to the mission gate.

Mrs. Craig curbed her vexation as a heron folds her wings, and although Bita as usual went through the routine of the mission life—prayers, choir practice, marketing, the family meal, and the common civilities were kept up— there was a sharp undercurrent of tenseness between them.

Hoping perhaps to wean Bita from her infatuation to something finer and nobler, Mrs. Craig took her to tea one afternoon to the home of a native gentleman. This man held a handsome post in one of the Civil Service departments. He was a shade darker than Bita, his wife some shades lighter, a pretty honey-coloured woman. And he had a young brother who had just graduated from a local college and who also expected to enter the Civil Service.

This man owned one of the best houses in Jubilee and possessed a fine library where he always entertained his friends. Beautifully bound Collected Works of Great British Authors. Novelists, Essayists, Poets in fine glass cases ranged round the walls. Always attracted by books, Bita went to examine the cases.

Remarked Mrs. Craig to the host: "You have a splendid collection of English authors. Which is your favourite?"

"Oh, they are all the same to me. I admire them all."

"Really! I have very strong preferences. For instance, I consider Wordsworth our most perfect mind in poetry. So austere and dignified. Sublime. Such a salutary love of nature. Of course you know about his 'Excursion.'"

"No. When did he make it?"

While Mrs. Craig explained the "Excursion," Bita attracted to the fiction drew out *Gulliver's Travels* and found the pages uncut. That did not make her think that her host never looked into his books in spite of his "they are all the same to me." A good book may be put away for a considerable time before the owner gets to reading it. And he may even never read it. She had had that experience. But turning to the imposing set of Walter Scott she pulled out one volume after the other and all were uncut. She tried the Dickens and the result was the same.

"My wife and I don't read much besides the newspapers,"

their host was saying to Mrs. Craig. "But it's nice to furnish a room like this with fine books and bookcases. It is the fashion and gives distinction."

"I think reading good books should be a *moral* necessity to every literate person," Mrs. Craig said coldly.

The Jubilee market was both the beginning and ending of the friendship between Bita and Hopping Dick. One day she dallied with him for such a long time that Rosyanna became impatient.

"Miss Bita, you know well dat a hab fer get back an' get lunch ready."

"You don't need to wait," Bita said sharply. "I have done all the marketing necessary for today."

Rosyanna sulked off. It was the first time since she had been going to the market with Bita that they had not returned to the mission together.

Rosyanna went home and prepared and was ready to serve the lunch and yet there was no sign of Bita. Mrs. Craig, going into the kitchen enquired for Bita. And Rosyanna replied that she had left her at the market with Hopping Dick.

Mr. and Mrs. Craig lunched without Bita, Priscilla commenting upon her absence and informing her husband of the cause of it. They agreed that it would be necessary to have a serious talk with her. And after the lunch was finished, Mrs. Craig told Rosyanna that she need not keep anything waiting for Bita but that she should clear the table and go on with her work. . . .

Meanwhile Bita had left the market with Hopping Dick to go strolling through the town, lingering along the main street and looking into the windows of the few interesting shops. Mischievous persons who saw them said that they were looking over the wedding trousseau.

After this window-shopping together Hopping Dick accompanied Bita to the gate of the mission, and there she lingered with him for another spell, quite aware that Mrs. Craig was looking at them from the veranda. Surely, thought Priscilla, the girl is doing everything to irritate and offend me. I have brought up a bird to pick out my eye.

She withdrew from the veranda as Bita approached. Bita was hungry and went directly to the dining-room as she entered the house, and finding no food there she repaired to the kitchen. The kitchen, according to the almost universal Jamaica custom, was a separate building from the house. Rosyanna was cleaning up and Bita asked her why she had not left her lunch in the dining-room.

"De missis har tell me fer clear off de table," said Rosyanna.

Bita's face changed; "Well, I am hungry and have to eat all the same. Give me some food."

"Me no hab nuttin' at all. Ah sarve lunch one time a day an' eberbody done hab them lunch at de right time."

"I don't care a fig about that," said Bita. "I want to eat." And she went to the range and began opening the pots.

"Deah's nuttin' in mi pots them," cried Rosyanna. "Ef you be'n want fer eat, a wha' mek you no did come home wid me from de market? What's it you fin' in dat Johnny Delgado to be talkin' widim?"

"That's none of your business, you old clucking hen!" said Bita.

"An' you'll be a cluckin' pullet yet by de time dat Jubilee cock done finish wid you," replied Rosyanna.

Bita turned and gave Rosyanna a sharp slap in the face, crying: "That will teach you to hold your dirty tongue."

Rosyanna began to howl and Bita was as quickly ashamed of having struck her as she had done it. Right then she felt she would like to sacrifice a thousand Hopping Dicks to undo it.

"I am sorry, Rosyanna. I beg your pardon," she said.

But Rosyanna blubbered: "Me no want no pardon from you."

The uproar brought Mrs. Craig out of the house into the kitchen. Her blue eyes turned to a cold glint as they took in the situation and in a hard voice she told Bita to go into the house.

This time Mrs. Craig brought her husband into conference to try to bring Bita to reason. But however contrite Bita might have felt about striking Rosyanna, Mrs. Craig's attitude hardened her and she was sullen and intractable. It was unaccountably strange that towards this woman who had extended to her the facilities for developing those remarkable traits of sometimes unfeeling haughtiness that often distinguish the highly cultivated, Bita should have always a lurking hostility.

"All these disgraceful happenings are the result of your infatuation for that worthless young man," said Mrs. Craig. "I don't think it is necessary for me to repeat all that I have already said to you about him, Bita. You are no longer a little girl but a grown young woman. You must choose between this man and your future welfare. You will have to decide *now*."

"I am sorry for the trouble," said Bita. "But I must

blame myself and not Mr. Delgado. He is not the cause of it."

"But he is," said Mrs. Craig. "And if you had listened to me and had nothing more to do with him, this would not have happened."

Bita remained silent but in an unyielding attitude.

Mrs. Craig continued: "If you will no longer listen to me, if you think I am not capable of giving you motherly advice, then I ask you to think for your own self. Think of what people are saying about you."

"They can say nothing except that I am friendly with Mr. Delgado."

"And that is enough for a man of his reputation and a girl in your position. You are not like Belle Black. She can be friendly with such a man. But you are like my own daughter. Could you imagine a girl like Miss Alder acting as you? And you are much more cultivated in every way."

Miss Alder was a year out of a young ladies' high school. She was the only daughter of a quadroon widow, a large landowner and perhaps the only one of her class who was a member of a nonconformist church in Jubilee. Periodically mother and daughter came to the mission for tea and periodically also Mrs. Craig drove out to the estate on a return visit, sometimes taking Bita.

"I do not ask you to consider me at all. But the work of the mission and your connection with it. The duty we have to perform before God."

Mrs. Craig lifted her eyes to the ceiling, then dropped them upon Mr. Craig like a signal for him to speak. Gravely Mr. Craig supported her, urging Bita for her own good and the peace and happiness of the mission household to have no further relations with Hopping Dick.

At that moment one of the dance tunes from the night of the party came singing in Bita's head:

"Just going to do the thing I want,
No matter who don't like it."

"If you are loath to tell this man that you don't want to associate with him any more," said Mrs. Craig, "I'll ask Mr. Craig to do it. To tell him that his persistent attentions are disgusting and harmful to you."

"But I don't want to say that," said Bita. "I like Mr. Delgado. Like him much more than I ever did Herald Day. After all he is a biped and not a quadruped," she blurted out.

The direct reference to the affair of Herald Newton Day brought Mrs. Craig to her feet. "You shall not speak to me in such a manner. I will not permit it," she said and marched from the room.

That day she telegraphed Jordan Plant:

"Bita ruining her reputation with worthless man. Please come at once."

In sending the telegram Mrs. Craig felt convinced that it was impossible now for Bita to continue living at the mission, whether she stopped her nonsense with Hopping Dick or not. The differences between them and the encounters had been so sharp that the even rhythm of the mission-house had become broken and upset. Bita could never again take the place in that life that Mrs. Craig had made and reserved for her. Mrs. Craig could never now accept her as her own daughter in Christ. She realized that her experiment had failed. And so her telegram was really a command to Jordan to come and take his child.

24

JORDAN PLANT READ THE TELEGRAM TO ANTY NOMMY and decided that it was better for her to represent him at Jubilee. She was more than mother to Bita, and Jordan thought that in such a situation she might be more diplomatic, understanding and acting better than he. He felt helpless.

The telegram arrived on Friday and, there being no school on Saturday, Teacher Fearon offered to drive Anty Nommy to Jubilee in his gig.

Bita had kept to her room for two days suffering from heartache and headache. That evening when Anty Nommy entered her room she broke down sobbing uncontrolledly saying that she and Hopping Dick were being persecuted because they loved each other. Anty Nommy assured Bita that she was not going to join in the persecution, but as her aunt and mother she had come to Jubilee to help her and find a way out of the impasse.

Bita threw herself face down on the bed and cried: "I love him! I love him! And I won't let you all separate us."

Anty Nommy declared that she would be the last person in the world to come between two people who were in love, for love was too precious a thing to fool with. She only wanted Bita to be reasonable and let her try and straighten things out without compromising the Craigs and bringing any scandal (of which they were so afraid) upon the mission.

"I don't care about the old mission anyway," said Bita. "I don't want to stay here any longer. I want to go home."

"Awright, darlin'," said Anty Nommy. "Doan' be ober-rash an' I wi' try an' mek everything awright."

She begged Bita to think kindlier of Priscilla and tried to show her that however stern she may be, the woman who had taken her as a girl and supported and educated her until she was a fine young lady must be, after all, her best friend. Perhaps she was right about Hopping Dick and that he was not the right type for her. But Bita replied that Hopping Dick was much righter to her than Herald Newton Day who had been Mrs. Craig's first choice.

Next Anty Nommy went to talk to Mrs. Craig, listening patiently to all she had to say. For Mrs. Craig Bita's infatuation for Hopping Dick was bad enough but what was infinitely worse was her behaviour to her. She told Anty Nommy that never in all her life had she been taunted and spoken to the way Bita had done. She could never understand a girl like Bita really falling in love with a man like Hopping Dick and to account for it she had come to the conclusion that Bita at bottom was a nymphomaniac.

The sounding and pronunciation of that word was stupendous to Anty Nommy and in spite of the sad occasion she was pleased to think that it meant that Bita was a wonderful person. So after relating the conversation to Bita and trying to get her to see the matter from Mrs. Craig's angle she ended by saying: "And she said dat she be'n t'inking dat youse a 'nymph fer manaxe.'" And Anty

Nommy was at a loss to understand why the phrase should have sent Bita into such a fury.

Anty Nommy came to the decision that she would have to see Hopping Dick herself. So she went with the coachman, Jerry Muggling, in search of him. During the time of her convalescence when Hopping Dick was at Banana Bottom with Belle Black, Anty Nommy had been introduced without remarking him much and had never dreamed that Bita could have gotten entangled with him. She felt that Bita should look higher, not from Mrs. Craig's pious point of view, but from a worldly one, just as her son Bab was aiming higher in preparing for the Civil Service.

Anty Nommy found Hopping Dick in his yard looking over a flighty colt that his father had brought home from the Bay Ridge horse-market. She told him straightly what had brought her to Jubilee and had a brief but probing talk, looking him over (mentally) and comparing his high and low points just as he had the beast's. Then she invited him to come to the mission-house in the afternoon.

At first Mrs. Craig protested against Hopping Dick's coming to the mission-house, but Anty Nommy persuaded her that it would be best to bring him into conference with Bita and make them face realities. So Hopping Dick came, Anty Nommy convening Bita, Priscilla and Malcolm and she acting as pretor.

Anty Nommy presented a résumé of the trouble, setting forth the friendship between Bita and Hopping Dick, Bita's present feelings and Mrs. Craig's opposition. She asked Mrs. Craig if her summary was correct, and Mrs. Craig approved it. So did Bita, who, now as bold as a lioness, seized the moment to declare to all there concerned that she was still very much in love and determined to have Hopping Dick.

Thereupon Anty Nommy demanded of Hopping Dick if he was also in love with Bita and he admitted that he was. Anty Nommy said that she was acting with the full consent of Jordan Plant and that they were not opposed to Bita and Hopping Dick loving each other, only they proposed that to put an end to an unpleasant situation Bita and Hopping Dick should get married at once.

Mrs. Craig's face turned frigid. How could Anty Nommy propose such a plan! Ruin the girl completely! Was Anty Nommy too ignorant to realize that Bita's high training had removed her life far from her peasant way of thinking and that it was not a thing to dispose of lightly like that of any ordinary Negro girl?

Bita, although taken entirely unawares by the promptness of Anty Nommy's decision and was confused, said that she was ready to be married immediately. But Hopping Dick was trapped and squirming in his place.

"I can't get married now," he said. "I don't hab no house."

"Then when can you?" demanded Anty Nommy. "Bita har spile harse'f. Becausen a disayah trouble she cyant stay yah any longer. She hab to liebe yah. Will you promise fer marry har in 'bouten a month?"

Hopping Dick had never thought that his little philandering would have carried to such a crisis. He had been prancing proud of the opportunity of going about in the company of the most cultivated Negro girl in Jubilee. How it had enhanced his prestige among his associates of the Saturday-night dances and card parties and in the grog shops!

But for all his vanity he had never entertained the slightest possibility of Bita becoming his wife. Bita was piquant to him as the young lady of the Jubilee mission. He had never thought of her out of that setting, much less that he would be called upon to remove her thence—to what other? Yet there he was faced with the necessity of that.

How could one in his station dream of marrying a girl like Bita who had been brought up to refinement and accustomed to large comforts and nice things. He couldn't take her to live with his mother in their little two-roomed house. And how would he provide for her? He who was still indirectly supported by his father.

He thought of the formidable cost of a marriage and a wedding feast. In a Negro village a good wedding feast meant a treat for almost the whole village. There would have to be fine and costly pinnacling cakes, roasting pigs, fowls, rum, wine. And all the necessary clothes!

No! He wouldn't attempt to spoil Bita's life at the mission for anything in the world. Even if he should be deprived of associating with her he preferred to visualize her as the fine lady of the mission rather than as the wife of Hopping Dick. In fact it was impossible for him to visualize a Mrs. Hopping Dick just then even if his imagination were raised to the ninth degree.

"Well, ah waiting on you to declare you'se'f," said Anty Nommy.

"Me!" replied Hopping Dick. "Ah couldn't think 'bouten marrying anybody when ah doan' have nuttin'."

A glint of a smile warmed Malcolm Craig's grave face and Priscilla's relaxed its rigidity as she thought that Anty Nommy was shrewder, after all, than she had guessed.

They were a little baffling, those dark folk. As a whole they seemed so insouciantly ignorant and unaware, yet as individuals they were sometimes capable of devilish ingenuity.

Crestfallen and ashamed, Hopping Dick withdrew out of Bita's way for ever. But there was no alternative for Bita now but to leave the mission. That was as inevitable to her as to Mrs. Craig. The breach between them had widened beyond closing and it was impossible for either of them to get back over it to resume the old nice and formal way getting along together. Bita's only regret was that, now that the final break had come, Hopping Dick should have been the cause of it and that people should link the departure that she had long ago contemplated with equanimity with a person she had been badly mistaken about and for whom that warm desire that had gripped her was already a thing to smile faintly about.

The next day the Craig carriage was gotten ready to convey Bita and Anty Nommy to Banana Bottom. The trunks would follow by dray. Jerry Muggling brought the buggy from the stable round to the veranda and Priscilla and Malcolm with dampened spirits went through the formality of seeing Bita and Anty Nommy settle into their places and bidding them good-bye.

There was a great lump in Priscilla's throat and a feeling of deadness in her precise spirit as Bita drove away, leaving a sensation as if the wheels had rolled over her paralyzed body and as if she were crushed into a little nothingness in an eternity of futility.

She had no heart left for that civilizing work. She was strangely a stranger in that tropical strange land, remote even from Malcolm Craig who was born there and had accepted it naturally as his own. But she had never been acclimatized, never really understood the people. She was weary and disheartened and communicated her feelings to her husband.

But Malcolm Craig did not share his wife's attitude, even though his work had suffered from disappointments and failures. He was nearer to an understanding of the people and saw them not merely by the dim candle of the church but in the whole light of humanity. He too had sometimes experienced a wave of futility, but never so overwhelming as was Priscilla's now. He had never been like her so absolute about God's will and man's destiny.

He had often had his doubts about his work. Wondered if he might not have served himself and man better if he had remained a layman. When he was a boy he had wanted to be an engineer—a builder of bridges. He had never once had a boyish dream of wanting to become a preacher of religion. But he had arrived finally at choosing that largely to please his father and to keep alive a tradition.

And now he was secretly wondering if it were not better for Bita to break away then. Perhaps she would realize a completer life in a different sphere. Who knows but that many of those natives whom they were seeking to advise as mentors and ministers might prefer their own particular patterns of life and living and do better in their simple way perhaps than many of their guardians and teachers?

Thus thinking, he tried to console Priscilla. But she was also thinking of the natives living their own life in another train—more as godless and immoral creatures who accepted Christian salvation without understanding or change of heart or habit.

She recalled the experience of the Church Sisters' Sewing

Circle which she had organized. And how one day she became aware that spools of thread and balls of wool and cases of needles were disappearing from the mission work-basket. And although she often observed quietly, she never could detect how. Once a gift of a fine box of knitting-needles was sent to her by a friend of missions in England. She placed it in the work-tray upon the large sewing-circle table. And soon she noticed that the knitting-needles were disappearing pair by pair. She never used a one herself. But fascinated by the manner of their disappearance, she always opened the box after each meeting of the sewing sisters only to find that another pair had mysteriously gone. And that was kept up until only the box was left.

As she thought of that box of knitting-needles and the other articles that the sewing sisters had spirited away, the cells of Priscilla's being began filling with bitterness. Since she had never detected the light-fingered ones at work, she was never sure if it were one or all of her black sisters who were so dexterously playing that game of souvenir-snatching and she had developed a kind of loathing for the whole coloured circle, feeling that in spite of their lip service to Christian principles, they were a different people—they could never be to her like her own—not even to think of that exclusive group to which she belonged.

And cruelly the conviction forced itself upon her that she had spent a lifetime working without faith. She had married and entered into that work in obedience to the spirit of tradition, for her family was an historical one, proud, famous, honoured, some even ennobled emanci-pators. And she had carried out her part of the tradition, but without faith, much less love, for the work and the people. And all that she had undertaken individually for

Bita and Herald Newton and generally for the people was lacking in the pure wine of faith and the saving principle of grace.

And so when Malcolm spoke consolingly, Priscilla did not conceal what she was thinking but freely exposed her thoughts and stated the affair of the Sewing Circle.

"But perhaps it might have been only one person responsible," said Mr. Craig. "A case of kleptomania."

Mrs. Craig was amazed at her husband: "Kleptomania, Mr. Craig! How could such a crime of high society exist among such backward people? It was just plain downright stealing."

25

THE DROUGHT WAS IN ITS THIRD YEAR BEFORE THE PEOPLE
actually realized that it was one of the most catastrophic
in the annals of the island. The well-watered and fertile
mountain valley of Banana Bottom was one of the last
regions to be affected by its blight. When the Banana Bottom peasants were still having a fat enough time, thirsty
and underfed people came in droves from the dry and stony
districts, bringing mules and donkeys to carry water and
loads of juicy mangoes, succulent velvety star-apples and
massive sweet-smelling soursops.

But now with the drought unabating the fattest districts were drying up. In Banana Bottom, noted for its
nigger yams as well as its bananas, the thick and heavy
vines of the yams were wilting in the sun, the long green
banana fronds were turning yellow and shrivelling up,
young coffee leaves folded up as if they were singed by a
bush fire, the long stalk leaves of cocoes and tanias, always
lush, were empty of juice, the fox tails turned from silver
grey to dry brown, the trailing ferns lost their furry quality, little springs gave up the last water to the sun, expos-
ing their clay-baked bellies, rivers sank beneath their
pebbly beds.

The giant bamboos seemed begging for rain with their
crests bowed against the floor of the firmament. The green
paled from the fronds of the tree fern. In the killing hot

air the flowers of the hibiscus were like bloodstains in the sun. In the scanty seed trees the blue quits and swees had lost their delight in chirping and preening and the lovely tails of the humming-birds, long and beautifully curved like blades of guinea grass, drooped sadly down from the leathery purple sheathes of the banana blossoms.

The people prayed for rain. From all over the island earnest prayers were directed to heaven. In all forms. The parsons summoned the people to prayer. The churches were filled with praying people. And outside the churches certain natives prayed in their own way, with the Obeah priests working their incantations. But no rain fell.

People sickened from drinking bad water and eating poor food and among the children there were outbreaks of rickets and yaws. When the crops failed each family of the better-off peasants had bought a barrel of wheat flour and a sack of cornmeal, which the housewives turned into all kinds of food: dumplings, johnnycake, corn pone, corn cake, puddings, porridges. But hardly into the common baked bread. The peasants were not used to that. Their bread was the vegetable roots and fruits of the field: yams, yampies, sweet cassava, cocoes, breadfruit, vegetable pears. Loaf bread for them was a delicacy as cake is to wheat-bread peoples and specially reserved for Sundays, wedding feasts and other special occasions. As a change from the native foods rice was favoured instead of wheat, the natives having learned the use of it from the Indian coolies. For those peasants who were too poor to buy individually many of the churches purchased, out of a general members' contribution, a few barrels of meal and flour which were doled out in portions to them.

Among the masses the tribulation was accepted as a

visitation from God and because of their sins. Native prophets sprang up everywhere predicting worse times. The religious feeling attained its zenith and it was taken at its tide by a saver of souls, a Briton named Evan Vaughan, and turned into a mighty movement.

The revival of Evan Vaughan dwarfed all the little native outbreaks. He had come to the colony as a young officer of the Salvation Army. But after a few years' service he had left it and attempted to establish himself in secular enterprises.

As the island was wholly agricultural it readily offered ideas for industrial developments that were not so easy to put into practice. And so, many attempts at building factories had petered out to nothing. Evan Vaughan's first attempt at business was the setting up of bread-making machinery on a large scale in a populous inland centre. But that kind of affair which did well in the city with its European colony and cosmopolitan life had no kind of a chance in the country. And the country people eating baked white bread preferred the well-kneaded compact loaf, like Spanish bread, to the light and loose steam bread. Thus Evan Vaughan failed in his attempt to turn the people from the cheap and wholesome tropical breadkind to a general consumption of cheap white bread.

His other attempt was a factory for making jams and jellies from native fruits. The natives themselves made delicious stuff out of guavas and naseberries, tamarinds, cashews and mangoes, besides the rich fat from the oil palm and the custard from the cocoanut palm. But the factory was not a success because the class of people who bought conserves preferred the imported and more refined brands with which they were familiar.

And so Evan Vaughan's little factory-making went the way of many other essays to develop a native industry in that warm agricultural land. Optimistic persons had sponsored various enterprises such as large-scale manufacture of furniture from the fine native woods, and cigarettes from the excellent native tobacco, but all such things could be imported cheaper than they could be made. American pine easily undersold the native hardwood, and English cigarettes the local article. And such was the power of mass production and tariff prices that American tinned milk and wheat flour, to name but two things, sold cheaper in the colony than they did in the United States.

Evan Vaughan having failed in his plans to minister to the material needs of the people, the thought of his first love, in that time of desolation and distress, must have decided him to return to the spiritual. He started his Big Revival at one coastal end of the island and carried it triumphantly across the plains and mountains to the other. The majority of the nonconformist preachers competed with one another to invite and surrender their churches to him. The colourful soothsayers and magicians were scattered in confusion before the power of the white prophet of God.

Yet the secret of his power was not easily discernible. He was a very small man, almost dwarflike, meagre, with the face of a cat or an old doll, not lighted by any kind of colour. His ordinary voice remained always on the same dead monotonous level, never mounting or falling with emotion, not even when he was making his greatest soul-assaults. Yet that voice was able to shake hundreds of hefty peasant men and women and bring them trembling and weeping to confess their sins at the Penitents' Form.

The Church of England clergy notably had held out against the Revival, warning their parishioners against it. Also a number of the non-conformist preachers, mainly those who were the proud descendants of the pioneers of Emancipation.

Among them was Malcolm Craig, who refused Evan Vaughan the coveted tribune of the Jubilee Free Church. But he was welcomed at the Ark. And many of the Free Church folk flocked to the Ark to stamp and shake and shout salvation. But none of them really deserted the Free Church this time. They remained faithful members although at night they delighted in going to the Ark where they could blow off their emotion whooping and wailing.

From Jubilee the Revival came over the mountains to Banana Bottom. Eagerly the Reverend Lambert put his church at the disposal of Evan Vaughan. And he was the first with his family to go down to the Penitents' Form. As an example and for sanctification he declared. His example was followed. The Reverend Lambert had the satisfaction of seeing men and women who had lived without the form of religion for years humble themselves at the Penitents' Form—couples who had been happy living without wedlock, harmless old rummies, members of the Saturday-night dancing set.

The young village abandoned its tea-meetings, dances and picnics for the salvation meetings. Couples who had been living in concubinage for years, some having even grandchildren of the free union, now became ashamed and miserable sinners and voluntarily separated until they should be married. So numerous were the "Revival" marriages that the church kept a stock of dollar rings on hand for them.

Yoni came out of her retirement to participate and play a leading rôle in the Revival. Bita was one of the few who held out against the gospellers despite the special pleading of Evan Vaughan, the Reverend Lambert and Yoni. The Reverend Lambert carried on about Bita as if her individual soul was worth more than that of all the young village together.

Bita's return to Banana Bottom had started many rumours, of which the commonest was that she was pregnant and because of that had been sent away from the mission. But as the weeks went by without her showing the signs of pregnancy her return home was attributed to something else.

Jordan Plant had accepted Bita's coming home with sympathy. Whatever regret he felt was from practical reasons. For Mrs. Craig had a fortune of her own and he thought that if Bita had remained under her tutelage and married from the mission to somebody whom the Craigs approved she would have been provided with a dowry.

But the presence of his only child, now a cultivated young woman, in his own home made him happy. She had grown out of that soil, his own soil, and had gone abroad only for polishing. Her choosing of her own will to return there filled him with pride; so strong was his affection for the land. His secret hope was that Bita and Bab might have developed an affection for each other and decided to settle down together upon his place.

But Bab had emigrated to the United States a short time after Herald Newton Day's departure for Panama. The competitive examinations for the local Civil Service upon which he had fixed his hopes had been abandoned for a system of selection. The selection was made by the special recommendation of people in respectable and responsible positions. And the result of this new order was to limit the minor Civil Service posts to the light-coloured middle classes and bar aspirants from the black peasantry.

A group of the nonconformist ministers and especially the descendants of the pioneers had registered a telling opposition to the change. But the times had changed and some of the strongest Government support had come from a group of black men, most of whom had near-white or white wives and light-coloured children.

One of these men was a member of the Legislature and a noted orator, although the thought behind the glittering display, when not empty, was always commonplace. He had been picked up straight off of a plantation by the missionaries and educated for the ministry. He had a magnetic voice and could stir audiences mightily and he had won the appellation of the silver-tongued parson. He had charge of one of the largest and best-paying churches in the colony. From that it was only a step to become a representative of the people in the island's Legislature. His wife was a lady from Great Britain who had come out to the island as an officer of the Salvation Army. And they had a large family of freckled reddish-coloured children.

This reverend black man, who represented a constituency about seven-eighths of which was black peasants, was the most eloquent advocate of the change. With his silver tongue he derided the idea that Civil Service posts should be given to peasant youths fresh from the huts, who possessed no "background" but were clever enough to pass the examinations. Civil Service candidates, he said, should come from respectable and refined homes.

The fact was that perhaps because of their lack of

refined things and sharpened by adversity, the black candidates often won the examinations way ahead of their more socially-favoured competitors. At this time it was remembered by aged white-headed blacks who knew the early origin of the honourable and reverend black legislator that he had not even had the benefit of a hut as "background" but that the missionaries had found him when the roof over his head was the trash-house of the sugarcane plantation and his bed the trash-heap.

Bita settled down quietly to the rural life of Banana Bottom, helping Anty Nommy to superintend the household, the drying of ginger, coffee and cocoa, the preparing of cassava and arrowroot starch, besides practising her music and taking long afternoon walks.

Much of her time was also spent with Squire Gensir. He always called at her house and she often went to Breakneck to play the piano. Sometimes Teacher Fearon accompanied her in the early evening after he had finished his monitor's classes and he and Bita and Squire Gensir had interesting discussions about the topics of the times.

The question of the hour then was Indian coolie and Chinese immigration. After the emancipation of the Negroes the big planters instituted a campaign to import indentured coolies and were able to convince the Government that that was necessary for them to carry on. The Negro labourers, intoxicated with their new freedom, had demanded the extravagant sum of a minimum wage of one shilling a day on the plantations. The planters raised their hands and their voices in horror. The plantations would all go to ruin if such large wages were paid. And so the coolies were substituted for Negroes. They were contracted for a period of about five years at sixpence a day and their women and children received less. It was always a debatable question whether the planters gained by the transaction for, as an agricultural laborer, a Negro was said to be able to do the work of from three to five coolies. But on the other hand the coolies, unlike the Negroes, were bound to the plantations for a number of years at a fixed price and whatever they lost in quantity the employers must have benefited by their sure, steady labour.

Anyway, the coolie contingents arrived every year and every year larger numbers of young Negroes emigrated to the Panama Canal Zone and the banana and cocoa and coffee plantations of Central America. And there was much feeling among the native workers against the coolies. And now that the island was in the grip of hard times there was a big agitation against the importation of the East Indians as well as the immigration of the Chinese.

The Chinese were in a different category. Here they were not chop suey venders nor laundrymen. They established small grocery shops all over the little towns and villages and prospered so excellently that they were able to drive large numbers of their native competitors out of business. Advocates of free trade and unhampered and unlimited immigration (as contradistinguished from subsidized importation of indentured labourers) maintained that the native shopkeepers should demonstrate their ability to do business by open competition with the Chinese.

But the small native shopkeepers argued that the Chinese were not open and fair competitors. They were strange and tricky dealers who employed petty and obscure means of trading that were foreign to the black dealer. The popular talk was that the Chinese thrived upon wholesale adulteration of common foodstuffs: butter, lard, cooking oils, flour and other daily necessities. Nevertheless the native consumers passed by their own countrymen to get the Oriental bargains.

In the city one of the biggest merchants was a Chinaman and the most popular tavern-keeper was of the same nationality. And in an island that had been from the beginning of its civilized history a cradle of experiment in unique human types the offsprings of Chinamen and Negro women were the latest and most striking contribution.

Liberal sympathy and support were not extended to Indian coolie immigration. To the descendants of the pioneer missionary families and other vigilants of human rights it was just another form of chattel slavery under cover of indenture, with the slaves strange brown men instead of black. The coolies had no choice about their toil. They were contracted in India, shipped across seas and herded off to the various estates, where barracks were provided for them. They lived very frugally, cut off from contact with native life, wore scantier clothing than the Negroes (often only the bright-red loin cloth which the natives called coolie-wrapper) and their diet consisted primarily of rice.

However, one substantial although scarcely remarked result of the imported indentured labor was the more intensive development of the hardy Negro peasantry. The Negroes in general would not work for the coolie wages. There was a steady outflow of them to the Central American jungles where their labour was indispensable to break the virgin soil for the vast banana and cocoa plantations that the Yankees were making. As workers their hides were better able to withstand the jungle fevers. And those who stayed at home worked miracles with the axe and the pick, the fork and the hoe, tilling the most difficult pieces of mountain land, bringing green growths out of stony forbidding hillside patches, eking out funds to buy the crown lands that were cut up for small proprietorship— striving and struggling against descending to the coolie level of the plantations, which to them was like a return to chattel slavery. In this they were aided by relatives, returning emigrants from Central American countries, many of whom invested their savings in small parcels of land.

However, the East Indian coolies as a people were not disliked. Their presence cast a kind of spell over the natives. Though some of them were quite black, their features (so different from the Negroid) were attractive to the Negroes and men and women possessed a neat gliding walk that was in marked contrast to the haunchy animal movement of Negroes. On notable holidays the Indians were often invited to assist at the native sports as athletes and fakirs, doing sleight-of-hand tricks, demonstrating somersaulting and Yogi exercises.

Nearly all the villages had their debating and sometimes literary societies. And the two subjects most debated then were: That a stop be put to Indian-coolie immigration and a check to Chinese immigration. The result was sometimes favourable to the Chinese, never to the Indians.

Teacher Fearon was the moving spirit of the Banana Bottom Debating Society. He, however, was more hostile to the Chinese than to the Indians. He was the product of a tiny town. His father had been a coachman to a local Government official. His elder brother, once a prosperous grocer, had gone bankrupt—ruined he lamented by Chinese competition.

The discussions between Teacher Fearon, Squire Gensir and Bita were sometimes exciting. Bita's sympathies, perhaps because she had travelled a little and gained a little practical knowledge of immigrant life, were on the side of free immigration. So were Squire Gensir's. But they were both against the method of importing coolie labour.

Perhaps Squire Gensir, because of the disparity of background, tradition, and race between him and Bita, was more susceptible than the circumstances warranted to the affinity of her mind with his, considering that she was also a member of the human family. He suspected too that he was in a measure morally responsible for her breaking away from Jubilee and that the beginning of it was the night when he encouraged her to let herself go dancing at Kojo Jeems' tea-meeting. He marvelled that Bita was devouring his profoundest books on religions and their origins and scientific treatises—the theory of the universe, the beginning of life, the history of civilizations and the physiology of man and nature, and that she did not merely parrot the ideas she picked up but interpreted them intelligently.

On her side Bita appreciated him more for his sensitive feeling and interpretation of music. Although his knowledge of the famous great composers was exhaustive and discriminating he was none the less enthusiastic about the lesser and sometimes anonymous ones. He was ever alert and quick to seize on the best, the original in popular songs, simple melodic strains and spontaneous chants, and he was the first to write down the folk songs of the peasants.

His ear was as keen as his memory was prodigious. Often he had Bita confused about the identity of composers when she mistook an obscure passage of Brahms' for Mozart, or Chopin's for Beethoven. But he assured Bita that that was a matter of extensive technical knowledge and that it did not betray a lack of true musical feeling and appreciation.

His ear was as keen as his memory was prodigious. Often he had Bita confused about the identity of composers when she mistook an obscure passage of Brahms' for Mozart or Chopin's for Beethoven. But he assured Bita that that was a matter of extensive technical knowledge and that it did not betray a lack of true musical feeling and appreciation.

26

SQUIRE GENSIR DETESTED THE SPIRIT OF THE REVIVAL but regarded it humorously as a spectacle. And one evening he proposed to Bita that they should go to the church together.

Evan Vaughan had hit upon the spectacular plan of keeping a candlewood torch burning high up on an iron pole before the church. The torch was lit upon the falling of night, when the ringing of the bell had ended, and the light could be seen from the villages for miles around shining over the high banana trees, the sentinel-like tree ferns upon the hillsides and the giant bamboos in the ravines and brightening the white roads going down the valley.

Bita and the squire arrived late. Inside the building was brightly lighted by a central chandelier and lamps of glass and tin set upon brackets ranged round the walls. It was a large church with a gallery seating hundreds of people. Malcolm Craig's father had built it as a main mission to serve the entire region.

The church was packed, with the crowds overflowing into the mission yard. The two outstanding features of the gathering were the little white man perched like an idol upon the high pulpit and the responsive singing of the people below. In his unchanging monotonous voice Evan Vaughan called: Come! Come! Come! No colouring nor movement in his pale cat's face (only sometimes a few tears rolling down it), his single gesture a steady—rather stiff—outstretched hand.

Yet he compelled men and women, groaning, moaning and shouting, fighting the devil in them, down the aisle to the Penitents' Form, crying to the Lord to wash them in his blood and keep their bodies unspotted from sin.

> "Lord, wash me in thy blood again
> And make me wholly clean,
> So I may live to praise thy name,
> Unspotted from all sin."

Evan Vaughan was helped by a small company of his Sisters in Christ who had left their homes to follow him from various districts in which he had preached. To them was added now Yoni Legge of Banana Bottom. Nearly all these young women were proud to testify that they had fallen from grace, but that the Revival had redeemed, sanctified and lifted them up again. They were quite intelligent and had been outstanding types in their respective villages as assistant school-teachers, choir-singers and seamstresses. And generally the chief sin that had overcome them was their becoming *enceinte* without marriage rites.

That had diminished in some degree their privileged positions in the village, especially when in most cases the trouble entailed the loss of their jobs. And if they were noisily eloquent in renouncing all worldly things now it may have been because they were aware that however much they were redeemed and saved spiritually they would never again recover their little material places lost. And so now they went with Evan Vaughan from district to district proclaiming the power of spiritual things over all.

At a signal from Evan Vaughan in the pulpit, his Sisters

in Christ would scatter among the congregation, each pleading with an individual to persuade him to go to the Penitents' Form. Sometimes many of them would bear down and concentrate upon a difficult individual moaning and groaning, clapping and chanting:

"This message is for you.
Bow down to Jesus, bow.
His love is great and true,
He calls and wants you now."

The eldest Miss Lambert was on her way from the parsonage to the church when she spied Bita and Squire Gensir in the crowd and took them through the jam to a seat beside Teacher Fearon. At that moment there were three of the Sisters in Christ working upon a famous rum-fighter named Delminto who came from the near-by village of Bull's Hoof. The man was resisting with strained face and muscles taut. But at last he threw up his hands and cried: "Oh, Lawd, h'ep a poah sinner!" And shouting and swaying he went as if he were struggling against ten men down the aisle to the Penitents' Form.

Looking down over his great excited flock Evan Vaughan's eyes came to rest upon Bita and Squire Gensir. He had heard about the atheist of Breakneck and had never dreamed that such a man would attend one of his meetings. He had also heard that he was held in the highest esteem by the peasants. And he thought it was a God-sent chance to undermine his reputation by a public exhibition of him.

In the lull that followed the confession of the rum-fighter at the Penitents' Form Evan Vaughan pointed his little hand in the direction of Squire Gensir and cried in his dry voice: "The fool hath said in his heart there is no God." And he ranted away on that.

"God is a spirit and learned books and high birth do not make it easy to find the narrow way to him. Indeed they make it harder. Did not our Master say to Nicodemus, the learned man: 'You must be born again to enter the Kingdom of God,' and to the rich and high man: 'It is easier for a camel to pass through a needle's eye than for a rich man to enter into the Kingdom of God'? It is better to be humble and ignorant and believe in God by the grace of Jesus Christ than to be high born and educated and living without salvation. For the life of the unbeliever is empty and barren. He may appear a fine man in people's eyes but he is like a beautiful allspice tree that never bears seed because God has cursed it."

Evan Vaughan paused and a mighty AMEN was echoed by the multitude.

"Let the bold and brazen man deny God. We who love and believe in Him will remain humble and ignorant as little children. Our Master said that of such was the Kingdom of Heaven. 'A little child shall lead them.' Then let us not be timid and afraid before high education and aristocratic birth. Let us proclaim the simple truth of salvation even to the most learned scholars. Those to whom God has given the gift of brains. Who have misused that gift in trying to penetrate the secrets of God. And when they are baffled they say in their stubbornness of heart: There is no God.

"St. Paul was one of the wisest men that ever lived. And our Master humbled him and told him that he could not kick against the pricks."

Stretching out both hands to Squire Gensir, Evan Vaughan cried: "I appeal to you, sir, before this humble congregation: In the name of Jesus, acknowledge God and be saved."

And in a twinkling six excited Sisters in Christ bore down upon Squire Gensir, exhorting, shouting and singing:

"Lord, save this white man,
Lord, save this white man
From serving the devil and drifting to hell;
Lord, save this white man."

That was the *pièce de résistance* used upon the sinners and always changed a little to suit the person concerned. If it were a girl: Lord save this poor girl. Or a youth: Lord save this young man.

The entire congregation turned towards Squire Gensir, wailing and shouting: "Lord save this white man." Bita and Teacher Fearon were ashamed and the squire was very annoyed, although he maintained an air of indifference—a kind of Chesterfieldean demeanour—with a faint trace of a smile.

For years he had lived among these simple Christianized Negroes who had tolerated his non-belief without understanding it as much as he had their belief in Obeah. And as they had been reticent and unaggressive about their fetish practices, so had he been about his ideas. The hill folk respected his learning and refined bearing and a mutual admiration and liking had sprung up between them. And now this little revivalist was endeavouring to spoil that relationship by making him out a common blasphemer. For the ordinary peasant's practical conception of a sceptic or an atheist did not extend beyond blasphemer.

Conspicuous among the Sisters in Christ, Yoni Legge turned her attention to Bita. "Do, Bita dear. Come to Jesus. Come right now. He will do for you what he did for me if you only take him now. You know I was wayward, abandoned and lost in sin. But the Lord has saved and washed me in his blood. Come, Bita, come."

Yoni broke down and wept profusely. She was reinforced by others of the Sisters in Christ. But Bita would not be persuaded.

From down in front of the platform, where most of the church officers were officiously gathered, Jordan Plant kept his eye upon his daughter. He himself had held out against the Penitents' Form, insisting that he had grown up and been baptized in the church, always a Christian, and could see no reason why he should go to a Penitents' Form when he had never been a backslider.

But the Reverend Lambert overrode all objection, setting an example by kneeling down first at the Penitents' Form and inviting all the officers of the church to follow him in the name of the Lord. Jordan Plant did as the rest but without conviction and not confessing anything. He was closer in spirit to his friend Malcolm Craig's ideal of Christianity than to Evan Vaughan's. And his pride was kindled to see his daughter holding out against the Revival spirit.

Standing close to the Reverend Lambert when the Sisters in Christ began their crusade against Squire Gensir, Jordan Plant had reacted against the exhibition and remarked to his minister that he did not think it was the right thing to do. Squire Gensir there in the church appeared to Jordan Plant like a guest just as when he came to his house and conversed with him and his daughter.

But the Reverend Lambert thought otherwise. He had always felt a little coldness in Squire Gensir towards him and had a suspicion that Squire Gensir did not appreciate him enough as an educated man, a man of God, and the spiritual head of Banana Bottom. So he said: "Why not? Mr. Vaughan is right. That man needs to be saved like any other sinner. God is no respecter of persons."

Wildly the congregation wailed: "Lord save this white man!" Squire Gensir became the central figure in the building. All faces were turned his way and the tendency of the excited singing and swaying crowd was to converge upon him. And at one time there was a something in the air as if that entire dark congregation was motivated to lay hands upon him and make him one of them.

But at that moment there was a commotion at the lower end of the church and a thin little black women with bright bandanna upon her head and tied under her neck entered at the back door beating a drum and followed by other women and a few men all bearing supple-jacks and singing:

> "Rolling rolling rolling down
> Ages rolling, rolling ages
> Rolling along for a golden crown,
> Silver shoes and silken clothes
>
> "Rolling along for a golden crown
> Golden wages, see my wages,
> Angels are climbing up and down
> Heaven's ladder, shining golden
>
> "Feeding on honey and milk and wine
> Flowing flowing, rolling rolling
> Better than best and superfine
> Rolling rolling rolling along."

A space was cleared around the leading woman; who handed the drum to an assistant to beat as she crouched low and began jumping like a frog, bouncing from one point to another. Some of the older Negroes remarked that that was the real old-time revival.

As the congregation, forgetting Squire Gensir, seemed to be turning away from Evan Vaughan to this more primitive excitement, he descended from the pulpit and hurried to the scene. He detested the drum and thought it was a barbarous thing, maybe because it reminded him of something in his Salvation Army past that he would have liked to forget. So he went up to the circle and cried: "Stop that drumming and put that woman out. That is not God's spirit but the devil's."

The woman and her company were retired from the church to a spot outside where the little children used to hold ring plays, but she carried a great portion of the congregation with her. Bita had separated from Teacher Fearon and Squire Gensir and was borne along with the fervid crowd.

With the drum tom-tomming the little woman started rolling and jumping again while the people sang the Rolling Chant, her immediate followers standing around and resting their hands upon their twisted supple-jacks. Higher and higher the chorus rose, the spectators joining until it drowned the singing from the church. As the chorus swelled, the tune quickening, the woman bounced faster and faster round the circle until she seemed compressed into a milkwiss ball, and at last with a great shout she fell down like a dead person amid cries of: "The Spirit! The Spirit! The Spirit is come."

A woman of the band stepped forth with her supple-jack and began whipping the fallen leader while the singing rose upon jubilant notes and others began rolling and jumping. And when the woman moaned and murmured under the supple-jacking the people said that the sounds were the voice of the Spirit.

At last the woman rose up and started prancing and brandishing her supple-jack, shouting intelligible phrases. With an eerie shriek a little girl fell down swooning into the ring and the risen leader began supple-jacking her. A youth fell down, then another person and others until the whole band of supple-jackers were busy whipping the fallen while the singing rose to weird piercing heights and the place was transformed into a whirling fury of dancing.

In the midst of them Bita seemed to be mesmerized by the common fetish spirit. It was a stranger, stronger thing than that of the Great Revival. Those bodies poised straight in religious ecstasy and dancing vertically up and down, while others transformed themselves into curious whirling shapes, seemed filled with an ancient nearly-forgotten spirit, something ancestral recaptured in the emotional fervour, evoking in her memories of pictures of savage rites, tribal dancing with splendid swaying plumes, and the brandishing of the supple-jacks struck her symbolic of raised and clashing triumphant spears.

The scene was terrible but attracting and moving like a realistic creation of some of the most wonderful of the Annancy tales with which her father delighted and frightened her when she was a child. Magnetized by the spell of it Bita was drawn nearer and nearer into the inner circle until with a shriek she fell down. A mighty shout went up and the leading woman shot out prancing around Bita with uplifted twirling supple-jack, but a man rushed in and snatched her away before she could strike.

27

A FRIEND FROM GINGERTOWN HAD BROUGHT ANTY
Nommy a bundle of branches of a new kind of rose of
comparatively recent introduction into the island. And she
had just finished setting them in a plot of ground against
the east side of the veranda, and sitting on the veranda she
was contemplating her work, puffing at her smoke-aged
clay pipe with satisfaction, when she was struck with
delight by Jubban singing a lilting new ditty in the
paddock:

> "Work, work, with hand and haht, mi boy,
> Work, work, no mind how sick you feel,
> For time may come you can enjoy
> You' lady sweet, mi boy,
> If you only put you' shoulder to the wheel."

Jubban was grooming the mules with curry-comb and
brush vigorously and yet so lovingly that the brutes
were as gentle and docile as sheep under his hand. Not
everybody could lightly groom those animals. There was
Mayfly, the perfect shaft-mule, always dependable in
making the steepest mountain grades over the market
routes even when the side mules faltered. But only Jubban
could pick the ticks from under Mayfly's tail and groom
her there. Any other person who wanted to do that had
to rope up Mayfly's hind legs. Once Jordan Plant, thinking
that because he was Mayfly's owner he ought to be able

to handle her as much as his man, tried to rub her behind. But Mayfly kicked him so viciously in his groin that he was laid up helpless in bed for over a week.

Jubban had a way of coaxing and taming mules and horses and making them work willingly. He was frequently solicited by the peasants to break in their young colts. For a colt broken in by him would turn out a better worker than one by a person who did not possess his sense of horses. So famous had Jubban become as a good drayman and handler of mules that he had been presented with a medal by the Society for the Prevention of Cruelty to Animals.

Jubban possessed a deep, rich tuneful voice, splendid for the easy-singing native jammas and shay-shays. And he sang triumphantly as if he had faith in his singing. He was never so happy as that day on which Bita gave him a cake that she had made herself, a sign that she appreciated his having picked her up that night when she fell down in a trance at the fetish dance. Since then she had been speaking to him in a different manner from the old impersonal way, as if instead of seeing him merely as an outsider who worked for her father she had come to recognition of him as a responsible person in the family.

Jubban did not imagine that he had performed an heroic act when he snatched Bita away from under the uplifted whip. He was familiar with the doings of such fanatic circles, when young persons gripped by the religious spirit would pitch down like dead and be supple-jacked by the older initiates until they were all one united circle.

It had a mighty influence, that sing-and-drum dancing, and sometimes members of nice native families who never participated in such affairs except as spectators would lose control of themselves in the contagious clamour.

When Bita had recovered her senses under the mimosas where she had been taken, she was at a loss to explain what had happened to her. She remembered experiencing an overwhelming mesmeric feeling and a sensation of becoming a different person in a strange place and suddenly there was a lacuna and she was conscious of nothing more.

Later when she discussed the incident with Squire Gensir, who had also followed the supple-jackers and witnessed what had happened to her, she declared she was ashamed. But was surprised when the squire admitted that he too had registered a similar overpowering feeling. He said that the supple-jackers had more authentic power in them than a thousand Evan Vaughans and had assaulted his emotional senses like a magic tempest.

"So you weren't touched at all by Evan Vaughan?" said Bita.

"Nasty little vile-speaking ranter," said the squire. "Hypocrite and humbug."

And now that Bita was definitely settled at home, a troop of suitors found their way to Banana Bottom as fantastic as those who besought the hand of Portia.

In little Gingertown here lived a light-brown and local Government official who frightened his two spinster sisters by announcing that he intended to make Bita his wife. The two sisters began mourning for their brother and bewailing their predicament because of the disastrous possibility—a brown man marrying a black woman.

What did it matter that the sisters were ladies of slender education and no accomplishment or self-improvement?

Their complexion was the colour of a ripe banana peel—not a fine ripe one like those that mature and yellow upon the tree in Jamaica, but rather the kind that is harvested green three-quarters fit so it can reach the far foreign market without rotting, and therefrom becomes a little bruised and blotchy.

And Bita was black—to be precise she was the quiet restful colour of dark blooming brown. But officially and generally that was called black. And that made a great difference in Jamaica, where there had been established a tradition by which all the little white-collar jobs were considered the special plums of the light-brown natives who came like a dam between the black masses and imperial authority.

However, when the little light-brown official did (through the Reverend Lambert) get an introduction to Bita he discovered an unresponsive heart and was rejected as ineligible—to his amazement—and also his sisters' who now were eloquently wrathful that any black girl, even though she were highly educated, should refuse an offer of marriage from one of the brown plums—their perfect brother.

Following him Bita also disappointed a young dark-brown preacher from the seaport of the Jubilee region and who was recommended by the Reverend Lambert, a pharmacist from a thriving railway town, the schoolmaster of Bull's Hoof and the black overseer and lessee of the vast Cane River Estate, whose absentee owner lived in England.

Anty Nommy marvelled at the many very eligible candidates for Bita's person who found some means or reasons for visiting the Plants, and was puzzled by Bita's indifference. It was as if the Herald Newton Day and

Hopping Dick incidents had left her with a definite reaction against cocksure and glib, suave and self-righteous, little, educated persons.

The Revival had upset the common ways of life among the rural folk. Business was bad with the grog shops, the Saturday-night dances were discontinued, tea-meetings were rare. The entire region from the Ginger River Valley to the Cane River Hills stretching beyond across the Garden of Jamaica was subdued under Evan Vaughan's revival spirit. Only a few scattered intransigeants of the ungodly set carried on with the old pleasures. But it was almost as difficult to find girls for dancing as to plunge into a pool full of fish and catch them with the hand.

However, one outstanding triumph of the Revival in Banana Bottom was the salvation of Hopping Dick. Because of the severity of the drought in Jubilee, Mr. Horse-dealer Delgado had asked his Banana Bottom relatives to receive his wife and family until the coming of rain while he itinerated in the interest of his profession.

And so Hopping Dick had accompanied his mother to Banana Bottom. There he had caught the Revival fever, having succumbed to the earnest pleadings of Sister-in-Christ Yoni Legge, by whom he was tenderly led to the Penitents' Form, where he confessed to his wild and reckless living and terrible small-town sins, calling upon God for forgiveness.

Old Deacon Delgado was so touched by the conversion of his relative that he offered him a good piece of his Banana Bottom land as a hope that it would materially effect the permanent salvation of Hopping Dick if he would till and stick to it.

It was a remarkable happening for the village, the converting of the dandy Hopping Dick from town to country and God. And it began auspiciously. The great Delgado clan of cultivators started off their kinsman with gifts of yam-heads and yampies, cockstone peas and Congo peas, corn, coffee and plantain and fat banana suckers. And other enthusiastic church folk added contributions of breadkind—seeds and young plants.

So changed was Hopping Dick, that when he met Bita, although he removed his hat with the old smart gesture, it was with such a contrite bewildered expression (as of a converted soul who regretted the past and had taken vows for the future) that Bita was constrained to smile.

But the Revival had not done so well by Teacher Fearon. The choir practice, his one esthetic joy, had been quite ruined. Nearly all the members of the choir had become full of holiness and the aim of the girls now was to follow the example of Yoni and qualify as Sisters in Christ and shout salvation songs instead of learning new anthems and choruses. Besides, the schoolroom where the choir practice was held was often requisitioned for the regular chapel meetings, as the church was entirely given over to the Revival.

However, Teacher Fearon sometimes asked Bita to play when the schoolroom was free in the late afternoon. Another August would soon come round again and he hoped to give a concert for the holidays, if the Revival spirit left any enthusiasm for it.

And one evening, while they were going through a selection from Judas Maccabæus, Crazy Bow appeared in the main doorway and marched straight towards Bita. It was the first time Bita had seen him at close quarters since her return from abroad. His lean face was arresting because of the wrinkles like enormous welts swollen upon it. And his great untrimmed shag, always exposed to the sun and the rain, was fully of nappy grey. But strangest of all were his eyes. They appeared as if a glassy film had grown over them and as if they never saw or cared about anything near but were always fixed upon a far-away object. Of Bita he showed no signs of recognition, nor did he speak. But when he stretched out his hands and touched the organ, she vacated the stool and he sat down and immediately began playing.

Bita had really never felt any resentment towards him at any time, but now she was gripped by a deep sorrow that a human being, a rare artist, should be deprived of the ordinary faculties. But the thought came to her that perhaps he did not realize the lack of them and was possibly a greater performer for that.

How bewitching was his playing! No wonder he had magnetized her into that trouble of his adolescence. If only she possessed a little of the magic of his natural genius.

Crazy Bow played the entire oratorio of Judas Maccabaeus and a few folk attracted by his mighty performance came tiptoeing into the schoolroom. And the news spread about that Crazy Bow was playing and soon the schoolroom was filled with a silent attentive audience, happy that the Good Spirit had visited their great musician and brought him home to them. For they did not often have the privilege of hearing him, since he was always wandering and it was seldom now, when he came home to his native village, that he was moved to play.

From Judas Maccabæus he turned to the Spirituals: "Peter, Go Ring Them Bells," "Jordan's River," "Swing

Low, Sweet Chariot," "Go Down, Moses." And he made the people weep, recreating again the spirit of the ancient martyrdom that still haunted the crumbled stones and rusted iron of many a West Indian plantation.

But again he changed with chemical quickness and was rattling off picnic and tea-meeting tunes, jigs, mintoes, quadrilles, schottisches, so rollicking that the folk turned mercurially from tears to shaking their legs and castanetting their fingers. Then abruptly he finished and rushed rudely from the building through the admiring throng and away.

That performance of Crazy Bow's was his grandest and last in Banana Bottom and it broke the spell of the Revival. He left the village that very day upon another of his long ramblings across the island. The next news that Banana Bottom heard of him was bad. It was from Jubilee. He had gone to the mission there and played the piano and had been given food. Patou appearing in the dining-room while he was there alone, Crazy Bow attempted to strangle him, but was prevented by the intervention of the coachman, Jerry Muggling. It was said in extenuation that Crazy Bow had been irritated by Patou making a fluttering noise and blinking at him like a bird.

Anyway, he was again considered a dangerous person by the local authorities and so he was arrested and sent up to the madhouse. And after a few violent weeks there he died in the straitjacket.

28

THE LARGE PROPERTY BETWEEN BANANA BOTTOM AND Breakneck was known as Castleground and belonged to Busha Glengley. Formerly and for many hoary years before the Emancipation it was the entailed property of an English family. But, possibly through modern changes in inheritance laws, it came into the real estate market towards the end of the nineteenth century and had been purchased cheaply by Busha Glengley.

It was not very valuable property. The most fertile section of it was subject to periodical inundation, when the crops of tenants were destroyed. The richest part of it was a large but rather inaccessible mountain forest with magnificent growths of the finest West Indian hardwood: candlewood, broadleaf, ebony, sweetwood, bullet tree, mahogany, mahoe, cedar, fiddlewood, satinwood, lignumvitæ and a host of lesser ones. There also were found the best of the supple-jacks, also the milkwiss vine which festooned the trees and which the lads scoured the forest to find to drain the vine of its milk, which was boiled down into rubber and made into balls for local games.

Between the forest and the village lay the big savannah, mostly barren sand, except for patches of fox tails, clumps of cocoa plums and sage and the little growths of a species of dwarfish palm. Branching off from the main road from Bull's Hoof, a footpath went across the savannah to meet

the road to Jubilee. It was older than the main roads and
had been in use ever since there were villages in the hills.
By taking it foot travellers going by Bull's Hoof towards
Jubilee gained over three miles. And it was also an old
custom of the village folks to pasture horses and mules
and donkeys and goats in the savannah.

Bita loved walking and always went for long promenades
across the savannah. And often she made use of the short
route in going over to Breakneck. One afternoon while she
was walking along the edge of the forest she saw a man
cantering back and forth over the savannah as if he were
training for some event. It was Arthur Glengley, that son
of Busha Glengley who superintended his father's properties.

Marse Arthur, as he was called locally, espying Bita,
turned his horse into a dashing canter towards the forest.
Upon reaching her he reined in his horse sharply and the
handsome brute reared and pranced nobly upon his hind
legs. Marse Arthur saluted with a sweep of his hat, dis-
mounted, patted the horse's neck, quieting him, and began
conversing with Bita. Marse Arthur had heard about Bita
and the country folk's gossiping of her, and although he
had never met her he knew at once who she was. For he
did not visit Banana Bottom often but only at the time of
the quarterly payment of rent when he rode up to receive
the collections of rent from the local overseer and spend a
day going over the property, receiving such tenants who
had complaints to make direct to the owner.

Marse Arthur was known in and around Gingertown
as a true son of his father, and if his amorous affairs were
less spectacular, he was, after all, only a junior and employé
of his father. He had his father's looks. The same round

healthy pink face, betraying not the slightest sign of mind, restless eyes and fleshy mouth. The only signs of his Negro origin from his mother's side were the rough kinky texture of his hair and the heavy lips. He had only the rudiments of learning as he had shown an early aversion to books, which neither public nor private teachers had been able to overcome, and he was more himself and at ease speaking the Negro dialect than cultivated English.

He possessed the same hearty, genial and commonplace manner of his father and his attitude towards the tenant peasant was not snobbish and haughty. Although he was determined and hard-fisted with them as executive head of his father's estate, he was very affable—particularly towards their young women.

And he was the idol of many of the brown and black country girls who worked as domestics in Gingertown, who were always breaking their hearts and one another's faces as well in street battles over him.

Marse Arthur opened the conversation with the universal "fine day" and carrying it on commented upon Bita's liking walking, her being able to settle down to life in the remote country, after having been educated abroad and her knowing Squire Gensir. They were now walking in the direction of the village and he suggested to Bita that they should go again towards the forest, which was very beautiful at that hour, brooding under the hovering twilight.

Bita replied that it was growing late and that she preferred to go straight on. He tried to bring the conversation down to an intimate level and into a familiar channel, but Bita would not give him any help. An instinctive dislike of him had possessed her and she was irritated that he should have taken it for granted that it was interesting to walk and talk with him. His brittle voice was unpleasant to her and his small-town dialect so different from the peasants' way of speech; their brief concise phrases, words dark and yielding as the soil and green as the grass wet with dew, pliant as supple-jacks and juicy as mangoes, sifted and moulded to give expression to simple Negro tongue.

Baffled by Bita's fencing, Marse Arthur was nevertheless undismayed and sharp with eagerness and as they arrived at a point near the Cane River where the path went deep down between high banks, he grabbed Bita firmly by the breast, pressing her against the bank and tried to kiss her. The sensation of his fingers like claws closing upon her teats had the opposite effect of what Marse Arthur expected. It was a trick he had tried upon apparently reluctant Ginger-town girls who had finally yielded. But it only infuriated Bita. She would not let him have her mouth, but kept turning her head, foiling his every attempt and one moment it caught him violently under the chin and his tongue was caught by his teeth.

"Be damned wid you!" he cried, releasing Bita with a push. "Wha' de hell you putting on style. You ought to feel proud a gen'man like me want fer kiss you when youse only a black gal."

"But this is a different black girl, you disgusting polecat."

"Diffran'!" sneered Marse Arthur. "S'pose you t'ink's a blarsted big diffrance becaz youse ejicated. T'ink youse as good as Lady ———.* But fer all you ejication an' putting on you nuttin' more'n a nigger gal."

Bita did not reply. She started to go, adjusting her hat.

* The Governor's wife.

But Marse Arthur was as red as a tomato and barred her way.

"If you touch me again, I'll jab you in your face with this hatpin," she said, drawing it from her hat.

"Try it!"

"You'll be sorry about this when my father sees Busha Glengley."

"Gawd damn you' fadah an' de debbil tek him sowl."

He advanced upon Bita again and gripped her wrist. He was full of hate and wanted to humiliate her.

"Go away, I say!" she cried viciously clawing at his face.

Right then Jubban appeared upon the bank above and jumped down upon Marse Arthur's neck. . . . Riding across the savannah to pasture the mules, he had discerned Marse Arthur's horse which had clambered up the bank to crop the overhanging fee-fees and had turned from his course to investigate.

"Wha' you mean by? What right you hab fer interfere heah, you facey fellah?" Marse Arthur asked, picking himself and his senses up.

"Ah wonder how come you tink Miss Bita one a them Gingertown wench them!" said Jubban. He was not aggressive nor felt like fighting or hurting Marse Arthur. Cases of adult rape were of rare occurrence in the colony and when they occurred they were mainly among the English soldiers stationed inland far from the city—a group of them sometimes intimidating a peasant woman upon the lonely country road and taking her into the bush.

But incidents similar to the encounter between Marse Arthur and Bita were frequent enough among the young country folk and did not create any sentiment of popular disapproval. For it was not considered an unusual practice for a black rustic to accost a maid and force her to love if he could. Many a love match had begun that way, some ending in happy union.

But Marse Arthur, bastard near-white son of a wealthy country gentleman, enjoying all the local privileges of his birth and position, was terribly wroth that Jubban, a hired drayman, should have dared to intervene in such a matter and put his common hands upon him.

"Doan' dare talk back to me, you stinkin' dutty mule boy!" he cried. "I wi' teach you you' place, mi man." And he lifted his horsewhip of three plaited supple-jacks to strike Jubban. But Jubban rushed him, gripping his arm and twisting it so that Marse Arthur dropped the whip, gnashing his teeth in pain.

"Ef is fight you want now, fight!" cried Jubban

"I wouldn' dutty mi hands them on a jigger-foot drayman," said Marse Arthur.

"Jiggahs on you, but mi feets em cleaner than you' mouth," said Jubban. "You t'ink ah 'fraid a you 'causen youse a son of a backra? Ise a drayman but a man all de same an' it wi' tek a bigger one than you to lick mi black bottom wid a supple-jack."

Marse Arthur was settling his planter's helmet straight upon his head. The white helmet was symbolic in a way of the big landed estates that had swallowed up the best of the rich tropical earth in the halcyon days of freebooting. It rested upon the head of busha and planter like a halo of protection. Under it slave-owners and slave-drivers had goaded the black herds to toil. And under it in spite of changing times they still remained the lords of the tropics.

Perhaps it was only as a symbol that the helmet infuriated Jubban, for he had never worked for the planter class. He knocked it off Marse Arthur's head and with a kick sent it rolling towards the river.

"Now gwan after it an' mek it quick," said Jubban, "or ah'll mek you go the same fashion."

Without replying, Marse Arthur went after his helmet. Jubban with Bita clambered up the bank to the mules and rode away towards the forest to pasture them. Looking back from a distance they saw Marse Arthur riding away.

"Guess him t'ink you was lak a one a them gals 'pon him daddy's estate," said Jubban.

"Thought wrong that time," said Bita.

"De backra mens t'ink all black womens them nuttin'." said Jubban.

"The Glengleys are not pure backra," said Bita. "But what's the difference? They all have the same mind. . . . He couldn't hurt me, really, but I loathed his touching me, the slimy white hog."

She asked Jubban not to relate the incident to anyone. When she got home she had the house girl sweep and dust Jubban's room. It was in the outbuilding, adjoining the storeroom for produce. And after the girl had finished, Bita gathered a bouquet of sunflowers as large as saucers, arranged them in a prized China-blue vase she had purchased in Dresden, and set it in Jubban's room. That did not escape Anty Nommy's observation and gave her cause to think, especially as she had remarked Bita coming in with Jubban and both conversing intimately.

Bita went to her room to rest and to think. She wanted to dismiss the incident as trifling, only Marse Arthur's phrase, ". . . only a black gal," rankled. It rankled the more because she knew that it was a common phrase that might be flung at any decent Negro girl anywhere. . . .

She thought how the finest qualities of mind or brain or heart were the attributes of only the rarest spirits, who may spring like flowers in the commonest as much as the most exclusive places, in the proud domain as well as the peasant's lot and even in hothouses. How then could any class or people or nation or race claim a monopoly of a thing so precious and so erratic in its manifestations? Oh, she marvelled at the imbecilities of a sepulchre-white world that has used every barrier imaginable to dam the universal flow of human feelings by suppressing and denying to another branch of humanity the highest gifts of nature, simply because its epidermis was coloured dark.

"Only a nigger gal!" She undressed and looked at her body in the long mirror of the old-fashioned wardrobe. She caressed her breasts like maturing pomegranates, her skin firm and smooth like the sheath of a blossoming banana, her luxuriant hair, close-curling like thick fibrous roots, gazed at her own warm-brown eyes, the infallible indicators of real human beauty.

"Only a nigger gal!" Ah, but she was proud of being a Negro girl. And no sneer, no sarcasm, no banal ridicule of a ridiculous world could destroy her confidence and pride in herself and make her feel ashamed of that fine body that was the temple of her high spirit. For she knew that she was a worthy human being. She knew that she was beautiful.

She reached for the book of Blake's poems that she had borrowed from Squire Gensir and turned to one of the poems that he had once read to her, finely without comment:

THE LITTLE BLACK BOY

My mother bore me in the southern wild,
And I am black, but O! my soul is white;
White as an angel is the English child,
But I am black, as if bereav'd of light.

My mother taught me underneath a tree,
And, sitting down before the heat of day,
She took me on her lap and kissed me,
And, pointing to the east, began to say:

"Look on the rising sun,—there God does live,
And gives His light, and gives His heat away;
And flowers and trees and beasts and men receive
Comfort in morning, joy in the noonday.

"And we are put on earth a little space,
That we may learn to bear the beams of love;
And these black bodies and this sunburnt face
Is but a cloud, and like a shady grove.

"For when our souls have learn'd the heat to bear,
The cloud will vanish; we shall hear His voice,
Saying: 'Come out from the grove, My love and care,
And round My golden tent like lambs rejoice.'"

Thus did my mother say, and kissed me;
And thus I say to little English boy.
When I from black and he from white cloud free,
And round the tent of God like lambs we joy,

I'll shade him from the heat, till he can bear
To lean in joy upon our Father's knee;
And then I'll stand and stroke his silver hair,
And be like him, and he will then love me.

A splendid poem, she thought, lying naked on the bed,
yet not one to be recommended to an impressionable black
child. For it was murder of the spirit, she reasoned, to cultivate a black child to hanker after the physical character-
istics of the white. Rather teach it to delight in its own
created self upon the earth, in heaven—and in hell.

But away from petty picking into little pieces a poem
magnificent as a whole, to speculate about its great creator.
What a marvellous universal mind was this William Blake's.
A precursor of and king among the futurists, Shakespear-
ean in comprehension. How perfect of music and phrasing,
and far-reaching the implication of that thought: When
he from white and I from black cloud free. . . .

It was like an uplifting outburst from Beethoven, a
winged wonder, cutting its way like lightning across the
chaos of the human mind, holding the spirit up, up, aloft,
proving poetry the purest sustenance of life, scaling by
magic and all the colours of passion the misted heights
where science cannot rise and religion fails and even love
is powerless.

Oh, if only she could rest her spirit tranquilly there,
upon thoughts where petty passions could not penetrate
nor inconsequentials intrude. But such is the composition
of the human mind that even in a tragic moment the most
irrelevant banalities sometimes will invade the domain of
the highest thought.

Thus Marse Arthur's sottish remark pursued Bita
there: "Only a nigger gal!" Like a wicked imp created for
irritation and mischief, that worthless phrase hovered above
her loftiest thoughts and would not away, flitting
around, and darting down into her deepest thinking and
spoiling it. She closed her eyes to shut it out and forget,

but still she saw it (like a little poisonous insect buzzing around a fine healthy body and seeking some vulnerable spot into which it can inject its venom).

The constant image of the ugly little thing so insignificant and yet so insistent brought sharply home to Bita the sense and humour of the ridiculous in all things and she exploded with laughter, loud, lilting, riotous shaking, rustic black laughter until the little thing was frightened, fits of laughter, gales and torrents and storms of laughter until it was scared and vanished to hell away.

29

THERE WAS A RUMOUR OF RAIN IN THE AIR ALTHOUGH there had been no sign of a token. Everybody felt confident that the drought was ending its term. The peasants had never known or heard of one that continued longer than three years. But the Indian coolies and Chinese shopkeepers said that they had known of five and seven years drought-and-famine in their countries.

During the high tide of the Revival, Evan Vaughan had praised God for the drought and demanded his congregations to join him praising God for it, because it was God's way of chastening man and preparing him for blessings. Evan Vaughan's God had been good enough to him, after all, because, wherever he went upon his spiritual mission, in spite of the stringency of the times the people made special general and generous contributions for the decent maintenance of himself and his Sisters in Christ.

The first serious setback to the Revival in Banana Bottom was when Sister-in-Christ Yoni Legge was discovered gestant. It was Sister Phibby who made the discovery. Something in Yoni's posture kneeling at prayer-meeting one morning made Sister Phibby so curious that her clairvoyant eyes were able to see clear through Yoni's corset.

When Yoni stood up to sing, "Praise God, from Whom All Blessings Flow," Sister Phibby studied Yoni's embonpoint, making sure that she had not been deceived by her eyes. And after the prayer-meeting was over, as soon as she had gathered her shocked senses together, Sister Phibby started out for Ma Legge's home, not unrejoicing on the way that whether there was Revival or drought, so long as the thermal spring in man was not entirely exhausted *her* work (even though the work of the Lord failed) would always go on.

In Ma Legge's yard, sitting in the shade of the beautiful cone-shaped red-pear tree, Sister Phibby expounded her theory of Yoni's state. At first Ma Legge was vexed, finding it impossible to believe that such a thing could have happened to her daughter during the period of her sanctified excitement, but hurrying to the house, followed by Sister Phibby, where Yoni was in negligee, she was confronted by the naked fact.

Yoni broke down sobbing before her mother's questioning, confessing to her condition.

"But, oh, mamma, mamma, he not no mortal do it, but an angel done it! An angel, mamma, an angel done it."

"You blasphemous t'ing!" cried Sister Phibby with upraised hands and eyes upturned to the thatched roof. "Ain't you afraid de Lawd Gawd strike you down? Ain't you ashame' fer tek'n' a taffy goat for Gawd's angel?"

Ma Legge groaned deep down in her heart. Upon further investigation it was revealed that Yoni's angel was no less a personage than Hopping Dick. It was a sad thing to do so soon after Yoni's rehabilitation and Hopping Dick's conversion and baptism in the Cane River, but both of them had to be dropped from churchly fellowship.

A temporary action, however, by which the sinners retained the active sympathy of the church members, for it was arranged that Yoni and Hopping Dick should get married. Immediately it would have been if Yoni had not objected to a cheap-and-poor Revival tail-end marriage. She wanted a picture-for-the-eye wedding which neither Ma Legge nor Hopping Dick could afford right then. It was altogether more respectable to Yoni's mind to have a little black bastard at the breast before the parson tied the knot than to stand the stigma of a cheap little wedding.

Sister Phibby's tongue soon spread the news of Yoni's hysterical and blasphemous outburst and the village ballad-ists, remembering how joyfully Yoni used to shout singing: "There are angels hovering round" to carry the tidings of a converted soul to heaven, now celebrated Yoni's preg-nancy with a parody of that revival song:

> "There's an angel hovering round,
> Look out, sister, look out!
> There's an angel hovering round,
> Oh, mind what you' about!
> There's an angel hovering round,
> Beware, sister, your doom!
> There's an angel hovering round
> To break into your room."

The day of the Revival was over. And when the emo-tional fog had lifted it showed that there were many other converted couples who had gone the way of Yoni Legge and Hopping Dick. In spite of the distress of the drought Banana Bottom began adjusting itself and settling back in its old ways again. The business of the grog shops began to brighten and tea-meetings were announced.

The most interesting tea-meeting was that to which Bita had been invited at Bull's Hoof. It was being held by the daughter of the backsliding rum-fighter Delminto. She had lived for some years with an aunt in the city of Kingston and was considered very up-to-date. She gave dances in her father's house at holiday time. And when she visited Banana Bottom for concerts and picnics she sometimes stayed overnight with Bita.

Bita was happy over the invitation to the tea-meeting. There was nothing to restrain her now from doing the things that did not go against her conscience. No overhanging thought of what others would say and of living to be an example for others. And she met with no opposition from her parents. Jordan and Nommy Plant seemed not only entirely unconcerned with Bita's daily life, but it was remarkable the manner in which they realized that she was no longer a child and deferred to her judgment and respected her individuality.

. . . .

The annual Conference of the Free Churches was being held that year and at that time in Gingertown. And Jordan Plant was the delegate from Banana Bottom. Malcolm Craig, on his way to the conference, passed through Banana Bottom and offered to convey his friend Jordan Plant in his carriage to the town. Malcolm Craig was wearing crêpe upon the sleeve of his black coat. For Patou was dead. He had died just as he reached his majority, from a complaint the peasants named realistically knot-guts. And although the parents had often longed for death to end his pitiful state, Mrs. Craig, who had never been very robust in that climate, had been badly shaken by the event.

Malcolm Craig expressed himself very happy to see Bita again, having a long talk with her about her life in Banana Bottom and her hopes for the future. He was able to see

at once that life in Banana Bottom was more congenial to
Bita than at Jubilee. In talking to her father Malcolm
Craig was apologetic about the unhappy termination of
Bita's connexion with the mission. But Jordan Plant assured him that all was well so far as he was concerned and
reiterated his appreciation of the splendid thing Malcolm
and Priscilla had done in taking Bita as a little girl and
giving her a complete education.

Before his departure for the conference Jordan Plant
in anticipation of rain had started burning bush for corn
and peas planting. Many other peasants followed his example. The ground was cleared and the brush spread over
it until it was brittle dry, and then fire was set to it and
for many days the skies of Banana Bottom were filled with
brown-black, blue-black smoke and the nostrils of the
people were tickled by the smell of crackling stubble.

Once an agricultural instructor visiting the village during a great bush-burning season had dissuaded some of the
peasants from burning the cut bush, pointing out that that
method spoilt and impoverished the land. They took his
advice and ploughed the bush under.

But Jordan, who had by far the greatest portion of
ground cleared, insisted upon burning it before digging.
The result was his reaping the finest crops while his neighbours', who had followed academic advice, failed, being
partly destroyed young by insects. For light burning destroyed insect pests and worms and the ashes were fine
fertilizers.

On another occasion the same instructor admonished a
peasant with a bundle of young cocoa plants which the
peasant had rooted up without ceremony from the soil for
transplanting. The instructor told the peasant that such

carelessly handled plants would not thrive. The peasant replied that he would make them. He planted the lot and a year later when the instructor again visited the district, they were developing into sturdy cocoa trees.

Thus sometimes even trained instructors had to learn from the ignorant instinctive man. For the culture of the soil was so like the culture of humanity, varying according to country and climate. Simple and complex. Obvious and subtle. Easy and difficult. Natural growth, artificial growth, abnormal growth. Plants ramming their roots in the rich soil and reaching up into the air in the fulness of their strength, others neglected, choked by weeds and stunted, and some beginning vigorously and later losing their sap and vitality to gormandizers.

The same age-old soil nourishing a variety of plants—the great common instructor imparting general knowledge to all alike—the scientific investigator as well as the ignorant soil-taught cultivator.

Nevertheless the Agricultural Society, since its inception, had by lectures and demonstrations rendered invaluable service to the peasantry. They were learning better to rotate and diversify their crops (although the boom in bananas had turned the heads of many of them to planting that fruit only). And they were learning better to combat the various plant diseases and to experiment in pruning and grafting to grow more excellent plants.

. . . .

On the afternoon of the tea-meeting Bita rode over to Bull's Hoof on her father's pony accompanied by Jubban, who rode a mule. When she arrived Miss Delminto sprang a surprise by asking Bita to be the queen of the tea-meeting. Bita consented.

Miss Delminto was a pretty and popular light-brown girl and many nice girls and young men from the regional villages were always attracted to her affairs. The name of the queen was kept a secret. Some guessed that it would be a girl from the city who was visiting Miss Delminto. But nobody had an inkling that it would be Bita, who was regarded as a kind of honourable guest.

Because of the mystery about the queen, the usual side-show of seeing the veiled queen upon her throne in her boudoir was exciting and profitable. A price of sixpence was charged to enter the boudoir, one shilling to kiss the hand of the queen and ten shillings for any person who wanted to have the veil lifted a little so that he could kiss the mouth of the queen.

The price to pay to kiss the queen was usually about half-a-crown, but this time Miss Delminto had put an amount that was almost impossible for any peasant lad, so that no common yokel could take advantage of it.

Even though the mystery of the queen fired the young men's spirits any gallant who paid as much as half a pound to kiss her would quite likely have no money left to participate in the evening's biggest event—the bidding of the cakes. And a gallant who could not bid a cake for his sweetheart at a tea-meeting would be cutting no figure at all.

Many sixpences and shillings were placed in the pewter plate upon the table at the door of the queen's boudoir. But only one person dared the price of a queen's kiss. And when Miss Delminto learned who it was she proposed to

Bita the substitution of another girl in her place. But Bita replied that the person who had put down that amount to kiss the queen ought to have the real one. She suspected that the person knew who the queen was and she herself was filled with curiosity.

When Bita saw Jubban appear in the plaited palm arch of the boudoir she was all a trembling piece of excitement. Jubban marched determinedly towards his desire, the veil was lifted, Bita gave him her mouth, and he planted a sweet kiss in it.

And now the real show was begun with a flourish of drums. (Kojo Jeems had been brought over from Banana Bottom to play.) A crier announced the coming of the queen. Some one demanded: "Who's the queen?" And a young lady recited:

> "The queen's a flower
> A sweet, sweet flower.
> But it's not the rose,
> Nor the lily-of-the-valley,
> Nor the night jessamine,
> Nor the hyacinth.
>
> "She's lovelier than
> The maiden-hair,
> She's brighter than
> The buttercup,
> She's daintier than
> The painted-lady
> And sweeter than
> The honeysuckle,
> Our lovely queen
> Our queen tonight.'

And now with a grand sounding of drum and cymbal, fiddle and flute the queen made her entry in a garlanded chair attached to staves and borne by four lads and surrounded by many charming maids-in-waiting. With the musicians leading she was paraded round and round the palm booth while the dancers lined up in pairs behind her to participate in the opening grand march.

Jubban as the spender of the largest single amount of money was entitled to be the partner of the queen during the grand march. Bita wanted Jubban to head the exhibition with her and encouraged him. But he was diffident and waived his rights. Jubban had a solid heavy set body and had never cultivated dancing. Coming as a stray boy to Banana Bottom and attaching himself to Jordan Plant's household, he had always remained rather lonely, outside of the groupings of the youngsters who were born in the region. Some of them had even nicknamed him Wanderbout. And as he grew older and became the trusted drayman of Jordan Plant, his friendships had been made mainly among other draymen with whom he became acquainted at the markets.

Bita was disappointed that Jubban did not lead her forth and have all the Banana Bottom dandies following behind him. Nevertheless she admired him for being himself and not trying to cut a figure as a dandy when he was not naturally that type.

She was touched by the manner he had chosen to reveal his feeling for her. He had taken his kiss without a word. But no word was necessary, for the kiss itself had spoken, warmly telling her more than speech could tell. And now she was struck again by the attractiveness of him, how, although he was always working in the sun and rain, day and night, his skin possessed a velvety indigo-black tone like an eggplant and that among all the men gathered there at that tea-meeting he was the most appealing.

The most popular dance tune of the evening was the parody: "There's an Angel Hovering Round." The original music was transformed into a joyous jigging, the dancers singing as they danced. A leading voice sang: "There's an angel hovering round," and the lads pointing mockingly at the girls shouted: "Look out, sister, look out," swaying with their partners as if they were swinging standing.

The girls shrieked wildly, joining in the refrain: "Look out, sister, look out," shaking fingers at and tapping one another with their fans. Even the drumsticks played an exciting part as Kojo Jeems with a flourish of notes tossed them into the air. And whenever the musicians stopped the dancers cried: "Encore for the Angel! Three cheers for the Angel!" And so the musicians had to repeat it again and again.

The windy afternoon had turned into a windier evening and in the middle of the night a high wind was driving over the hills and there was a promise of rain in that wind. And while the dancers were riotously jigging the rain fell out. The joymakers rushed away from the palm booth to shelter in the house, the kitchen, the outhouses, the horse-stable. And the tea-meeting was broken up.

The rain poured down as only tropical rains can, like armies of daggers out of the heavens. As if an Almighty Hand had torn open the enveloping clouds and let loose a vast unfailing dam of water.

All through the night it fell and in the morning the face of the country was changed and all the signs showed that the rainy season had come at last. The guests who had come from distant villages started home in the rain so that they could get across the fords before the rising of the rivers.

Bita also went. Jubban saddled the beasts. Miss Delminto took her father's waterproof coat and wrapped it around Bita. The lashing wind, the crashing rain, wrestled wildly over the hills. As Bita and Jubban started down the road a cry from the house made them look back to see the wind lift the flat roof of the palm booth and blow it down the other side of the slope to the gully.

Great tropical trees were swaying like reeds in the wind. Tree ferns and thatch palms fell as if machetes were laid to their roots. Cedar and torch trees, sweetwoods and other timber trees crashed in the forests. Breadfruit and avocado pears shivered and tumbled in the fields. Giant bamboos groaned and whined pitifully, rubbing against each other, and flung their grand lengths upon the earth. One dropped from a high bank across the road and Jubban had to dismount and remove it before he and Bita could proceed.

In the tilled fields the sugar-canes were strewn like straw and banana trees were flattened out like soldiers on their bellies at exercise. Fences were twisted awry and grass huts were lifted and blown along like chaff, leaving the dwellers naked to the merry elements.

With the blessing of the rain a destroying hurricane had visited the island, sweeping everything before it with velocity and fury. A devastating hurricane causing a little loss of life but big loss of property. A few fishing-boats surprised off the coast had capsized and their occupants were drowned. And a number of peasants lost their lives trying to ford the swollen rivers.

The soil softened, landslides came down into the roads, spreading away like enormous fans. In the little towns some frame houses were blown clean off their foundations. In the rural regions all the better houses of the peasants withstood the storm. These were all locally constructed and often the foundations were of wooden pillars of Jamaica hardwood driven deep into the ground. Such houses were better proof against earthquake and winds than the nicer frame houses set upon stone foundations.

The destruction of farm products was sweeping and paralyzing. Since the decade of the boom in the banana many peasants had taken to cultivating that plant only, to the exclusion of other crops. And now that all the full-grown and fruiting trees were destroyed whole families who had barely managed to subsist throughout the drought were right up against starvation.

Six miles from Bull's Hoof, where two rivers disappeared under the earth and where there were innumerable sink holes, the whole flat region was flooded and the road impassable. Boats were hastily built to convey the people across.

The great market traffic was interrupted.

And throughout the colony the hurricane and flood had wrought havoc. Telegraph poles were down and the country was cut off from the city. Because of this, although the hurricane was catastrophic in extent, native imagination had nevertheless invented exaggerated stories of it in many regions.

Thus it happened that one afternoon, in the closing days of the conference of the Free Churches, in the first newspapers to reach Gingertown from the city, Malcolm Craig read that the roof of the Jubilee mission had been blown off.

Malcolm Craig in common with the preachers and lay delegates gathered together at that conference had been very worried over the extent of the hurricane and its consequences following the long drought. But even the most sensitive and universal-minded of mortals may come short of realizing the full tragedy of an experience of suffering in which they did not actually participate. The bad news from Jubilee crowded out all other sad reports of the hurricane from Malcolm Craig's mind. He could not communicate by wire with the town and could think of nothing but the fate of his frail wife, whom he imagined dead or lying ill and helpless with the roof gone from over her head. And so summoning Jerry Muggling to harness the horses he left Gingertown for Jubilee, travelling by way of Banana Bottom and accompanied by Jordan Plant.

As they drove out into the country they noted that the Public Works Department was already on the job, for there were men at work throwing their axes into the trunks of obstructing trees and shovelling away the loose earth and stones of landslides. The hurricane had abated but the rain was still falling in intermittent and torrential showers. The waters of the Banana Bottom hills had come down, spreading like a sea over the wonderful Ginger River Valley.

The Ginger River, receiving torrents of rain water from its many tributaries, had risen and overflowed its banks. At some distance below the point where the Cane River emptied into it, there was a ford that was very dangerous in rainy season. A decade back a bridge had been built a little above it, but it had been broken in pieces and swept away by a previous flood. Hardly ever a rainy season passed without loss of life occurring at that ford. It had always been dangerous. A few hundred years before the conquistadors had called the Ginger River the Rio Peligroso.

Although the river there seemed to lie upon the plain like a large placid lake, its undercurrent was deadly. There was no visible warning of danger like that of a roaring river with strong currents. The peasants knew when it was unsafe to cross by comparing the old level of the ford to the new when the water rose.

The Craig carriage arrived there at twilight and when Jerry Muggling saw how high the river had risen he refused to try it. The coachman knew much more about dangerous tropical rivers than Malcolm Craig and told him so. But that merely exasperated the parson, almost unbalanced by anxiety over his wife. Malcolm Craig told the coachman that he would take the ford himself if the coachman refused. So declaring, Malcolm Craig ordered Muggling from the seat and took the reins himself.

Jordan Plant felt convinced that Muggling was instinctively right, but thought it would be cowardly to draw back and let his friend challenge the waters alone. And so he decided to accompany Malcolm Craig. But he took the precaution of removing his boots and coat. He could swim.

Glum and full of anxiety, Jerry Muggling watched Malcolm Craig drive into the ford. It was dark and he kept peering into the waters until he could see no more. The horses were a fine strong-working and good-teaming pair. But the undercurrent was swift and treacherous and told against them. In the middle of the stream they halted poised as if they were in accord in making a final determined stand. Malcolm Craig coaxed them onwards, but relentlessly the current turned their heads downstream.

The buggy was like a death trap as the waters pushed it down upon the animals. Jordan Plant leaped into the river, calling to Malcolm to do likewise. But Malcolm Craig was no swimmer and his clothes were a hindrance. Jordan gave him his left arm and struck out for the bank, but he was handicapped by Malcolm Craig's tight awkward grasp. They could make no headway against the current and the last thing the coachman heard was Malcolm Craig's voice above the waters crying: "Lord have mercy!"

Thus Malcolm Craig went down to his death carrying Jordan Plant. And all because of exaggerated news. For the solidly-built Jubilee mission and church (like most of the stout edifices erected by the pioneer missionaries with black labour) were untouched. The hurricane had struck only a gable-end of the kitchen, lifting the roof clear of Rosyanna's head.

It was from the city newspaper also that Mrs. Craig learned of the news of the drowning. Rosyanna served the fatal newspaper with breakfast to Mrs. Craig in her room.

Priscilla Craig had been unwell ever since the death of Patou and had taken to her room with the coming of the rains. When Rosyanna returned again to remove the breakfast things she found Priscilla leaning back in a rigid saintly posture among the pillows, the newspaper clutched in her hand.

Rosyanna ran bawling for help out of the mission, thinking Mrs. Craig was dead. It was the morning of the weekly sisters' meeting and the church sisters hurried from the annex where they were praying and into the mission. But Mrs. Craig was not dead then. She recovered from the stroke and breathed a few days longer. But she did not desire to live. She had always said that she would not care to live if Malcolm Craig died before her. She had allowed herself to be almost worried to death by disappointment over Herald Newton Day and Bita and the frustration of her planning.

The mourning church folk visited the mission, bringing gifts of gorgeous tropical fruits and flowers, but Priscilla Craig had no heart left for sympathy, no eyes for lovely flowers. Her thoughts now were only of her husband, to follow him, leaving all the prodigal glories of the tropics for ever. And she did. A few days after the burial of Malcolm Craig Priscilla's tired body was laid beside his in the mission graveyard.

30

MALCOLM CRAIG'S HORSES WERE FOUND NEAR GINGER-
town, trapped by the harness and the shaft which had
been wrenched away from the carriage. But his body and
Jordan's were recovered many miles farther down upon an
estate where the river divided and formed an islet. They
were taken in charge by a Congregational minister. Both
bodies were boxed. And as the place was near the railroad,
Malcolm Craig's was sent by rail to the station nearest to
Jubilee.

When the news of the drowning reached Banana Bottom,
Anty Nommy was all broken up and helpless with grief.
But Bita kept her head, and asked Sister Phibby to come
down to the house to take care of Anty Nommy and help
with the arrangements for the funeral.

Bita decided to go with the dray to get her father's body.
Before she went she asked Sunday-school Superintendent
Delgado to supervise the funeral arrangements, giving him
money to purchase the necessary things and pointing out
the place where the grave should be dug.

She left Banana Bottom with Jubban in the evening. It
was a long journey of about ten hours in the heavy rumb-
ling rattling dray. And all the way travelling Bita was
restless with a strong hectic feeling. It was the first time
in her life that death had come home close to her carrying
off at one stroke two beings with whom her life was inti-

mately linked and whom she loved. She knew that her father was dead and yet she could not really visualize him dead.

She crossed the Ginger River's cruel ford, now subsided into a shallow insignificant sheet of water. It was daybreak when the dray arrived at the lowland village. Bita shut herself in the vestry-room to remain a little while alone with her dead father. The fine traits of his face stood out sharply in death. A strong angular Negro face firm, purposeful with a sign of aggressiveness but nothing of meanness or deceit about it.

She tried to recall that elusive time of her childhood when she first became aware of him. She wondered if it were that day when blandly she pulled the cloth from the breakfast table, breaking with childish wantonness the special mug in which Jordan Plant used to take his coffee and chuckled over it. Yet she wasn't sure now if it was really a conscious remembrance of the actual scene or if it had grown fixed in her memory from Anty Nommy's relating it to her. For a child's actual experiences and those that are related by older relatives are so inextricably mixed in the dawning consciousness of childhood's memories that it is difficult to separate one from the other.

She remembered how her father had petted her. Distinctly she recalled the Sundays when he and Anty Nommy attended the sacrament of the Lord's Supper, and how her father always held her in his arms, and the magic ginger bun he used to extract from his pocket so that she should be quiet and not talk and try to put her hand in the pewter plate with the little pieces of bread when it was passed round. She couldn't remember how she did get to church. She only remembered being there in the interior. And one day her father gave a half of her bun to another child who was restless in its mother's arms and with a sudden sure gesture she scratched the other child's face, knocking the piece of bun to the floor. The other child had cried and Anty Nommy said: "Shame! Shame!" But she did not really feel ashamed until she grew to be a big girl and remembered it.

Now she thought too of the time when she was raped by Crazy Bow how strange and terrible her father's face had been, yet he had been so kind and more fatherly than ever to her. A fine father. And she had loved him deeply with a love rooted in respect. All the men that she really respected had something of his character: Malcolm Craig, Squire Gensir, Jubban.

Bita did not cry. She drew the sheet back over the face and left the room determined never to look upon it again.

It was the local custom that dead bodies should travel at night. Jubban fed and groomed the mules. The box was fixed in the back of the dray and at evenfall it departed. Bita rode in front with Jubban. The bed of the dray was covered with straw and Jubban cushioned bags upon it so that Bita could be comfortable.

And now after being alone with her father's body and communing with the past, the hectic feeling had left Bita and she was filled and brooding with a great peace. She was silent most of the time. The dray rumbled easily along, the mules keeping up a lively pace as if they were anxious and happy to get home. They passed the little white church of Gingertown in which the Free Church conference had been held and the notorious ford of the Ginger River, so low now that a dog could cross it without swimming.

It began raining softly, but there was no terror in the rain now. Just a fine sprinkling as if the dews were too heavy in the heavens and were turned into a drizzle.

Jubban unfolded the tarpaulin and covered the dray, raising it above the stanchions against the washboard in a slanting way so that the water could run off. Bita put her hand upon his shoulder and leaned upon him and Jubban shifted himself so that her head was pillowed against his breast.

The untimely death of Jordan Plant had set him seriously thinking and he had a feeling now of being a kind of protector of the house. And Bita was thinking the same thing. Almost unconsciously Jubban's hands encircled her waist and spontaneously their mouths came together and a sweet shiver spread through her body against the impact of his warm passionate person.

Jubban slackened the reins, hitching them upon a stanchion, and the mules marched slowly along of their own volition and Bita in Jubban's embrace was overwhelmed with a feeling as if she were upon the threshold of a sacrament and she yielded up herself to him there in the bed of the dray. It was strange and she was aware of the strangeness that in that moment of extreme sorrow she should be seized by the powerful inevitable desire for love which would not be denied.

She was not oblivious of her father's body in the back, but her conscience fortified her with a conviction of the approval of his spirit. He who had seemed to understand her all her life would understand now. Her spirit was finely balanced between the delicate sadness of death and the subdued joy of love and over all was the glorious sensation of life triumphant in love over death.

In the tropical flush of daylight the dray arrived at the Crossroads. All through the night a crowd of people had gathered together at Jordan Plant's house, watching and waiting, wailing and chanting. And before dawn some of them had wandered down to the Crossroads to meet the body.

The women crowded around Bita, weeping and commiserating her. And then she broke down and cried too until the procession reached the house. Bita went directly to her room and cried herself to sleep. Anty Nommy had overcome the first shock of grief and was up and helping in the house.

Jordan Plant's grave had already been dug in the garden beside the grave of his first wife. Preparations were made for immediate interment. The church members wanted a church service over the body, but Teacher Fearon said that the body should not be kept from burial a moment longer than was necessary and his counsel prevailed. And so the Reverend Lambert read the funeral service on the veranda of the house and the body of Jordan Plant was carried to the grave by six brother officers and buried beside Bita's mother just as the sun came in glory over the Banana Bottom hills.

31

BITA WANTED AN EARLY AND QUIET WEDDING, BUT SHE could not persuade Anty Nommy of the necessity of it and to agree with her. Since Jubban was Bita's choice instead of one of the more brilliant and better-off suitors, Anty Nommy felt not the slightest objection to him. Indeed, Anty Nommy liked Jubban as a man and preferred him infinitely to Hopping Dick. Only she thought that Bita with her high education might have done better and married a man of means and position. Jubban was superior in one thing. He possessed a deep feeling for the land and he was a lucky-born cultivator. No one could do better than he in carrying on the work of the soil that had absorbed Jordan Plant's being and kept his heart's blood always warm.

But Anty Nommy said the marriage should wait upon the memory of Jordan Plant. She could not bear a wedding in the house following so soon after a funeral. The tragedy was too fresh in her mind. People would talk. And why should Bita let people talk when she loved her father? And Anty Nommy would not hear of a quiet little wedding. It would have to be a big country wedding with a great crowd of people, and gorgeous feasting. The leading peasant family of Banana Bottom could not afford to disappoint the villagers by having a cheap insignificant wedding.

And so it was agreed that the marriage of Bita and

Jubban should wait for at least six months when the period of half-mourning was reached. Bita was relieved that Anty Nommy was not perturbed at all about her being pregnant. That was entirely a family affair, Anty Nommy said, laughing. Did she not herself give birth to Bab out of wedlock? And was she not as good a woman as any?

The knowledge of Bita's engagement to Jubban amazed all the nice little people between Jubilee and Gingertown and created a lot of windy talk. Those who had just a smattering of education and resented Bita's wider knowledge said that Bita was, after all, only a common peasant girl that had been taken up and made ladylike by a sentimental white couple and that she was reverting to type because it was too much for her to live up to the standard of being a lady. While girls with less education and chances were aspiring to ladylike living and trying to get away from their peasant origin, Bita had deliberately chosen to vegetate in the backwoods with a common drayman.

The months following the hurricane and floods were desperate hard ones for the peasantry. The hurricane had finished the work of the drought. For a short time the peasants lived on the stuff that was half-damaged by the hurricane and floods: felled bananas, plantains, sugar-cane, soursop, cassava and breadfruit.

But there was a great shortage of the minor foodstuffs that would have been so helpful to the peasants during the acute period of distress if they had not neglected them for the banana. Jordan Plant, as usual, had been a shrewd cultivator, never planting all of his best land with banana. He reared hogs and had planted a lot of corn and sweet potatoes for them. Sweet potatoes were sparingly used for human consumption and the custom, when they were fit to harvest, was to turn the hogs loose to fatten in a fenced field. But now the food of hogs was fit for the gods. Those who could were glad to buy sweet potatoes and Anty Nommy and Jubban sold a great quantity of them at moderate prices.

The transient Negro workers had had a fat season of work clearing away the wreckage and debris of the hurricane and flood. And when there was nothing left to do they used their savings to take ship to Panama.. The Panama Canal was the big hope of the poor disinherited peasant youths of Jamaica and all those islands of the Caribbean Belt that were set in the latitude of hurricanes and earthquakes—all those who did not like to sport the uniform of the army and police force.

After experimenting with different kinds of labourers to do the spadework of the Canal Zone, the Yankees had found that the West Indian spades were the most reliable.

With the hard times raging there was a big increase of predial larceny. The fields of the prosperous peasants were entered at night and yams and cocoes dug up and cocoa trees stripped. Proud young peasants of the hill lands who had always prided themselves on being able to live by the careful cultivation of their patches without descending to coolie labor in the lowlands, were now compelled to go begging for work at the gates of the plantations.

The planters saw in the visitation of the elements a salutary lesson—for the peasant workers. For although the plantations had been ravaged, too, the planters had reserves of food and money that the peasants had not. It was gossiped that some of them (among whom was Busha

Glengley) had declared that it was a good thing that the niggers should be forced down to coolie labor.

This angered the Banana Bottom peasants especially because, as a result of the incident between Bita and Marse Arthur, the short cut that the peasants had made use of since the days of slavery was fenced in by barbed wire, trespass signs were put up and the peasants were denied the ancient privilege of pasturing their livestock on the waste land.

Squire Gensir declared that it would have been illegal to fence off an ancient footpath in the "Mother Country" and he had a personal talk with Busha Glengley about the matter. Marse Arthur had thought that it was time to make money out of the waste land, and as he was the manager of his father's landed estates, Busha Glengley did not interfere. And the fence remained.

During that time of distress the agitation was redoubled and grew in bitterness against the immigration of the Chinese and the importation of Indian coolie labor. Meetings of protest were organized against the yellow and brown foreigners and the Legislature summoned to prohibit a further influx of them.

The newspapers were deluged with letters from native leaders and European residents about the means of helping the peasants and schemes to lessen their suffering and protect them from natural disasters in that blessed island. Some suggested a fostering of native industries and a system of tariff reform. Others put forward a plan of sinking wells in the dry districts and extensive irrigation works. While others said the peasants should be encouraged to diversify their crops so they should not put all their expectations upon the banana, which of all plants was the most susceptible to natural accidents such as hurricanes.

But a wag wrote that the only practical way of shaking the peasants' faith in the banana was for the Yankees to diminish their appetite for the fruit, and nobody wanted that. He also took the opportunity to say that it had been proven that the banana was the authentic fruit that tempted Eve to sin and brought about the expulsion of the first parents of mankind from the Garden of Eden. And as nothing could have been done to prevent man from taking risks in the beginning, so nothing could ever be done now nor in the future so long as man was man.

The time fixed for the wedding was drawing near. Yoni, who was nursing a plump little baby and was still unmarried, asked Bita if she had any objection to their getting married together. The two young women had become great friends again and Bita thought it would be a pretty thing to have a double wedding. And as Bita's house was larger and better appointed she suggested to Yoni to make one big wedding feast in her house.

Belle Black came from Jubilee to spend a month with Bita and help with the preparations for the wedding. And she and Bita and Yoni went up to the city of Kingston to stay a few days and buy their wedding clothes. When Bita was at Jubilee and visited the city with the Craigs, the party always stayed in a private house with white friends of the Craigs'. But travelling to the chief town independently, she was troubled about finding a decent place to stay in with her friends.

For all the respectable hotels and boarding-houses (most of them owned or managed by light-skinned coloured people) had developed a policy of excluding black or dark-brown guests. For such guests the hotels were either always filled up or if there were vacant rooms they were always reserved. In some quarters it was said that American tourists had determined the policy because they objected to the presence of dark-coloured persons in the hotels in which they stayed. Jamaica was developing a good business in American tourist trade and could not afford to ruin that business by being fair and decent to the people who made up the overwhelming majority of its population.

But the trouble went deeper than that in reality. The social life of the colony was rooted upon shade and colour prejudice. During the epoch of slavery the lighter-skinned offspring of white men and black women had privileges that the black slaves had not. Although the Eurafricans were slaves the majority of them were attached to the masters' households, while the blacks worked in the fields. Many of the Eurafrican children were sent abroad to be educated by their fathers and some in time came into possession of landed property and even became slave-owners themselves. Pretty and elegant Eurafrican girls invariably became the mistresses of white planters and it is recorded that they were even sold at fancy prices by their fathers for that purpose.

With their limited privileges, although they were not free, the Eurafricans constituted a group and looked down with contempt upon the pure-blooded Africans and in time multiplied in numbers to form a distinct middle class between the planter and governing classes and the slaves.

When slavery was abolished in the British West Indies the Eurafricans by their education and experience were in a favourable position to take advantage of the great social change. Many of the abandoned estates finally passed into their hands, the educated ones qualified for the higher professions and were employed in the Government services, and the smaller white-collar jobs such as those of clerks and shopgirls were reserved for the poorer ones. The women were no longer compelled to be the mistresses of white masters and the Eurafricans developed a strong group pride, marrying almost exclusively among themselves and reproducing and rearing their own kind.

But as the Eurafricans developed in wealth and power they also approximated to the social standards and attitudes of the white planters with little sympathy for the freed blacks and their problems, their struggles for social adjustment, and so there had developed between Europeans and Eurafricans on one side a system of social discrimination against the expatriate Africans.

Bita had been advised by Squire Gensir to go to a moderate-priced hotel in which he always stayed when visiting the city. He gave her a note to the owner. Squire Gensir was aware of the discriminations, notably in the city, against black persons, but the owner of that particular hotel happened to be a dark-brown man and he gave Bita a note to him. But this man, according to the general custom, employed as manager a light-coloured woman and he was away in the country when Bita arrived in the city with her friends.

The housekeeper was a haughty woman whose naturally snobbish manner became overbearing when she saw that her would-be guests were black country people who had presumed to think that they could find accommodation at the hotel where she worked. She did not politely say that there were no rooms vacant, but frankly told Bita that that hotel did not accept black persons as guests.

One such rebuff was enough for Bita. She went with Yoni and Belle Black to a cheap unpleasant hotel where decent black persons who could afford to pay for better accommodation were mixed indiscriminately with bad-mannered light-skinned ones and nondescripts who found there their natural element.

Bita wrote to Squire Gensir about her plight and he arrived in the city by the next afternoon's train. The hotel-owner had returned from his visit to the country. Squire Gensir protested to him against the manner in which the young black women were treated and said he was ashamed that such conditions should exist in Jamaica. The hotel-owner apologized, pointing out that he was not at the hotel when the incident occurred, ashamed that in a matter involving Negroes and mulattoes a white man had to intervene to obtain fair treatment for the Negroes. The housekeeper was discharged and Bita, Belle Black and Yoni were given accommodation in the hotel.

Smarting from the insult offered by the yellow woman, Belle Black was in a militant mood and staged a scene when she went with Bita and Yoni to sample the wedding fabrics. They had gone to a large shop in the main business street and as they needed a lot of things the head lady clerk had been assigned to wait upon them.

The head lady clerk was a very gracious, sunny-smiling light-coloured person and seeing that the girls were going to get a wedding trousseau she began exchanging pleasantries with them about marriage.

But while the lady clerk was attending to the girls an octoroon woman, an important customer, entered the shop and addressed herself to her. The woman was accustomed to being served always by that clerk and as she wanted only a small thing the lady clerk excused herself, asking the girls to wait awhile, and went to serve the constant customer.

In a resentful spirit Belle Black interpreted that as a slight towards her and her companions and she turned loose a mitrailleuse of angry protest in the shop.

"Wha' de debbil you mean leabin' us waiting yah fer sarve dat udder woman fust becausen har skin im yaller lak a boil' pumpkin? . . .

"Doan come givin' me any a you' p'lite excuse dem. We was de fust one heah an' we ought to be de fust sarve', becausen we money is as good as anybody elsen money. All unno mulatto niggers am all de same to me. You t'ink youse dat big t'ing dressin' up on six shilling a week, but lemme tell you I cyan't see you. In de country where ah come from you got to show some'n' moh'n a li'l' turn colour to make class. You got to be somet'ing, you got to hab somet'ing.

"Eh, eh! Ku yah though. Ah nebber heah nor seen such a shitination in mi life. Becausen you turn-colour niggers am wearing a standin' collar an' a silk blouse ebery day in de yahr you becomin' to t'inkin' youse de angels demself round' de t'rone of de Lawd Gawd. But lemme tell unno all dat you ain't nuttin' at all but a lotta cans full a somet'ing dat ain't sugar."

The manager of the shop tried to assure Belle Black that it was all a mistake, that he would never countenance any discrimination against black people in his shop because as a group they were his biggest and most important customers, and that the only colour that mattered in his shop was the colour of money.

The manager spoke truly, for prejudices and discriminations in business can easily stand an economic interpretation and the people who practice them are mean and violently unreasonable because they hate to refuse any kind of money and do so only because acceptance might cause them to lose much more than they receive.

But Belle Black was not appeased and calling Bita and Yoni to follow her she flounced out of the shop.

Came the wedding day. The double wedding. Bita and Jubban, Yoni and Hopping Dick. The marriage ceremonies were to take place at Gingertown. And there was to be a cavalcade. The peasants loved nothing so much as a wedding with many horses, and couples belonging to the same village and who were marrying often preferred to get married away from home at some important place to which they would go riding and return home triumphant on horseback.

Bita also desired to go to Gingertown because she did not want to be married by the Reverend Lambert. The Lamberts had been exceeding tongue-loose about her marriage to Jubban. During a discussion of the matter the Reverend Lambert, accusing Bita of burying her talent and education in the mud, had said that he would be ashamed to perform the marriage ceremony. This was repeated to Bita and irritated her. Also the elder Miss Lambert had said that Bita was a disgrace to all intelligent and high-aiming Negroes. Not only did Bita not want the Reverend Lambert to officiate at the ceremony, but she had not even extended the courtesy of an invitation to any of the family.

Teacher Fearon had pointed out to the Reverend Lambert that Squire Gensir approved of Bita. But that was no recommendation to the Reverend gentleman, who called Squire Gensir a decadent in the literal sense of the word. To the Reverend Lambert Squire Gensir, interested in the collecting of the transplanted African fairy tales and the ditties in dialect of the tea-meetings and of field workers and draymen, was in no sense an inspiring person. Squire Gensir was an unprogressive person, looking backwards, while the minister considered himself a progressive man, forward-looking. He believed in progress for Negroes and preached it according to the lights of his intellect and he could not see any indications of progress in Squire Gensir's work and his atheism nor that they could be beneficial to Negroes in any way.

The marriages were celebrated in the Congregational church at Gingertown. On the morning of the wedding Jordan Plant's yard, in which the guests had assembled, had the aspect of a horse fair with prancing and neighing stallions and fillies, pawing ponies, stout draught horses and mules.

There were not enough side-saddles in the hill region for the women riders and some who were expert used male saddles, riding sideways. Many used long Indian shawls as riding-habits to cover their frocks. The lovely shawls were much in use among the peasant women as a decorative article of dress.

As Jubban's best man Squire Gensir was among the guests and he was the poorest-dressed man there. While all the young and older men were suited out in broadcloth, serges, tweeds and cutaways and stiff-starched collars,

Squire Gensir was at his ease in a brown linen suit and soft shirt, the coolest of them all in that torrid climate.

The cavalcade proceeded in orderly fashion but at a slow enough and almost solemn pace to Gingertown. But it was a great ride back home. The company broke up into cantering and galloping groups along the long level stretches and some matched horses racing.

On the road between Gingertown and Bull's Hoof Bita was galloping along with Teacher Fearon and his wife, Squire Gensir and Jubban, when her horse suddenly bolted down a track leading to a valley. The road there skirted a mountainside and it was a sharp incline down which the horse abruptly started. Bita had a terrible jolt but managed to keep her seat and her head and hold on while the horse raced furiously down the dangerous track. She could not think of controlling him, but only to sit tightly. When the horse reached the gully in the valley he leaped clear of it, but the path turned up a hill and then Bita was able to control him. The men had followed her but were unable to make good headway down the narrow dangerous path. Now they came up alarmed at Bita's state and wondering if she were hurt. But Bita, smiling, demonstrated to them that she was all right by giving the whip to the pony and forcing him to take the hill at full gallop back to the main road.

The wedding feast was served in a vast palm booth erected over Jordan Plant's biggest barbecue. In it were fixed bamboo poles and beams upon which rough boards were laid on which the food was piled. Roast pigs, roast fowls, goat meat, broad dishes of yams, yamies, cocoes and ripe plantains. Fancy loaves of bread. Orange wine, port wine, kola wine, Jamaica rum. Ginger beer for children and teetotallers. And four pyramids of daintily decorated cakes: two for Bita and two for Yoni.

After the cutting of the cake, in which bridesmaids competed, the toasts were proposed with the drinking of the wine. Teacher Fearon was toastmaster and perfectly acted his part. He began by toasting himself first, then the brides and bridegrooms and all Banana Bottom. He called upon Squire Gensir, who made a short speech saying that although he was a bachelor in the bone he could enjoy a happy wedding. Superintendent Delgado also made a speech. But the toast of the toasts was Hopping Dick's. Evidently Hopping Dick thought it was his duty to say something for Jubban too who had waived his right to make a speech.

Hopping Dick spoke facing Bita, Belle Black and Yoni sitting together, and a little ways from them Anty Nommy and Ma Legge bearing in her arms the angel baby. "Ladies and Gen'lemens

"There is no moh wonnerful t'ing in a man life than de day when im get himse'f a wife. A man may go chasing over the wul' lak a tomcat, but de day will come him gwine fin' somet'ing fer hold him down at home. An' it'll be a most happy day ef him get the right pusson de right way. But nobody knows 'bouten dat in de beginning. Ef one yahr pass an' gone any a mi frien's them did tell me ah would be steadyin' mese'f an' hookin' up an' settlin' comfably wid a sweet-lovin' woman I woulda answer him: youse crazy all ways in an' out excepn' none.

"Yet heah I is now hand an' foot an' eberyt'ing in what ah use to say was no man's business. But it's bettah me boys: bettah than runnin' from pillar to post like a mawgar dawg, cracking ebery bone an' always hungry when de dawgs them dat stays at home am growing fat in one place eatin' outa de same ole bowl ebery day, an' a rovin' Rover jest goes on rovin' until him finish up wid gettin' dat tail cut off.

"Yes, ah tell you all, ladies an' gen'lemens, this is one moh mawhvellous mekin' an' turnin' day fer me. An' Ise got fer t'ank Gawd an' de Chu'ch and mi Christian bredderin an' Banana Bottom fer it. And as de udder bridegroom which is de biggest one him refusing fer say anyt'ing but jest contented enough an' nacherally fer gettin' Godsendin' him de most beautiful flowahs in Banana Bottom an' all a Jamaica (an' ah want nobody fer vex cause I say it's de trute) ah wi' jest say fer him dat him is de one luckiest man in de wul'.

"Jest lak a outside horse dat nobody woulda bet on winnin' de race; jest lak a pusson you nebber bliebe could do it walkin' off at de end of de show wid de prize. Yessir, ah got to tek off mi hat again an' mek a low bow to mi frien' de udder bridegroom. An' ah got to admit it him is a bigger affair than mese'f.

"What big-big mens, doctohs an' lawyahs an' teachahs an' preachahs b'en mout'-waterin' fer, beggin' an' beseechin' an' nebber could a get—dat was gived as a free gift to mi breddah bridegroom, Jubban. Ah must gib him de glad hand a congratulations." [Hopping Dick stretched across the festive board and grasped Jubban's hand.] "An' ah want fer declare publicly and graciously fer Jubilee an' all fer hear an' bliebe dat I doan' bear de biggest bridegroom no grudge. An' ah gwine to finish by callin' fer t'ree cheers fer de two bride an' de two bridegroom."

The guests cheered as heartily for the speech as they did for the brides and bridegrooms. After the feasting the boards were removed and the booth cleared for dancing. The dancing went on all the late afternoon until evening, when a great crowd which could not be accommodated at the feast came to Bita's house to dance. All the young village were there and the crowds overflowed the palm booth and the house and spread out on the barbecues.

That evening when the dancing was at its height one group of young men got hold of Hopping Dick and another of Jubban and repaired to the grog-shop proprietor's house. The grog shop was a part of the same building as the proprietor's house and the proprietor let in the company at his back door and served them drinks.

It was a custom to get a young bridegroom away from the bride on the first night of their marriage and fill him up with liquor, and if he got drunk he was locked in and left under the table to sleep all night by himself.

The lads succeeded with Hopping Dick. He drank round after round, mixing the drinks, wine, porter and rum, and regaled the young rustics with lively tales of the small town and its smarter life: of gay parties and drinking bouts, horse-dealing and card-dealing, how the town bucks used to get after the country girls in the market shed in which the girls came to rest and sleep on Friday nights in preparation for the Saturday market.

And while Hopping Dick was laughing with his companions over his jokes one of them shook off his cigar ash into Hopping Dick's glass. There was a saying that tobacco ashes in liquor could get a man drunk quicker than anything. The trick brought an uproarious outburst from those who saw it and Hopping Dick joined in slapping his thigh, thinking that the laughter was because of his joke. The trick was repeated more than once. At last Hopping

Dick, weary after a strenuous day's riding and feasting, was swaying sleepy drunk and the fellows laid him out under the table and soon he began snoring.

Jubban had drank nothing but orange wine, refusing to change or mix the drink. He was nice with the fellows, but he was never a man for gay company, and there was something about him that kept them from making as free with him as with Hopping Dick. Now he heaved up, shook himself like a bear, said good-bye to his cheerful companions and strode home.

Late that night or rather before dawn after the dancing was ended, Bita was wakened by subdued singing under her bedroom window. It was the village choir singing the anthem: "Break Forth into Joy." Distinctly she heard Belle Black's treble and recognized Teacher Fearon's voice. She shook Jubban softly out of his heavy sleep so that he too should hear.

That was Teacher Fearon's gift, Bita thought. How beautiful it was, that low singing below her window just before dawn! Oh, it made her happy. Those singing voices were the most beautiful gift of all.

The "Return Thanks" was the closing event of a country wedding. It always took place the Sunday following the wedding, when the married couple and near relatives proceeded in ceremonial fashion to the local church and returned thanks to God for the happy celebration of their union.

As Jubban's best man, Squire Gensir also went to church. And it was the first time he had ever entered a church to sit under a sermon since he became a freethinker. That day he presented his horse to Jubban. He explained to Bita,

in making the gift, that riding so hard the day of the
wedding had stirred up memories of his fox-hunting days.
They were disturbing and he had decided that he did not
need a horse any more. No doubt Jubban could make better
use of the horse than he.

Bita replied that if the memories were pleasant ones, she
thought it was fine to remember them. But Squire Gensir
replied that he did not want to be in constant contact with
things that reminded him too forcibly of a past he had
renounced.

Not long after that the squire announced that he would
have to return to England. Bita noticed that he was not his
usual quiet composed self. There was a trace of agitation
in him. He had been more than twenty years away from
England and he did not want to return there. He had
always said he wanted to end his days and be buried in the
tropical soil of his adopted land.

But a spinster sister to whom he was devoted and who
had been ailing a long time had expressed a desire again
and again to see him once more. Squire Gensir was con-
science-worried, for his relatives thought that the sister was
going to die. And so he felt that it was his bounden duty
to go.

He went promising to return again. The key of the
cottage at Breakneck was left in Bita's care, so that she
could avail herself of the use of the piano. The Negro village was sad about the going of Squire Gensir. But he
promised to return again. He said that he wanted to come
back again to finish his work on the native folklore. He
had already done three books, but he was planning a larger
and more comprehensive one. And besides his work he
loved that island and loved its common people as a whole

with their good qualities and bad, their earthy common sense and their gentle humour and futile superstitions.

But he never returned. . . .

One twilight Bita and Anty Nommy were startled by a sudden harsh cackling of many fowls and their flying up in the air and over the barbecue like wild birds. Anty Nommy remarked that that was a sure sign of death and began worrying about Bab somewhere in Panama or the United States, from whom she had not had any news for a long time. Bita mocked at Anty Nommy's superstition and said that if people were always sent signs of death one would have been received for the double drowning of Jordan Plant and Malcolm Craig.

But a few weeks later Bita had news of the death of Squire Gensir, and Anty Nommy, figuring up the days, said the death had occurred about the same time the fowls acted so strangely. But Bita was unconvinced.

Squire Gensir had arrived home in the late fall in time to see his sister die. Dreading a long ocean voyage in the winter, he had planned to return to the tropics in the spring. But the northern winter was too hard upon his ageing bones after his long sojourn in the tropics. And so he had succumbed under its rigours.

Bita's sadness was tempered by the knowledge that Squire Gensir may have had some consolation dying among his own people that he might have missed in his adopted land, the early associations and memories of childhood that cling to the stoic wanderer until the end. He had seemed to her, after all, in spite of his free and easy contacts with the peasants, a lonely man living a lonely life. And although the peasants admired him, his high intellect and acute intelligence precluded him from sinking himself entirely in the austere simplicity of peasant life.

Having the key to the bungalow at Breakneck, Bita continued to go there to play the piano. She had heard nothing definite from the squire's relatives and wondered what would be the ultimate disposal of the house and things. But one day she received a communication from a bank in the city. Squire Gensir had left her the lot of land and the house with everything in it and five hundred pounds in the local bank.

Squire Gensir had always felt that he was instrumental a little for Bita's turning away from the rigid life of the mission, asserting her independence and finally breaking with the Craigs. Touched by the gift and overcome by emotion Bita could not restrain her tears. She shut herself in her room and cried.

She thought of the effect the knowledge of Squire Gensir's bequest would have upon the Lamberts and all her other detractors. They would be sure to find virtue now in the manner in which she had acted. They had talked so much about her irreparable mistake when it became known that Mrs. Craig had given all her money to the Society for the Prevention of Cruelty to Animals. Now she felt that she was amply compensated for whatever material benefit she may have sacrificed by quitting Jubilee.

In the cool of the late afternoon Bita walked over to Breakneck and visited the Hut. The housegirl had been cleaning and dusting it regularly twice a week. Things were in their place just as Squire Gensir had left them: books and magazines, the rough, ink-stained writing-table and the piano.

It gave her an uncanny feeling to think that he would

never come back to touch those things again. Never sit down to the piano, and that she would never again hear his voice—that finest thing about his insignificant little body, which had opened the way for him into the deep, obscure heart of the black peasantry.

She sat down to the piano. But she could not perform anything. She could only think of the man. After all, he had been much stranger than she had really imagined. She could see him clearer now. How different his life had been from the life of the other whites. They had come to conquer and explore, govern, trade, preach and educate to their liking, exploit men and material. But this man was the first to enter into the simple life of the island Negroes and proclaim significance and beauty in their transplanted African folk tales and in the words and music of their native dialect songs.

Before him it had been generally said the Negroes were inartistic. But he had found artistry where others saw nothing, because he believed that wherever the imprints of nature and humanity were found, there also were the seeds of creative life, and that above the dreary levels of existence everywhere there were always the radiant, the mysterious, the wonderful, the strange great moments whose magic may be caught by any clairvoyant mind and turned into magical form for the joy of man.

32

Before dawn on a Sunday Bita was awakened by the sound of the dray passing through the gate. It was Jubban coming home from the far market. The mules snorted hauling the dray round the house to the shed. Bita got up out of bed, wrapped herself in a shawl and went to set Jubban a little cold supper in the dining-room: cold Congo-pea soup with a piece of goat mutton, a slice of yam and a cut of banana pone.

She heard Jubban calling to the boy to wake up. The boy was sleeping in the outroom that had formerly been Jubban's. Now the boy was awake and up and was taking the mules to the paddock. Jubban came round to the back door of the house, outside of which there was a broad wooden bowl. He hauled off the heavy market boots. He washed his hands and face and after he washed his feet. Then he walked into the house and greeted Bita. She kissed him. His clothes smelled strongly of the cane sugar and the perfumed fever grass in which the breadkind for the market was laid.

Jubban sat down to eat and Bita prepared his favourite beverage: crude cane sugar and water with the juice of bitter oranges, while she asked about the market. Jubban answered that it had been good. For the past two years, ever since the hurricane, the market for breadkind had been excellent. He had taken sugar to the market and had sold it as high as five shillings a tin.

He told Bita about the trip to the market and back in a few phrases. He was not voluble. He talked in monosyllables of the dialect. But he expressed himself clearly. Bita appreciated his reticence, which suited her temperament for she was not a talkative woman.

Finishing his supper, Jubban went into the bedroom, took a peep at little Jordan sleeping in his crib and went to sleep. On coming home from the far market he usually slept until midday on Sunday.

Bita never could sleep directly after waking up at that hour. She went into the sitting-room and lay on the sofa and her thoughts flitted in disorder across the world. From Jubban to Jubilee, college days, travelling, Jubilee again, and back to Banana Bottom and Jubban.

Jubban. She was contented with him. She had become used to his kindly-rough gestures and they had adjusted themselves well to each other. The testing-time was over. Three years had passed since the memorable hurricane and flood. Intimate relations with Bita and the mastership of the house had developed in Jubban all the splendid qualities that were latent in him. His sureness and firmness about the things of which he was familiar, such as superintending the clearing of the land, planting, harvesting and marketing and the care and breeding of the live stock.

The land had prospered under Jubban's hand even more than under Jordan Plant's. Bita had purchased from the remnant of the Adair family the crumbling old " 'State House" and land that her father had coveted, for less than a hundred pounds, and now there were a few cows feeding upon that fine pasture grass. And Anty Nommy was pleased with the development of the property and as proud of Jubban as Bita.

Thinking of Jubban and how her admiration for him had slowly developed into respect and love, Bita marvelled at the fact that they had never said "I love you" to each other. The thing had become a fact without the declaration.

They lived their life upon a level entirely different from her early romantic conception of love. Once she had thought of love as a kind of mystical force, incomprehensible and uncontrollable. But gradually she had lost all that feeling of the quality of love, for it was a borrowed thing, an exotic imposition, not a real intrinsic thing that had flowered out of the mind of her race.

She had no craving for Jubban to be other than what he was, experienced no hankering for that grace and refinement in him that the local soothsayers said was necessary to an educated person. She liked to play for him for he had a natural feeling for music and showed appreciation of even the most difficult things. But he was in no way a hindrance to the intellectual side of her life. He accepted with natural grace the fact that she should excel in the things to which she had been educated as he should in the work to which he had been trained.

Her music, her reading, her thinking were the flowers of her intelligence and he the root in the earth upon which she was grafted, both nourished by the same soil.

Reaching her hand out to the bookshelf she drew out her college copy of the *Pensées*. One of the rare pleasures of adult life is returning sometimes to the scriptures of our formal education days and finding new interest and meanings in old passages.

Bita turned the pages of the *Pensées*:

> . . . la vraie morale se moque de la morale; la morale du jugement se moque de la morale de l'esprit.

That was one thought from Pascal that her philosophy teacher had never chosen to expatiate upon as a Christian gem. She had come by it all by herself. Squire Gensir had once said of it that it was more Pagan and Stoic than Christian. A thought like food. Something to live by from day to day. Unbounded by little national and racial lines, but a cosmic thing of all time for all minds.

Perhaps Pascal would have been incredulous if it had been prophesied to him that in future centuries a black girl would have found in his words a golden thread of principle to guide her through the confusion of life. And in a receptive and critical mood Bita turned the familiar pages, picking here and there an outstanding passage at random and thinking how like a risen river overflowing its banks was the man, bigger than the Christian creed in which he was confined.

Alone thinking contemplatively profoundly, the conviction came to her that clear thinking was the most beautiful of all things. Love and music were divine things but none so rare as the pure flight of the mind into the upper realms of thought.

Well, she thought, if my education has been wasted it is a happy waste. They were right perhaps who said it was wasted who believed that the real aims of education were diplomas and degrees and to provide things of snobbery and pretension like a ribbon on the breast and a plume upon the hat to dazzle the multitude.

The *Pensées* fell from her hand. . . . She had fallen asleep.

Bita was awakened by little Jordan's bleating in the yard, and looking out of the window she saw him, his shirt wet and yellow with mango juice, writhing indignantly in Anty Nommy's arms, angered that Anty Nommy had taken him away from under the kidney-mango tree, thus preventing him from overstuffing his belly with too many of the ripe fruit that had fallen during the night. The sun was up and Anty Nommy was preparing breakfast.

"What a pickney, though! What a pickney!" Anty Nommy was saying and playfully slapping little Jordan's bottom. "Showin' you' strengt' a'ready mi li't' man. Soon you'll be l'arnin' fer square you' fist them off at me."

THE END

backra: native appellation for white and used mostly in an invidious sense—commonly written *buckra* but really pronounced *backra*

bammy: delicious cakes made from the rough residue of the bitter cassava (*Manihot utilissima*)

blackhatch: common name for the tallest and stateliest of the tree ferns

breadkind: general name for the staple vegetables and fruits

cat: the tamarind switch or its equivalent, used for flogging prisoners in Jamaica: cat is an abbreviation of the cat-o'-nine-tails and is employed as noun and verb

chewstick: the stem of an acid climbing plant with which the peasants clean their teeth; also used to flavor ginger beer

cho-cho: a vegetable apparently kin to the melon family, much valued by the peasants

cocoaplums: an indigo blue berry, favorite among children

cotta: a rough chaplet made of dried bark, leaves, or straw used by the peasants in bearing loads upon their heads

disayah: this here, this one

duppy: ghost

dutty: dirty

facey: brisk, forward

fass: impudent, officious

fee-fee: flower of a wild vine children use as whistles

jamma: field and digging song

jesen: just

jippi-jappa: local name for hats similar to Panama hats

john-tubit: little singing bird

knot-gut: fatal constipation

ku: look

milkwis: a forest vine from which a substance like milk is extracted and made into rubber

nummo: no more

Obeah, Obi: West Indian form of African magic

pickney: pickaninny

pindar: a sort of peanut

ping-wing: a wild plant, cousin to the pineapple

quattie: a penny ha'penny

saal (in mi saal)*:* having a good time

sandplatters: sandals

shey-shey: barbecue song and dance

six-months: poinsettia

stucky: sweetheart

supple-jack: a climbing forest vine excellent for riding-whips and walking-sticks

taffy goat: ram

trash-house: a shed in which the refuse of the sugar cane is stored after the juice has been pressed out

tup: a penny ha'penny

unno: you; all of you

wut: worth

wimme: with me

yah: here